D1278858

NONSENSE AND WONDER

NONSENSE AND WONDER

The Poems and Cartoons of Edward Lear

by **THOMAS BYROM**

A **Brandywine Press** Book
E. P. Dutton
New York

Quotations from Lear's diaries, letters, and manuscript poems are by permission of the Houghton Library, Harvard; the National Library of Scotland; the Pierpont Morgan Library. The correspondence between Emily Tennyson and Lear is in the Tennyson Research Centre, Lincoln, and extracts are quoted by permission of Lord Tennyson and the Lincolnshire Library Service.

This book was edited and produced by
The Brandywine Press, Inc.
Clarkson N. Potter, President

Design by Ellen Seham
Typography by David Seham Associates, Inc.
Printed and bound by Westbrook Lithographers

Published, 1977, in the United States by E. P. Dutton,
a Division of Sequoia-Elsevier Publishing Company, Inc., New York,
and simultaneously in Canada by Clarke, Irwin & Co., Ltd.,
Toronto and Vancouver.

Byrom, Thomas.
Nonsense and wonder.

"A Brandywine Press book."
Bibliography: p. 239
Includes index.
1. Lear, Edward, 1812–1888. 2. Poets, English—19th century—Biography. 3. Artists—England—Biography. I. Lear, Edward, 1812–1888. Nonsense and wonder. 1977 II. Title.
PR4879.LzZ59 760'.092'4 [B] 77-14560
ISBN 0-525-16835-4

10 9 8 7 6 5 4 3 2 1

First Edition

For my father, my mother and Joya

Nluv, fluv bluv, ffluv biours
Faith nunfaith kneer beekwl powers
Unfaith naught zwant a faith in all.

—Edward Lear

In Love, if Love be Love, if Love be ours,
Faith and unfaith can ne'er be equal powers:
Unfaith in aught is want of faith in all.

—Tennyson, *Idylls of the King*

Contents

Acknowledgments

I wish to acknowledge my debt to Vivien Noakes, whose thorough and sensitive study, *Edward Lear, the Life of a Wanderer*, has given both substance and inspiration to my first chapter, and has guided me throughout. The facts in my sketch of Lear's life are mostly hers; the mistakes, and the interpretations, are mine. I recommend her biography to any reader who seeks a deeper understanding of Lear. I must also thank her for her wise and helpful criticisms.

I wish also to thank William Alfred, Jerome H. Buckley, David Jarrett, Mary Jarrett, and most of all Robert Pear, who first at Harvard and then at Oxford helped me through several drafts.

Chapter One

A Sketch of Edward Lear's Life

One day in the middle of October 1866, Edward Lear took the train to visit his sister in the country. He was delighted to hear his fellow passengers talking about his *Book of Nonsense,* and how it had brought pleasure to thousands of families. Then, to his dismay, a somber gentleman began to explain that the author was not Edward Lear, but Edward, Earl of Derby. Lear was just an anagram, a ghost of scrambled letters, a jumble.

"This is quite a mistake," interrupted Lear. "I have reason to know that Edward Lear the painter and author wrote and illustrated the whole book."

"And I," said the gentleman, "have good reason to know, Sir, that you are wholly mistaken. *There is no such a person* as Edward Lear."

"But," said Lear, "there *is*—and I am the man—and I wrote the book!"

They all started to laugh at this wild claim, until to prove himself Lear took off his hat and showed his name and address on the inside, in large letters, and then flourished a marked handkerchief, and lastly, one of his cards, whereupon, as he told a friend, "amazement devoured those benighted individuals and I left them to gnash their teeth in trouble and tumult."[1]

He celebrated this small triumph with a sketch in which he represents himself as a serious person, properly drawn, and the gentleman as a cartoon figure.

At first Lear seems to be making fun of the gentleman. But is he? If we look closer we observe that he has also made himself ridiculous in his own eyes. He has exchanged identities with the gentleman, making a gentleman, grave and respectable, of himself and a fool of the gentleman. When we realize that Lear is happy to share the folly, we begin to feel the depth and the warmth of his joke. All his nonsense does just this: it turns criticism into love.

Edward Lear made an art of folly. He became the first nonsense poet, and he was the originator of a whole school of nonsense cartooning. He was our first absurdist, with Lewis Carroll the spiritual father of a movement in European culture which embraces Flaubert, Jarry, Kafka, Ionesco, Beckett, Pinter and many modern painters. He was also an ornithological draftsman of the first rank and a highly gifted water-colorist.

Only in his chosen profession, as a painter of landscape oils, did he fail—in his own as well as in public esteem. Determined to paint from life, he traveled to the most outlandish places and sketched thousands of scenes in pen, pencil and wash. Back in the studio he tried to transfer these bold, delicate and spontaneous compositions onto large canvases. But his line stiffened, the tones became ponderous and the colors garish. He was a much better painter than most, but somehow his skills failed his vision. With care, he lost fluency. With study, he lost depth. Oil smothered his sense of wonder.

If this was his greatest folly, it was still folly for a larger, albeit hidden, purpose. The point lay not in the studio work but in the travels. Lear sought out the strange and exalted corners of the Victorian world—Athos, Olympus, Arcadia, the Nile, the Holy Land, the Himalayas—not just for excitement or novelty or to advance his career, but because these outward journeys were also inward ones. He was looking for a sublime, not merely to paint it and sell it, but to possess it.

Ironically, it was in his nonsense poems and cartoons that he eventually found what he was looking for.

1812 to 1837

Lear was born in Holloway, London, on May 12, 1812, the twentieth of twenty-one children. Dickens, whose gift for the absurd he shared, was born a few months earlier. Tennyson, whose friend he became, was two years old. Byron, whose life he in some respects imitated, was in his mid-twenties. And the Regency was in its second year.

His father, Jeremiah, was a stockbroker. The family came from Dorset and had prospered in eighteenth-century London as sugar refiners. His mother, Ann, was Northumbrian. Many of her children died at birth, but Ann, Sarah, Henry, Mary, Eleanor, Jane, Olivier, Harriett, Cordelia, Frederick, Florence, Charles, Edward and Catherine survived. Several children appear to have died unnamed, and there was perhaps a second Catherine. All we know of Cordelia Lear are her dates. But we can guess that she was nearly as well acquainted with death as the original Cordelia. Edward was lucky enough to have been born next to last.

In 1816 Jeremiah Lear, having switched from sugar to stockbroking, fell upon hard times. His house was let and the family split up. Ann, who was the oldest child, was given charge of four-year-old Edward; she was to look after him for the rest of her life. A few years later, Jeremiah secured a bank loan and the family reassembled in Bowman's Lodge, their Holloway home, where they continued to live, though in reduced circumstances, till Edward was fifteen.

He was affectionate, lonely and plain. From the age of five he suffered from fits of epilepsy, which he called "the demon,"[2] and from about the age of seven he had bouts of severe depression, which he called "the morbids." Like so many eminent Victorians, he was of a manic-depressive temperament, and his childhood was darkened by poverty and loneliness. Harriett taught him his manners. Eleanor gave him drawing lessons, Charles bullied him. His mother evidently had no time for him. Ann became his real mother, his nurse and protector. She took him on trips to Margate for his health (at a time when Keats had moved there for the same reason). She gave him his first school lessons: probably she used the common primers—*Magnall's Questions* and *The Child's Guide to Knowledge*—evangelical, catechizing, question-and-answer guidebooks. Later, he was to feel grateful that he had escaped formal instruction. Ann read him the classical myths and the Bible. When he was ten or eleven, he discovered for himself the Romantics, and like the adolescent Tennyson, he wept at the news of Byron's death. Ann probably encouraged his love of poetry, and she also taught him to paint flowers, butterflies and birds in a special room opposite the nursery, called "the painting room."

His diary speaks briefly and darkly of two childhood traumas. When his cousin Frederick Harding died, Lear wrote: "It is just 50 years since he did to me the greatest Evil done to me in life, excepting that done by C:—and which must last now to the end—spite of all reason and effort."[3] Frederick, his mother's nephew, had been bought out of his regiment and was staying with the Lears in the spring of 1822. It was on April 8, Easter Monday, 1822, that the event to which Lear refers took place. Frederick probably made some kind of homosexual assault, and it left Lear deeply troubled—he often marked the date in his diary when it came around. The "Evil" done to him by "C"—perhaps his brother Charles—may have been something of the same kind. Clearly, Lear blamed an aberrant streak in his sexual nature upon these pederastic experiences.

About the age of eleven he was sent to school, but we know nothing of his formal education except that it was very brief. In the same period, his sister Sarah married Charles Street and went to live in Arundel. Edward visited her often and spent much of his time in the South Downs, a countryside he greatly loved, as did Samuel Palmer and the Pre-Raphaelites. Sarah's household was the first in which he was able to make friends outside the family. His gift for nonsense probably first developed among these, "my Sussex friends," who thought him "3 parts crazy—and wholly affectionate,"[4] and who assured him (a nonsense compliment) that he could "do nothing like other people."[5] The phrase sticks to him like a bur to wool. He was to make his name doing nothing like other people. Among these first friends was a family called Drewitt, and Lear seems to have written his earliest poems for one of the daughters, Eliza—his "Ode to a Chinaman," "Miss Maniac" and "Peppering Roads." He began also to make connections among the older and wealthier people, members of the gentry and aristocracy, in whose company and under whose patronage he was to spend most of his adult life. William Turner's patron, the Earl of Egremont, lived nearby at Petworth, a grand country house where Lear first saw a real collection of paintings. He was introduced not only to Egremont, but also to other patrons of Turner—Walter Fawkes and Lord de Tabley among them. He probably thought of trying for art school, even the Royal Academy. But the family was too poor for that. In the autumn of 1827, Jeremiah Lear retired to a house in Gravesend, taking with him his wife and one daughter, Florence. Again the family was scattered, this time for good. At the age of fifteen, Edward found himself abandoned by his parents and wholly dependent on Ann, who had inherited a small income.

She never married, and devoted her life to bringing him up and sending him out into the world.

They moved into rooms in Gray's Inn Road, and Edward started to earn his living by doing drawings and colored work for shops—"uncommon queer shop-sketches"—and by making "morbid disease drawings"[6] for doctors and hospitals. Soon, however, he found himself specializing in birds. There was a vogue for illustrated zoology books. Audubon had begun his work in 1820, and in 1825 Selby and Jardine had published their *Illustrations of British Ornithology*. By the time he was sixteen, Lear was working for Selby, to whom he had been introduced by Mrs. Godfrey Wentworth, the daughter of Walter Fawkes. It was she who first took him to the Zoological Gardens in London. In 1829 he drew the blue and yellow macaw for a visitors' guidebook, *The Gardens of the Zoological Society Delineated*, and in 1830 he started a project of his own—drawing parrots from life. He spent hours in the parrot house taking measurements and making sketches and color notes. Occasionally he made swift caricatures of the fashionable people staring in at him. He transferred his drawings into negatives on lithographic plates, and by the autumn had prepared two of a projected fourteen folios, entitled *Illustrations of the Family of Psittacidae, or Parrots*. Lear's skill was quickly recognized. On November 30, 1830, a day after the first two folios were ready, he was made an associate of the Linnaean Society. He was only eighteen. Among the subscribers to his project were Lord Egremont and Mrs. Wentworth, and his most important patron of all, the president of the Zoological Society, Lord Stanley, Earl of Derby, on whose private estate at Knowsley, outside Liverpool, there was one of the best menageries in Europe. Lear never finished the full edition, despite the encouragement of William Swainson, a friend of Audubon. He stopped at the twelfth folio, which was issued in April 1832.

Lear was now a tall and ugly young man of twenty. He had a few friends his own age. William Nevill and Bernard Senior, from Sussex, were perhaps the closest of them. With Bernard, he spent days and nights on the town and contracted syphilis. It is as well to remember, when we read the later lyrics about disappointed love and follow the course of his homosexual infatuations, that Lear was by no means a virgin; he seems to have sown his wild oats with conventional vigor. He was still close to Sarah and he often visited her. Once in the country, he would dabble in verse again: imitations of Byron on the glories of ancient Greece, anapaestic celebrations of the South Downs, brief Romantic lyrics. At the end of 1831 he moved with Ann to new lodgings on the eastern side of Regent's Park, only a few minutes' walk from the zoo. She remained kind and protective. He, by now, was chafing impatiently in her company.

He found fresh work illustrating the *Transactions of the Zoological Society, The Zoology of Captain Beechey's Voyage* and *The Zoology of the Voyage of H.M.S. Beagle,* the ship on which Charles Darwin had served as naturalist. He also drew pigeons and parrots for the Naturalists' Library and did lithographs for Bell's *Tortoises, Terrapins and Turtles.* Through this work, he met John Gould, an entrepreneur who profited from the vogue of zoological books. Gould could not draw very well, so he set Lear to work with his wife Elizabeth on the illustrations for his *Century of Birds from the Himalayan Mountains* (1831). He was ungenerous enough to sign his plates "J. & E. Gould"; Lear is nowhere acknowledged in the book, and he was, not surprisingly, annoyed with Gould. But he swallowed the insult and accompanied him on a tour of Continental zoos in the summer of 1831 in Germany, Switzerland and Holland, and contracted to work with him until they finished *Birds of Europe.* Lear showed himself especially skilled at drawing ravens and owls. Often he gave them a sagacious look. He seems to have felt as dark as a raven, as blind as an owl and as gaudy as a parrot. But he was also, like them, a creature with a deep and mysterious nature—wise and exotic.

In 1832, Lear was invited by Lord Stanley to Knowsley on a commission to draw his private zoo. For three generations thereafter, the Earls of Derby were to be his chief patrons. At first he took his meals belowstairs with the steward, where he entertained the Earl's grandchildren with impromptu nonsense and cartoons. Soon he was invited up to eat with the adults and the high society, and he rapidly became a successful court jester, a role he was to play over and over again in many of the great country houses in England. Unfortunately, he destroyed the diaries of these years, but his letters to Ann indicate that he was a great social success and made many useful connections. But he did not like the usual kind of aristocrat. "The uniform apathetic tone assumed by lofty society irks me *dreadfully,*" he wrote to a friend.[7] He hated snobs, philistines and idlers, and felt that upper-class Englishmen were too often all of these.

His closest friends at Knowsley were children, whose company he had never before had the chance to enjoy—his brothers had emigrated to America with their families, and Sarah's two sons were nearly his own age. He adapted the traditional limerick form and produced for the young Stanleys his first "nonsenses," which were received with "uproarious delight and welcome."[8] Over the next ten years, he added to and perfected them, and eventually published them in 1846 as the first *Book of Nonsense.* They mocked the fashionable goings-on upstairs and rhymed in seesaw fashion about queer people in queer places, and they ended with both a soothing refrain and, often, a farcical bump. But they also had a dark side, and in some ways these were sad years for Lear. His father died of a heart attack in September 1833. Florence, Cordelia and Catherine died about four years later. The eerie closeness of death which he felt as a child now became all too real. In the next quarter-century, he watched himself outlive his huge and scattered family. He was also frequently lonely at Knowsley, among children and aristocrats, with no real company of his own age and class. So it is not surprising to find in the limericks, alongside a quiet satire on the follies of fashion, darker feelings of isolation, a preoccupation with death, and the acting out of the role of the eccentric, the childlike uncle who has infinite license, but who would rather surrender his freedom for the bonds of some real affection.

He worked at Knowsley till 1837, and left many of his drawings behind in the library. Some of these were reproduced in *Gleanings from the Menagerie and Aviary at Knowsley Hall* (1846).[9] Meantime, he was still working for Gould, and in 1835 he had enrolled in Sass's School of Art in Bloomsbury, where students were prepared for the Royal Academy entrance examination. But his financial situation made it impossible for him to think seriously of embarking on the ten-year course. In the summer of the same year he traveled to Ireland with Arthur Stanley, later Dean of Westminster, and the following summer, 1836, he spent sketching and walking in the Lake District.

By October he had decided upon his profession. He would be an itinerant landscape painter. He broke off his association with Gould. He felt his eyes had been weakened by too much close draftmanship, and his asthma and bronchitis worsened with each winter. He was now determined to go somewhere warm and dry, and to sketch large scenes out in the open. The Stanleys gave him some commissions and sent him off to Rome. He had just turned twenty-five.

1837 to 1849

Lear left England at the end of July 1837. Ann went with him as far as Brussels. She did not see him again for four years, and she lived the rest of her life alone. He was clearly relieved to break from her at last, but he felt almost as guilty about her solitude as he felt sad at his own, and he wrote to her often.

He spent several months wandering and sketching his way down through Luxembourg, Germany and the Alps, and he arrived in Florence—"all a hurly-burly of beauty and wonder"[10]—in late autumn. There he met English artists who put him in touch with friends in Rome, which he reached early in December. He took rooms near the Piazza di Spagna and joined the café society of expatriated artists. He began to gather small commissions easily enough because the city was full of wintering English high society. He found himself moving freely among bohemians and aristocrats. But for all the bustle, novelty and independence, he felt very lonely. Indeed, this was his first taste of a loneliness that was to dog him through the long years of exile to the grave. But it was a loneliness which at some deep level of his nature he freely chose—he needed a solitude to commune with and to free himself. He loved sketching the Campagna just outside Rome, a ruined wasteland of olive trees and rocks, hills and low horizons, a pastoral landscape conspicuously desolate. From time to time he thought of marriage. But there were his epilepsy and the uncertainty of his social position, and perhaps also the fear that a wife might desert him as his mother had once done.

Despite his troubles, he had a happy and busy time in the next few years. There was more work in the winter months than he could easily manage. He returned home in 1841, and life looked bright. He saw Ann and then went up to Knowsley, where he worked on lithographs of his drawings of Rome; in the autumn he made a tour of the Lowlands with Phipps Hornby, a cousin of his patron Robert Hornby. *Views in Rome and Its Environs* was published by Thomas McLean the same season. The views are competent, in the manner of Claude Lorrain,[11] but the perspective is frequently awkward and the human figures are positively clumsy. Lear could not bring himself to draw people well, and this was by no failure of skill, but by some deeper inhibition. His landscapes always look as though he preferred them empty of human life. He invariably reduces his figures to stiff puppets, the ghosts of stick-men.

He returned to Italy at the end of the year and settled into his Roman life, with expeditions to Sicily in the spring of 1842, and to the Abruzzi and the Adriatic coast in the summer of 1843. He was now firmly set in his chosen career as a wandering "topographical landscape painter." He hurried busily through ever wilder landscapes, capturing the scenery in hundreds of sketches. These are often magically light and vivid, reflecting the joy he took in his bright and energetic tours. But once in the captivity of his studio, they were turned into dark and sometimes stilted lithographs for his travel books, where often we have to look to the vigor and novelty of his prose commentary to tell us of the love of nature which inspired them.

In May 1844, when he turned thirty-two, his mother died in Dover. She had borne twenty-one children in twenty-four years, had seen thirteen of them die, and had raised the survivors in uncertain financial and domestic circumstances. She can hardly be blamed for deserting her youngest son, but desert him she did. In his letters and papers, he mentions her only half a dozen times, and even then peremptorily. He hardly knew her, and we cannot tell whether he loved her. But we can guess that a great part of his sense of alienation came from her neglect. He had been an orphan in a family teeming with children; Ann had succeeded in making him at least an only child. It was little to make a life out of, and his feelings are clear enough to read in the nonsense poems in which he writes of family life—both the limericks and "Mr. and Mrs. Discobbolos, Part I" and "Part II." When he received news of his mother's death, he wrote to Ann inviting her to come and stay with him. But she preferred to remain at home.

In the spring of 1845 he met Chichester Fortescue, the first of three men (Fortescue, Franklin Lushington and Hubert Congreve) for whom he seems to have felt a homosexual love. It is possible that he had already had a homosexual relationship with a Danish painter, Wilhelm Marstrand, in Rome in the early forties. Fortescue was ten years Lear's junior and had just taken a first in classics at Oxford. Later he had a solid political career as a Liberal, and he was ennobled by Gladstone for his services. He was a modest, introspective man with a love of the arts, and he and Lear at once became fast friends and always remained so. Lear showed him around Rome and took him sketching. Fortescue wrote in his diary: "Lear a delightful companion, full of *nonsense,* puns, riddles, everything in the shape of fun, and *brimming* with intense appreciation of nature as well as history."[12] Their correspondence covers forty years, and it is full of affectionate nonsense.

Lear decided to spend the summer of 1845 in England. It was his second trip home. He took rooms at 27 Duke Street, St. James's, and from there visited his friends, among them the Stanleys. He was working on two projects: a book about his travels in the Abruzzi and a collection of his limericks. On February 10, 1846, Thomas McLean, who had brought out his *Views in Rome* in 1841, published *A Book of Nonsense* in two volumes at 3s. 6d. each. There were seventy limericks in all; Lear chose the nom de plume "Derry down Derry" and placed on the title page a limerick explaining how the book had come about:

> There was an Old Derry down Derry,
> Who loved to see little folks merry:
> So he made them a book, and with laughter they shook,
> At the fun of that Derry down Derry.

It seems to have sold moderately well even though McLean was not a publisher of children's literature. A new edition was issued in 1854, this time with the verses arranged in five-line italic form; in the first, they were in sloping capitals and three lines. In 1861, Routledge, Warne and Routledge, publishers specializing in children's books, bought it up and reissued it—and then, at last, it began to sell fast. There were other early editions, but their history is obscure since they were quickly read to pieces in the nursery, and it was not until the tenth edition in 1863 that copies were sent to the copyright libraries.[13]

Meanwhile, in April 1846, McLean published the first volume of *Illustrated Excursions in Italy*. It was dedicated to the Earl of Derby, and it so impressed the Queen that she summoned Lear to give her drawing lessons. He gave her twelve, at Osborne and Buckingham Palace. In August, the second volume of *Illustrated Excursions* appeared, just after the last lesson; and later in the summer, Lord Derby brought out *Gleanings from the Menagerie at Knowsley Hall.* Though he had made only £100 out of all three books, Lear must have felt that this had been his most successful year so far. In December he left for Italy.

Back in Rome he found plenty of fresh work to busy him. But he was short of money—"tinless," as he called it—and the winter turned out to be very harsh. Heavy snows kept him indoors and aggravated his epilepsy. Moreover, after ten years the city had lost some of its excitement for him. He began to think of returning to England for good. Yet, with the constant stream of English visitors, he could at least be sure of making a living in Rome—England was a riskier proposition. For the moment, he decided to stay in the south, and in the spring of 1847 he set out on a sketching tour of Sicily and Calabria with a painter friend, John Proby. In an inn on this tour he overheard himself described as "nothing but a damned dirty landscape-painter,"[14] and thereafter he adopted with delight the title of Edward Lear, Dirty Landscape Painter. Toward the end of their trip they saw the first signs of the nationalist revolution, and so they hurried north and reached Rome in the middle of October. There Lear opened his studio for the winter season, worked on his summer sketches, and entered into the old routine of rising early, working hard and dining out. Inevitably, he grew depressed, and again he thought of going home. He wrote to Fortescue that he felt "the days of possible Lotus-eating are diminishing, and by the time I am 40 I would fain be in England once more."[15] But in February 1848, he met Thomas Baring, later Earl of Northbrook and Viceroy of India, and they quickly became the closest of friends—"an extremely luminous and amiable brick,"[16] Lear called him.

By March 1848, Venice and Milan were in revolt. Lear packed his belongings and hastily accepted an invitation from the president of the University of Corfu to come and stay, and possibly teach. But instead of settling on the island, which he reached in April, he found himself accepting a fresh invitation from an old acquaintance, Stratford Canning, who had been appointed Ambassador to Turkey, and who asked him to join the diplomatic party on its way through Greece to Constantinople. For the next fifteen months, Lear was to wander restlessly around the Mediterranean, using Corfu as his base. He had soon set up his sketch pad in the Acropolis, "in a wilderness of broken columns," where "owls, the birds of Minerva, are extremely common, and come and sit very near me when I draw."[17] He slipped out of Canning's entourage to go on a few weeks' tour with another old friend, Charles Church, the nephew of the commander of the Greek forces in the War of Independence, in which Byron had fought and died. But he came down with malaria at Thebes and had to be taken back to Athens. He recovered quickly and followed the Cannings to Constantinople, only to have a relapse at the embassy.

He lay in bed, gazing out the window at a long towpath, wondering what to make of his life. Revolution had put Rome out of reach. He was enchanted by Corfu—"a Paradise,"[18] he told Ann—but he was not sure if he could settle there. It seemed he would have to return to England and give up being a society painter and a wanderer. Hard study was what he needed, he felt, so that he could master at last the human figure and hence "carry out the views and feelings of landscape I know to exist within me."[19] He had never before understood so clearly the difference between what he could do and what he wanted to do. But by the end of August he had recovered completely, and instead of acting upon this new insight, he set out on a hazardous journey which took him right across Greece and Albania to the Aegean. After some exciting adventures, he reached Yannina in early November, with 219 sketches and a log of his journey.

Ann expected him back in England, but the thought of an English winter was too much for him. He accepted yet another invitation, his third since he had fled Rome. Another old friend, John Cross, asked Lear to travel with him, at his expense, to Egypt and the Holy Land. Lear eagerly took up the offer and left for Cairo. When he got there, he found Cross had gone ahead to Palestine, and his fever returned. He decided to go back to Greece by way of Malta.

In Malta, he met—by a happy and terrible chance—Franklin Lushington. Slowly he fell in love with him. It was perhaps the strongest affection of his life; it was to give him a few hours of ecstatic happiness—and many more of misery and frustration. Lushington did become his closest friend. But, like Fortescue, he was ten years younger than Lear, and he was by nature stern, inexpressive and quite unable to respond in kind to Lear's feelings for him. He had been at Rugby under Dr. Arnold, and at Trinity College, Cambridge, where he got a first in classics and was made a Fellow. His brother Henry had been, with Hallam and Tennyson, one of the Cambridge Apostles; his brother Edmund married Tennyson's sister Cecilia—his is the wedding celebrated at the end of *In Memoriam*.

Lear and Lushington decided to go together to Greece. They arrived at the beginning of spring and spent a few happy weeks traveling in the Morea, south of Patras, in a landscape which, like the Campagna outside Rome, was both verdant and desolate. Lear found himself wandering, at last, in the literal Arcadia, in the company of the ideal friend. He was ecstatic—they were probably the happiest days of his life. "As for Lushington and I," he wrote home to Ann, "equally fond of flowers, we gather them all day like children."[20] They visited the temple of Apollo, and Sparta, Mycenae and Argos and then turned north through Attica to Thebes, where Lear had caught malaria the year before, and journeyed on to the home of the gods, Parnassus, and to the Oracle at Delphi.

When Lushington left him at Patras, Lear continued north on his own. He had failed once already, on his Albanian tour, to see the grandest of holy mountains, Athos; now he was determined to perfect his spring by reaching it and drawing it. He wandered through the Vale of Tempe and came to Mount Olympus, which he sketched thoroughly. But suddenly he grew sad. He was reminded—why, he could not understand—of all the bleakest and loneliest places he had ever visited, both in England and on his many travels. Bewildered, despondent, he gave up his attempt to reach Mount Athos and turned back. He decided to go home to England.

1849 to 1855

It was Lear's third homecoming. He arrived at the beginning of June 1849 to discover that an old family friend had left him £500 in her will. It was just enough for him to lay the ground for the serious study of art which he had decided upon when ill with fever at Constantinople. At least now he could make a real effort to find out what kind of an artist he might become and what art might mean for him. He was already thirty-seven, a late age at which to embark on a ten-year painting course. Still, he enrolled once more at Sass's in Bloomsbury, with an eye to the Academy entrance examinations. It was fifteen years since he had studied there.

He spent the summer of 1849 drifting from one country house to another. He visited Lushington in Maidstone, but found him taciturn and withdrawn. Here he probably met Tennyson for the first time, on the eve of his fame. They became uneasy friends. Later, Lear was to find in Emily Tennyson his closest confidante and staunchest ally. He went up to Knowsley and was warmly received. He wrote telling Fortescue how happy he was. In September he returned to town, took rooms off Oxford Street and started at Sass's.

On January 16, 1850, Lear learned to his intense delight that he had been accepted by the Royal Academy, along with eighteen others, as a probationer till April. His fellow students were mostly twenty years younger than he, and he made good fun out of the situation, depicting himself in a Thurber-like cartoon as an old duffer teased and tormented by infant schoolmates. On April 26 he was accepted for the full course. But he never finished it. He was to remain for about two and a half years, off and on, working in the Antique School, trying to master figure drawing by sketching classical statues. He felt he would have done better at night school, drawing from the life. Unhappily, he was too stubborn to abandon his course, and he never learned the skills which he felt might show him how to animate his work. He fell back upon the notion that his failure was purely technical. It was the kind of easy way out that meant only more hard, useless, blinding work.

Money, moreover, was an ever-present problem, and he was forced to return to the old, distracting projects. In 1851 he brought out his *Journals of a Landscape Painter in Greece and Albania*, and he followed it quickly with *Journals of a Landscape Painter in Southern Calabria and the Kingdom of Naples* (1852). The first was an immediate success and won him a certain amount of recognition—though, cruelly enough, very little money. But it inspired Tennyson's poem "To E.L., on his Travels in Greece," no small consolation. He spent the summer holidays of 1851 in Devon. It rained and he felt lonely. Lushington joined him in August for a walking tour through Cornwall, but Lear was too depressed to be good company. Back in London he tried to turn some of the Greek sketches into oils—only to fail. He had returned from his exile with the resolve to make a fresh start. By the end of 1851, he found himself more bewildered and clumsier than ever. He persevered in the Antique School but felt that life was slipping away.

He was rescued by the Pre-Raphaelites. They mended his spirits, if not his art. In the summer exhibition of 1850, when they had come out into the open, Lear had had one of his oils hung for the first time—a study of Claude Lorrain's house on the Tiber. The public reacted with fury and disgust to the work of the Brotherhood; but Lear admired their naturalism and especially their sense of color. They had the sort of brightness he had long admired in Turner's work. He came to know Robert Martineau, and early in the summer of 1852 Martineau brought Holman Hunt to Lear's studio to look at his work. Hunt felt that he needed to paint oils not from sketches, but directly from the landscape. He had been planning to go down to Fairlight, in the hills behind Hastings, and he suggested that Lear accompany him. Lear could teach him Italian, and he could give Lear hints about painting.

It was a happy prospect for Lear. Here were new friends, fellow artists of the first rank who were affectionate and willing to help. Lear scouted the countryside and rented Clive Vale Farm. Hunt arrived with William Rossetti, who proved warm and lively company. Lear was shy at first; this was the first time he had shared close quarters with anyone, and he no doubt feared that his epilepsy, which he kept a secret, would be discovered. But he soon relaxed. He followed Hunt into the field for ten days, and entered notes on his painting technique in a comical *Ye Booke of Hunte*. Millais spent a day with them, and Martineau also came down for a visit. Tennyson was invited, but could not come. They were all eager to illustrate his poetry, and some of the Brotherhood did so for the Moxon edition of 1857; Lear's illustrations, in quite another vein, became one of the grand projects of his life. He never finished them, but a few were published posthumously in 1889.[21]

Over the course of their month together, Hunt and Lear forged a genial and close friendship, one that was to prove lifelong and that had none of the covert feeling that troubled Lear's relationships with Lushington and Fortescue. Lear taught Hunt a great deal about poetry and music, and Hunt acknowledged as much, although privately he had no very great opinion of Lear's painting. Lear declined to think of himself as a Pre-Raphaelite Brother, but called himself a Son instead, and nicknamed Hunt "Daddy," with Millais and Woolner as his "Uncles." They were all much younger than he, and therein lay the joke, which he repeated in the limericks, where certain Old Men and Young Ladies behave like children and an avuncular and singularly childlike nonsense poet presides over all.

In the autumn of 1852 they left the farm. Lear stayed on in Hastings to paint a fig tree in the garden of Frederick North, the local member of Parliament, one of whose daughters, Catherine, was to marry John Addington Symonds. Lear and she were close friends later, and wrote light verse together. Marianne, the younger sister, was Lear's special friend at this time, and she recalled in her memoirs how he would wander into the sitting room at dusk and sing Tennyson's songs for hours, "composing as he went on, and picking out accompaniments by ear, putting the greatest expression and passion into the most sentimental words. He often set me laughing; then he would say I was not worthy of them, and would continue with intense pathos of expression and gravity of face, while he substituted 'Hey Diddle Diddle, the Cat and the Fiddle,' or some other nonsensical words to the same air."[22] Lear set many of the poet laureate's lyrics to his own airs. In 1853 he published some of them, including "Tears, Idle Tears" and "Sweet and Low," the cover sheet of which is visible in the foreground of Holman Hunt's painting *The Awakened Conscience* (1852). They were the only settings favored by Tennyson himself. In fact, the tunes sound rather conventional and sentimental to the modern ear.

Lear returned to London in February 1853, and took new rooms at 65 Oxford Terrace. At first, things seemed brighter for him. He was working on paintings for the two major London exhibitions at the Royal Academy and the British Institution. He sold a large work to Richard Bethell, later Lord Westbury, the Lord Chancellor, and with a new sense of independence and direction, he finally left the Academy school. Hunt was now his sole tutor. In the spring, the British Institution accepted his *Mountains of Thermopylae*, and he felt greatly cheered; a few weeks later, the Academy agreed to hang *The Quarries of Syracuse*, although Lear was not entirely pleased with the way it had turned out.

Just as it looked as though he was about to become a settled and happy professional painter, "the morbids" returned. He helped his sister Sarah and her husband pack up and set sail for New Zealand. She had been his only real sister and he was distressed to see her go. He spent the rest of the summer in a state of misery. He went down to Windsor and tried to finish a commission to paint the castle; then he went to Leicestershire to work on one of his larger oils, of the temple of Apollo at Bassae, which he had visited on that idyllic expedition with Lushington. He wrote to Emily Tennyson how tired he was and how much he longed for both the sun and a regular living. With his depression, his health began to deteriorate. He felt that his four years in England had been too confining. His study at the Antique School had been a mistake, the whole Academy plan had been abandoned, the human figure remained a mystery to him. His landscapes were still empty of life. However close his comradeship with the great Brotherhood, the exhilaration soon wore off and the truth showed through—he could not paint well, and life remained utterly bewildering. He needed warmth, distant lands and empty horizons—the large spaces of exile—for room to reflect, and perhaps also to forget.

He made swift plans to visit Egypt and Palestine. Hunt agreed to join him when he had finished *The Light of the World*. On December 6, 1853,

Lear set sail for Alexandria. It was five years since his first visit to Egypt, and he was dazzled. He saw the sights of Cairo for a few days and then joined a large party of English tourists who were going up the Nile. The teeming river life fascinated him, and he started painting again, though he felt that water colors could not do justice to the vividness of the landscape. He soon disliked his bourgeois companions, and felt lonelier than on any of his rougher, solitary journeys in the past. They diluted his excitement with their insipid chatter and shallow curiosity. He was not a tourist! He went with them as far as Aswan and the first cataract, and then left them to visit the oasis home of Isis at Philae, a "fairy island" like Corfu. He stayed there for ten days, camping out happily in the great temple of Isis. On the journey downstream, he spent another ten days exploring the ruined temples at Thebes and the tombs of the Valley of the Kings. He grew a beard and for the first time let it remain when he returned to civilization. Hunt was waiting for him in Cairo when he arrived in the middle of March 1854.

Then, suddenly and inexplicably, Lear decided not to accompany Hunt to Jerusalem, but to ship home instead. Once before, in 1849, he had planned to go with a friend to the Holy Land, and had come this far only to turn back at the last moment. He made the excuse that he had run out of money, when both he and Hunt knew perfectly well that he could easily borrow, as he had done many times before. Rather, there was something about Egypt that made him pause. To go on, or to turn back? To commit himself to real self-discovery, or to prefer the safety of home? Twice more he would behave in exactly the same way.

He reached England at the end of April 1854, his fourth homecoming. In a few weeks he had finished the commission Lord Derby had given him to paint Windsor Castle. But his chest began to trouble him, and he left England in August for a walking tour of the Alps with his old friend Bernard Senior. He wanted to go with Lushington on a tour of the Pyrenees, but Lushington's sister fell ill in Malta and he had to fetch her home. Lear's spirits were raised a little by the Alpine sublime, however. In six months he had exchanged a view of Philae for a view of Interlaken. Whatever it was he was seeking, he had been seeking it actively; and for the moment he had succeeded in shaking off the depression that had settled so heavily on him the previous year.

But back in London for the winter of 1854–1855, the morbids returned with a vengeance, and "the demon" with them. It was perhaps the worst winter of his life. His lungs were in such poor condition that he had to spend most of his days indoors, where he toiled without much success on the large oil of Bassae and turned out £5 "pot-boilers" to pay his way. He now understood—clearly and forever—that he could not stay in England another winter. He was condemned by ill health, depression and financial necessity to a life of exile. It would be a mistake, perhaps, to exaggerate the extent to which either Lear's health or his ambivalent feelings about the high society in which he moved determined this condition of alienation. He was in many ways a remarkably strong man, and intensely companionable. Perhaps he could have made a place for himself at home if he had really wanted to. But there was a deep longing in him for foreign landscapes with their ruined temples, holy mountains and desolate pastoral expanses. He was compelled to leave England for reasons deeper than he could admit or recognize.

In June 1885 he went to a stag party which Wilkie Collins gave for Millais, who was about to marry Effie Ruskin. Afterwards, Lear wrote to Tennyson, "I feel woundily like a spectator—all through my life—of what goes on amongst those I know:—very little an actor."[23] It was the price he paid, this isolation in company, for being the court jester—always putting himself out to entertain, always unsure of the constancy or depth of the friendship offered him in return. He nearly went down to Farringford to stay the summer with the Tennysons. Instead, he chose to wander once more from place to place trying to be happy, without much success. Eventually, he turned up at Lushington's home, Park House, only to find himself unwanted. Frank's brother Henry was dying, so the household was worried and gloomy. When Henry died in August, Emily Tennyson wrote to Lear, guessing how badly he had been treated, "I have a dim sad feeling we must help each other and love each other."[24] She accepted his confidences and understood the depth of his love for Frank. She confided her own feelings of loneliness when her husband was away and exclaimed, regarding the bond between them, "Dear Mr. Lear why do I say all this to you but from a feeling you are not to be always 'alone' and you must now sympathize prophetically with me."[25]

In the autumn she invited him down with Frank and tried to interest him in a Miss Cotton. He was overjoyed to be with Frank and Emily; Miss Cotton left him cold. In his thank-you letter he wrote:

> According to the morbid nature of the animal, I even complain sometimes that such rare flashes of light as such visits are to me, make the path darker after they are over:—a bright blue and green landscape with purple hills, and winding rivers, and unexplored forests, and airy downs, and trees and birds, and all sorts of calm repose,—exchanged for a dull dark plain, horizonless, pathless, and covered with clouds above, while beneath are brambles and weariness.[26]

These seem to be some of "the views and feelings of landscape" which he had recognized, during his convalescence in Constantinople, "to exist within" him[27]—they are our interior views of his soul. The sad "English" view is easy enough to understand. But it is disturbing to notice that the happy "abroad" one, for all its brilliance and tranquillity, is remote and unpeopled. Lear's ideal, had it come true, would have disappointed him cruelly. It was perhaps just as well that he never mastered the human figure. Such was the emptiness in his heart, he would have drawn himself a ghost.

But there was Emily to confide in now, and his feelings for Frank to lead him on.

1855 to 1861

Early in 1855, Lushington accepted a post as Judge of the Supreme Court of the Ionian Islands. He was to be based on Corfu. For Lear, it was a happy turn of events. He remembered the island as a paradise. Perhaps he would be able to recreate the Arcadian spring of 1849. At least he would be able to escape another English winter, and in the company of the person he most cared for. He went to see Frank in the autumn and it was agreed that they should leave together.

On the overland journey Frank was kind. But after they had arrived, at the year's end, Lear saw little of him: he moved in higher, more official society. Lear found himself thoroughly alone. He was farther than ever from his Arcadia, and as the dream shattered, he was close to madness. He strode for hours up and down his room with tears streaming down his face. Or he lay on his bed and stared at the ceiling. For the first month, it rained incessantly.

Then life slowly improved. By the end of January 1856, he was caught up in the small social whirl of the island, and he began to sell his drawings. In February he turned down an offer to become director of the art department in the university: he valued his independence too highly. In April he moved to larger, lighter rooms, and waited for his canvases to arrive from England. He decided to paint a huge landscape from above the village of Ascension; his plan was to win instant fame in one of the big exhibitions back in London. And his spirits were greatly cheered by his springtime wanderings over the island.

He hired a Suliot servant, Giorgio Kokali, perhaps because Suliot guards had ridden with Byron in his last days. Giorgio stayed with him for twenty-seven years, his one lasting companion, yet hardly a companion. Though liberal for his time, Lear had conventional ideas about the nature of service. Giorgio had to keep his distance. About this time, too, Lear made friends with the Cortazzi family. The mother was English and a relation of the Hornbys, and Lear got on particularly well with the two daughters, Helena and Madeleine. He confessed in a letter to Holman Hunt that he had fallen half in love with Helena, who could recite the whole of *In Memoriam* by heart. She was a straightforward, independent young woman. She liked the people he liked and was interested in painting, music and poetry. He wanted to propose, but he hesitated and talked himself out of it. He worked on his Ascension painting and sent two oils to be hung in the London exhibitions.

In the middle of the summer, Lushington proposed a new expedition, and Lear suggested they make for Mount Athos. He wanted to try, for the third time, to climb it. They crossed over to the mainland in Frank's yacht *The Midge*, and Lear found the traveling much easier than on his 1848 visit. They walked fifty miles from Salonika, and arrived at last on the monks' territory at the foot of the oldest seat of the ancient gods, the summit of which could be seen from Olympus and the plains of Troy. Like so many of the places Lear visited, Athos was grand both by nature and by spiritual tradition. One recalls his pilgrimages, for such they were, to the temples of Isis at Philae and of Apollo at Bassae, to Parnassus and Olympus, his lingering in the holy cities of Rome and Constantinople, as well as his so far abortive attempts to reach Jerusalem and the Holy Land. Athos, and all the mountains, made Lear aware of his inner needs. They provoked spiritual reflections, they tugged at his heart, for he was a deeply, though informally, religious man. In this he was greatly influenced by his sister Ann, whose Christianity was of a loving and practical kind. He had no sympathy with the dissenting views of Ellen and Sarah, and he loathed the hypocrisies of churghgoing as he knew it at home and in the English communities abroad.

Athos inspired him, but it also greatly angered him, for it sheltered, in no fewer than twenty monasteries, a great number of monks who lived, so Lear felt, "in an atmosphere of falsehood and ignorance . . . falsehood, because I am positive that living alone—banishing all women whom God has made to be our equals and companions,—passing life in everlasting repetition of formal prayers—in fact—turning God's will and works upside down—I say this is falsehood—though it may be ignorance as well."[28] It is not hard to see why he was upset. He too was guilty of "living alone," and for spiritual reasons. He too was compelled to let the warm, human, intelligible world recede in order to contemplate the mysteries; and it had been harder for him, since he had not taken refuge in the safety of ritual or formal belief. He had remained more open, and in his wanderings he experienced daily the pains of solitude, never reconciled to the fact that it was through isolation that he knew he had to find himself, that desolation should breed wonder, that the truth he sought should lie beyond the safety and happiness of human society.

Unreconciled, still open, he preferred to flounder from one holy mountain to another, from one holy city to another, sketching, dabbing in a few pale elementary colors, bewildered in both his life and his art by a sense of something cruelly missing in moments which seemed most exalting. Hence the crude ghosts in the foregrounds of his landscapes. Hence the dependence of his art—the painting, the cartoons, the poems—on absence and loss; and beyond, on a sense of transport or wonder, a celebration of something just over the rim of what is seen and known, warm and intelligible. Lear was distressed by the monks and their mountains because they showed him the necessity and the uses of his own loneliness, and they spurred him on a spiritual pilgrimage which he knew to be more honest, as it was more painful, than theirs.

On his way home to Corfu, he paid a swift visit to Troy, returning at the beginning of autumn, 1856, in excellent health and happy mood. There was a large earth tremor just after he arrived, and he moved to safer rooms, near Lushington. But the judge remained cold, as Lear wrote mournfully to Emily. He quickly painted some local views to pay for his trip. Winter turned dark and miserable, and he felt imprisoned. He spent a few rainy days with Lushington in Albania just after Christmas, and this cheered him. By the time spring came round, he was feeling happier altogether. He had been brushing up his Greek. He was now fluent in the modern language, and his knowledge of the classical was good enough for him to read the New Testament in the original—the realization of an old ambition. And his Ascension painting pleased him.

With his life in its usual springtime appearance of good order, he thought of visiting the holy places of Palestine, which he had already missed on two occasions. He tried to persuade Clowes, a friend from Knowsley days, to come with him. But Clowes would not go, and so, starved for the company of his friends, he postponed the trip and decided to spend the summer in England. He wanted to publish his drawings of Mount Athos. He had been invited, also, to contribute to an international exhibition in Manchester. Just before he left, he sold the Ascension painting for 500 guineas. At least he had no need to worry about "tin" for a while.

He arrived in England in May 1857. It was his seventh homecoming since the first tour of Continental zoos with John Gould a quarter of a century earlier. He found Fortescue in love with the wealthy, twice-widowed Lady Waldegrave. She had houses in Oxfordshire and London and also owned Walpole's Strawberry Hill. Lear was introduced, and though he found her patronizing, she was at least a generous patron and gave him two commissions for paintings of Palestine. Fortescue invited him to his Irish estate at Ardee, where he spent a quiet and happy later summer, painting a little and taking long walks with his friend in the evenings. He talked constantly of Lushington, but Fortescue did not understand and encouraged him instead to pursue Helena Cortazzi. His old friend Robert Hornby died, and he was greatly saddened. One evening he sat up very late with Fortescue, reading *In Memoriam* aloud from start to finish. In October he went to see *The Quarries of Syracuse* hung in the exhibition at Manchester, and he visited Knowsley. He lingered late into the autumn, then reluctantly headed back to Corfu. He knew that the Cortazzis had left and that he could expect to be lonely. Moreover, he had not found the energy while at home to publish his drawings of Athos.

Lushington was more distant than ever. But instead of allowing sadness to sweep him under, Lear fought bravely against the morbids. He stayed indoors and read St. John in the Greek, as well as a book on Palestine, Burton's *Mecca*, and the Brontës, Shakespeare, Rabelais, Tennyson and Ruskin. He stopped going to church. He could no longer stand the hypocrisy and he was thinking more deeply about his beliefs. He told himself that if Helena Cortazzi had not left the island, he would certainly have proposed to her. Frank grew colder with each meeting, and Lear's only comforts were in his reading and in his preparation for his Holy Land trip.

Easter 1858 came round and he found himself with Giorgio at Jaffa, joining the Easter pilgrims on the road from Ramleh to Jerusalem. The countryside reminded him of the Roman Campagna. After a long, hard climb he at last caught sight of the Holy City, but "with a great hollow between *me* and *it*, as I expected."[29] Next morning, waking in Jerusalem, he had an epileptic seizure and later wrote in his diary, "O! the strange ups and downs." He climbed the Mount of Olives, "every step bringing fresh beauty to the city uprising behind."[30] One thinks of the young Wordsworth rowing away from the lake shore and watching the mountain rising sublimely from behind the lower bluffs. "At the top, by the Church of Ascension, the view is wonderfully beautiful indeed.—Turning round,—lo! the Dead Sea!—clear pale milky far blue, with farther off all rosy mountains—fretted and carved in lovely shadow forms,—this long long simple line melting into air towards the desert."[30] Two days later he sketched these "most curious and sublime views," though with little success, he felt. All he could get of them were "bits and wanderings."[31] This desert sublime puzzled him; there was something difficult, undrawable and indescribable about it. He went down to Bethlehem and visited Hebron.

Then he arranged an expedition south to Petra. It was an expensive and dangerous journey, but when he arrived it was more than worth the trouble. Here was Shelley's desert sublime! "The slow advance" through the wadi "chills with a feeling of strange solitude the intruder into the loneliness of this bygone world, where on every side are tokens of old greatness." The ruins of antiquity in the emptiness of the desert, old glories and unspeakable loneliness—it was "a magical condensation of beauty and wonder." But he discovered that he had not the art of Shelley to record it. He was too overwhelmed to do much sketching, for how could he represent "the sound of the clear river rushing among the ruins of the fallen city?"[32] During the night a band of Arabs gathered and demanded a levy for crossing their land. Lear refused to pay, but the next day more Arabs gathered, and after menacing him and his guards and taking all his money, they let him free to hurry back to Jerusalem. He was shaken but unharmed.

Back in Jerusalem the Easter crowds had gone and Lear had room to explore. But the poverty depressed him, and the Christian sectarianism, too. He went to Galilee and Nazareth and explored Jericho, but turned back when he was robbed a second time. On his birthday he took the steamer for Beirut. "Jaffa soon faded away—but only the long long long line of Judaean hills broke the blue of sea and sky. . . . Evening and night very long—and torturing. —I did not lie down till 12."[33] Two crosses, for two fits, follow this diary entry. In Lebanon he sketched the cedars in the mountains and then traveled inland to yet another holy city, Damascus. It was enchanting and he would have stayed, but the heat was too exhausting, and he returned swiftly to Corfu. It had been a brief and confusing expedition, exhilarating but also fatiguing and frustrating. It had hardly made the way clearer for him.

Once back in Corfu, the morbids descended again, and Lear found that Lushington had grown so tired of island life that he had resigned. In August 1858, they returned to England together. Lear went to stay at Campden Hill with Hunt, who cheered him up, and he visited Helena Cortazzi, who aroused in him his old feelings. But he did not propose. He fretted, and decided to spend the winter in Rome with Clowes. Corfu had yet to prove a success. This time, perhaps Rome would work for him. Before he left, he went to the zoo and drew the vultures.

He took new rooms near the Spanish Steps at the end of 1858, and made a real effort to settle firmly. He spent rather more than he could afford on furniture, and he summoned Giorgio from Corfu. On Wednesdays and Saturdays he held open days in his studio, but he managed to sell only a few of the Palestine and Egypt paintings, and he found his clients tiresome in the extreme. They were mostly "swells" and boors. He visited the Stratford Cannings, who were wintering there, and also the Brownings, only to be appalled by the crowds of sycophants and snobs who surrounded them. One afternoon the Prince of Wales, then seventeen, called and asked to see his work and seemed genuinely pleased. Then rumors of war sent his clients packing home to England. Lear was left with a two-year lease and no business. He scorned his client's alarm until war was declared at the end of April 1859, and then he too left for England. Gloomily he wrote in his diary, "I recall winters and lives in many places and remember as much ill in all, perhaps."[34]

Again, he went the rounds of the country houses, playing the court jester, infinitely obliging, cheerful company, but inside, weary and dazed. Lewes, Wells, Winwick, Farringford—a merry-go-round, and secretly a bore. But he had a happy time with the Tennysons, for once. Alfred took him on long walks and recited his new *Idylls of the King*. Lear entertained Hallam and Lionel, and he confided in Emily, who struck him as even more saintly than ever. He was in debt by now, but with each visit he collected fresh commissions. In midsummer he left London, which he found distracting, and took rooms in St. Leonard's in Sussex, in the countryside he had first loved, and there he set about to clear his debts. He rose at five for the first light and worked through till half-past seven in the evening. It was a very beautiful summer, and the unexpected warmth and the hard work buoyed him. In July Napoleon made peace with the Austrians, and it looked, for the moment anyway, safe to return to Rome. Lear went up to town to enlist subscribers so that the Fitzwilliam Museum in Cambridge could buy his painting of the temple of Apollo. It had become his tribute to Frank; and on December 9, 1859, he took the train up to Cambridge to see where it would be hung. He also had his musical settings of *Idylls of the King* published, and just before Christmas, was seen off for the Continent by Lushington himself.

Lear took the express to Marseilles and had a rough crossing to Civitá Vecchia. Winter in Rome was long and dull. He saw himself wandering away as far as Japan or New York, Paraguay or Tobago. But he stayed. He had his commissions to work on, the rent paid in advance and £350 saved up. He planned another large exhibition painting.

With the spring of 1860, he sent Giorgio back to his family in Corfu and returned to London. It was his tenth homecoming. In June he went with Frank to Farringford to visit the Tennysons. He was happy to see Emily—"she *is* an angel, and no mistake";[35] but when the photographer Julia Cameron arrived and forced him to perform his Tennyson settings on the piano, his spirits sank. Alfred made matters worse by discoursing after dinner on "criticism—alas!"[36] Lear could not stand his grumpiness. There was a disastrous afternoon walk: "we three set out to walk again, but AT was most disagreeably querulous and irritating and would return, chiefly because he saw people approaching. But FL would not go back, and led zygzagwise towards the sea—AT snubby and cross always."[37] Tennyson forced them to come back by a muddy shortcut, and was furious when they ran into some of the local villagers returning from church. "Verily," the exasperated Lear wrote in his diary before bed that night, "this is a wondrous man . . . So I came to bed!—and I believe that this is my last visit to Farringford: nor can I wish it otherwise all things considered."[37] But as he returned to town, he found how painful it was for him to leave Emily, and he felt he had perhaps been too hard in "not reflecting on much of AT's miseries."[38] Of his feelings for Frank, he wrote nothing. He went to see Ann. She looked old and worn.

In August he went to stay at Nuneham with Fortescue and Lady Waldegrave, who had been very pleased with the paintings of Palestine he had done for her. When he arrived, however, he found that the large house party, of which he had supposed he would be a member, was decamping to Strawberry Hill; he was expected to stay behind with the governess and to do two paintings of the grounds. He had never been so obviously snubbed even in the early days at Knowsley, and Fortescue seemed not to notice. Lear stayed on in misery for a few days, did a few drawings to work from, and returned to London, where he encouraged himself with plans for some large paintings for the exhibitions—a nine-foot *Cedars of Lebanon*, and a seven-foot *Masada and the Dead Sea*. He found some cedars at Walton-on-Thames and put up in a hotel nearby. He painted hard during the day, and at night set aside an hour for translating Plato and another for penning out his Mount Athos drawings. And, to amuse himself, he composed some new nonsense. He had been writing new limericks from time to time in idle moments on his wanderings. Now he worked at them with joyful diligence. He wanted to bring out a new and enlarged edition of *A Book of Nonsense*, and he decided to offer it outright to a publisher instead of publishing it himself through a printseller like Maclean. He worked on *The Cedars* till the year was over, returning to London in the middle of the winter.

In the spring of 1861 he rented new rooms at Stratford Place, and Ann came and sat with him while he worked. He held open days. At times the rooms were crammed, at times empty for hours. He would while away the empty moments drawing for his new nonsense book. Often he walked Ann back to Islington where she was living, and she told him about his brothers and sisters and of the family days before he was born. She was seventy and very frail. He was nearly fifty.

On March 4 she fell ill, and he went every day to her bedside to bring her flowers and hold her hand. "What a blessing you are here!" she said, "—not among the Arabs!"[39] Even at the end her first thought was for him: "Edward, my precious—take care you do not hurt your head against the bed iron."[40] On March 11, she died.

> Came back at 12. Still she breathed, but very feebly:—I could not go in again: it seemed so strange! a tearing and grinding my own heart: yet I would have done so, could I have done good. But I said—I will walk outside—and you, Mrs. Woollett, put down the blinds when all is over. At 12.15 they were closed!
> Had I believed she would have died, so, I would have sat still by her dear side:—but I feared it would have been terrible. Whereas, God be thanked for such a mercy—she died as a little infant falls asleep! Painless—motionless!
> As her life has been one of good and blessing so is her death.
> But she is gone. And I have now no sister Ann to love me and think of me.[41]

When he sorted through her belongings, he found she had kept everything he had ever sent her.

Emily Tennyson at once asked him down to Farryingford, but when he arrived he saw that he was not really wanted. Only she cared, only she received him with decency. He was put up in a nearby hotel. He slipped away without saying goodbye on March 24, and wandered from one friend's house to another, inconsolable.

1861 to 1870

About this time, Millais asked him to dinner. Lear came away disliking him, and feeling that his success—he had just sold *Apple Blossoms* for 450 guineas—was undeserved. Stubbornly, and in vain, Lear decided to ask 700 guineas for *The Cedars*. Millais was popular; Lear was practically unknown, and he was pricing himself out of the market. Perhaps it was a way of striking back proudly at a harsh world. In the summer of 1861 he made a brief tour of Switzerland and Tuscany. In August he went back to St. Leonard's and worked on paintings of Florence. *The Cedars*, on exhibition in Liverpool, was praised in the highest of terms, but no one bought it.

In October Lear tried to sell the expanded edition of *A Book of Nonsense* first to Smith & Elder, then to Routledge & Warne, but to his dismay neither publisher wanted it. So he arranged for Dalziel to make wood engravings of the drawings—they would be cheaper than lithographs—and to print and bind the book. Routledge then agreed to take one thousand copies for distribution. The book was issued at Christmas and it sold five hundred copies in a few days. But the reviews were bad, and when Lear returned to Corfu in the spring of 1862 after a dull winter, he had to sell the rights to Routledge for £125, since Dalziel was pressing him for money and Routledge had paid him none. He showed Routledge's receipt to his friends the Prescotts, and he was angry and distressed to see they considered the success trifling. By now, he was beginning to think of his nonsense as something more than a sideline.

He had two exhibition paintings that summer, but they were hung badly in dark corners. Worse still, Tom Taylor attacked *The Cedars* in the review columns of *The Times*. Lear was now in bad financial straits. He had not sold a large work since 1860, and his only income was £50 from Ann's small estate. He had invested a modest sum against the day when his sight might be too poor for him to paint, and he did not dare break into it. It had been folly indeed to spend so much time and expense on one huge painting in the hope of making his name and fortune in one coup. The exhibitions were over by October. *The Cedars* remained unsold. And, as it turned out, he had got the worst end of the deal with Routledge. *A Book of Nonsense* was to go through nineteen editions in his own lifetime but he got not another penny out of it.

There was news at once sad and happy when Fortescue confided in him that he was engaged to marry Lady Waldegrave. Lear's thoughts naturally turned again to marriage, and he went to visit his old friend Richard Bethell, now Lord Westbury, the Lord Chancellor, whose twenty-four-year-old daughter Augusta greatly admired him. She was warm, open and encouraging, but he did not get to the point of proposing to her. Instead, he returned for the winter of 1862–1863 to Corfu, where on his last stay he had met Evelyn Baring, a cousin of his old friend Thomas Baring, Lord Northbrook. They had become close friends. Baring was thirty years younger than Lear, and he was a strong and a warm man, easily able to understand the deeper side of Lear's nature.

Back on Corfu, Lear invented a new winter system of working, a kind of production line. He prepared sixty mounted sheets of paper, drew broad outlines on each, then filled in all the blues, browns and greens in order until each landscape was finished. He hoped to sell each painting for 10 guineas and to repair his broken finances at one stroke. He was surprised that under this new regimen he was more contented than he had felt for many years. If the production was mechanical, it was only superficially so, and he was imposing upon himself a speed and spontaneity which were the source of his real talents. In sixty days he had finished the sixty "tyrants," as he called them.[42] By the end of February 1863, they were all on display in his studio, which he opened to the public in March. It must have been a strange two months—sixty images growing with complete regularity before his eyes, all coming into full focus at exactly the same time. In a few days he sold a number of them for £120.

He began to get out more. Sir Percy Shelley, the poet's son, took him yachting and had his musical setting of "O world, O life, O time!" written down. He also became friends with a family called De Vere, and made many nonsense poems and drawings for the daughter, Mary. He had never had so happy a winter. He began to think seriously of settling in Corfu and of giving up his summer trips to England, since he saw his friends for only a few hours, if at all, and the expense was always emptying his pocket. At the end of March 1863, he dismantled his exhibition of tyrants and went on a tour of the Ionian Islands, drawing and preparing material for another travel book.

Back in England for the summer, he found that his large paintings which had been on display all year at Stratford Place had not been sold. He started work on the Ionian Islands book. He visited Ann's grave one day, and walking back through Holloway, he came upon his childhood home, Bowman's Lodge. It was up for sale for building material. He looked over it—his own room, Henry's, Mary's, Ann's, his mother's rooms, the nursery, the painting room, the "dark" room, the playground. It was full of names and fifty-year-old memories.

On December 1, 1863, *Views in the Seven Ionian Islands* was published on the basis of subscriptions which Lear had gathered arduously by writing six hundred letters. He was able to put aside £300 at three per cent, and just before the New Year he left for Corfu. In the spring of 1864 he went with Evelyn Baring to Athens. As their boat sailed away from Corfu, he wrote an early version of his nonsense poem "The Cummerbund" on deck under the stars. Athens disappointed him, so he took Giorgio to Crete—and there too he was disappointed. The island looked very barren, it rained, the ruins were invisible. But in mid-May, just after he had turned fifty-two, he reached Mount Ida and found himself looking down "on the birthplace of Minerva, and the burial place of Jupiter," and he felt that "few scenes can be grander and fresher than this."[43] On the morning of May 15, he climbed joyfully over the mountain.

> Corn—Corn. Anatolian sheep. Wide, gulfy, shadeless hills, hiding Ida . . . most lovely green undrawable vales . . . Lovely leafy thickets and glens. Birds! birds! . . . The vast multitude of blackbirds, nightingales, and many other sorts of birds is wonderful and most delightful, as is this mountain scene: sitting below oaks—a cornfield sloping down to the stream . . . It is noon; and considering how unwell I was yesterday—happiness abounds . . . 1 p.m. the longer one looks at this place—the lovelier it seems . . .

But in the afternoon the morbids returned: "1.30 . . . a kind of sadness—'tears, idle tears' comes over me, so much here reminds me of England, and of other days."[44] The birds, as always, transported him, but not for long. The sublime had once more turned out to be "undrawable," and too much like home to release him from the burden of past sorrows or to clear up his present bewilderment. In his drawings of Mount Ida there is too much foreground or middleground and too little of the mountain itself.

At the end of May 1864, he left for England. He kept his rooms at Stratford Place as a gallery for his large paintings, especially *The Cedars* and *Masada*, and for the work he hoped to have ready during the winter. He conceived of a large exhibition of small water-color drawings, to be ready by the next summer, and he visited all his friends. Then he went south to Nice in November, and took expensive rooms for the winter. The year before, he had run off sixty of his so-called tyrants. Now, planning to complete four times that number, he set out his paper in batches of eighty. On December 2 he had reached "the 18th Day of 240 Tyrants."[45] By the first of the year he had done 144 of these pot-boilers, as well as a number of smaller paintings of Nice, which he sold at £5 each to the local "swells." Lord and Lady Fitzwilliam paid £100 for a number of them, and he made friends with their son, and wrote for him, in February, "The History of Seven Families of the Lake Pipple-Popple," one of his nonsense prose pieces. He saw a little of Helena Cortazzi, who happened to be wintering there; but he no longer thought of marrying her. Gussie Bethell passed through on her way to Rome, and his affection for her deepened.

In April 1865 he was back in England, finishing his tyrants. They sold fast. The Prince of Wales bought ten drawings, and there was a fresh commission for a painting of Jerusalem. In the middle of the summer he went to stay with the Bethells with the intention of proposing to Gussie.

But he could not summon the resolve. When he visited them again in September, Gussie played the piano for him. Again, he nearly proposed. But he could think only of the danger that the marriage might not work, that there would only be greater misery. Perhaps also his love for Lushington and his epilepsy, still a secret, stood in the way. He faltered, accepted a commission from Lady Waldegrave to do a painting in Venice, and left to winter in Italy.

He disliked Venice, beautiful though it was. He saw his painting of the city as "Man-work—not God work,"[46] and he was interested only in the sublime, in landscapes infused with at least a hint of heaven. He moved to Malta, hoping to be closer to Evelyn Baring. But the Barings had sailed out to the West Indies to assist the commission set up to investigate Governor Eyre's suppression of the Jamaican rebellion. In three months, Lear's paintings brought in only £25. He sailed home in April 1866 by way of Corfu, and was freshly amazed at the island's beauty: "Can I give *no* idea of this Paradise island to others? Would Gussie like to live here?"[47]

He went at once to the Bethells on his return to England, and he dined several times with Gussie. But he did not have the courage to propose. He asked Lady Waldegrave for advice. She seems to have been an unfortunate influence in his life: she patronized him, and she had sent him off to Venice when he seemed on the verge of proposing the previous autumn. Now she advised him that since Gussie had no money, marriage would be impractical. If only Lear had asked Emily Tennyson instead.

In his anxiety he developed an itching skin and neuralgia. On October 1, 1866, he "rose early—and absolutely finished the last of the 240 Tyrants."[48] He gave a batch of 250 to Maclean's Gallery for exhibition during the winter. He also offered some new limericks to Routledge's. They refused him at first—and then accepted. He was depressed by the cold, the smoke, the damp and the darkness.

At the end of November he again visited the Bethells. In the evening, "upstairs—some music and some talk: little with Gussie—and perhaps 'so, best'."[49] After dining out with most of his friends, he suddenly set out on a fourth expedition to Egypt and Palestine—he could not live with these English failures—no wife, no lover, no fame, no money. Just after he left, a favorable review of the seventeenth edition of *A Book of Nonsense* appeared in *Once-a-Week.* At last he was winning a small fame, but not for his painting, not for his lifework!

In Cairo he found it would cost him nearly £400 to go up the Nile as far as the second cataract, so he wrote to eight friends asking to borrow £100 from each, confident that back in London his tyrants would sell. The brightness of the south and the teeming bird life of the river astonished him. "The myriads of pigeons! and when they fly, their shadows on the ground!"[50] The emptiness of the desert also astonished him, and the weight of the past. "Ruins of the Temples—about which there are no words to be used," at least not by "those who dare to think—or who cannot help thinking."[51] The sublime, natural and man-made, escaped him once again. How could he draw or tell of such things? The desolation was unspeakable, inside and outside. "Most lonely lonely river! The intense loneliness of the river! How can it ever have been what, when these temples were built, it needs must have been—a populous country? . . . cindery ashy hills east, sand ranges west."[52]

He revisited the island temple of Isis at Philae, and again he was overwhelmed. "I walk a little farther, and lo!—after 13 years—beautiful Philae once again!!—and more beautiful than ever. I sit and draw till 2. . . . The place seems to me, if possible more lovely than formerly; and one feels acutely how little one has done to represent such beauty. It seems to me my former drawings were not *severe* enough. . . ."[53] Abu Simbel was no less amazing, and so were Sakkara and Memphis and the Nubian desert, where again he found "loneliness extreme,—long lines of hill and river . . . a great expanse of sand—but all length and width—no height whatever. The paucity of people—of life amazes me."[54] As so often, Lear found his eye drawn horizontally off into the melting distance instead of vertically up, and the landscape was either empty of people or the people seemed merely picturesque. When he sat down to draw, the sense of wonder—in nature or in the heart—somehow slipped away. Was it severity he needed? Or new skills? Was it real inspiration he lacked, or craft? It was all very puzzling. Still, there was comfort and strength in the air. "The desert, this here perfect loneliness, is nowise sad to me:—its simplicity and silence give place to memory and thought—past and future—to act."[55] When he looked back he saw that the gloom was not unrelieved. "13 years ago! *what* changes! On the whole, I *am* happier but don't let us moralize: there are yet 215 miles to do."[56] Thousands, rather, but for now he had found space for the resolve to strive and to seek further. Meanwhile, he had started to read Pascal.

There had indeed been lighter moments of pleasure—and also vexation. An American cousin, Archie, had joined Lear for part of the expedition and had greatly tried his patience. He had turned out to be a typical tourist, fickle, inane and bored. Next to him Lear must have felt himself a real explorer. And in Luxor Lear had spent some time with an eccentric English resident, Lady Duff Gordon. One afternoon she took him to the English cemetery. They came home "round by the Nile;—the way in which she calls attention to the 'lovely rounded muscles and velvet skin' of naked men close by—and absolutely naked cox and all—is not what I like to admire in an Englishwoman."[57] Lear's primness gives him away—or is he teasing?

By April 1867 he had crossed the Sinai desert on camel and had reached Gaza. Jerusalem seemed even more beautiful than before, and Lear was deeply moved by the sight of Sephardic pilgrims praying at the Wailing Wall. The longness and the lowness of the countryside once more drew his attention: "lo! lo! the wide and lovely plain of Philistia, with the long long lines of Palestine landscape—green corn—downs—and far blue hills."[58] He pushed north to Nazareth and Galilee, only to find the road cluttered with Easter pilgrims. Suddenly he felt too exhausted to continue. His spirit—once more—had been mysteriously broken! He turned around and reached Alexandria by April 20.

Landing at Brindisi, he wandered slowly up the Aegean coast to the forest of Ravenna, through which Bryon had once ridden. At the beginning of June, Giorgio went with his family to Corfu, and Lear headed for England. And more failures?

His travels had become more frantic, his art less sure. Life, and the hope for a home and happiness and recognition, receded more and more swiftly.

The Cedars was still unsold, but enough tyrants had been bought to clear all his debts. When he made the rounds of his friends, however, he was depressed and petulant. His ties with them were weakening, and their ranks were thinning. At Strawberry Hill, Fortescue asked him to sing. For the first time in his life he refused. He was disgusted by the wealth, apathy and vanity of country-house society. Down at Farringford, he felt he should never have broken his resolve not to visit the Tennysons again. He also felt, not without some justice, that the laureate's poetry was growing stale.

Naturally his thoughts turned again to Gussie. He went down to the Bethells determined to propose. Unhappily, he decided first to consult Gussie's sister, Emma Parkyns.

> And then the talk with Emma P.—
> like a sudden spark
> Struck vainly in the night
> And back returns the dark—
> With no more hope of light.
>
> Yet after what she said a year ago—her "certainty that now A and I could not live together happily"—seems strange. Anyhow it broke up a dream rudely and sadly.[59]

Perhaps Lear would not so quickly have accepted her advice had not Gussie's father remarked emphatically to him at dinner, "She will never marry."[59] He wrote in his diary before bed, "What a horrible day," in large letters, followed by three crosses for three seizures. With her family evidently against the idea, Lear could never find the courage to propose. Lack of money was now no objection—that had been Emma's excuse before—since Gussie was to inherit £20,000 on her marriage. It is all too probable that she loved Lear and would have accepted him. But there were the demon epilepsy, Frank, the fear of desertion, the habit of solitude, the morbids: he could not ask her. He stayed on, and wrote for her brother's children "The Story of the Four Little Children Who Went Round the World." On November 7, 1867, he took his leave:

> Bkft—and much laughter: as far as I am concerned—crackling of thorns.—Had all this—could it have had—an earlier movement—well:—but now it is too late . . . a few words—but of little import with G . . . at 11 I left these splendid higgeldypiggeldy halls—Gussie and the kindly Lord W.—and all coming to the door, and so I went away—with the mind drearily tangled and numb.[60]

And then, "What is left now but to go abroad as soon as possible:—yet where to go?"

He went to Cannes for the winter. There he had light and air and clients. He sold little, but made friends with John Addington Symonds, who had married Catherine North. They talked of Byron and Shelley and the new poets Swinburne and Walt Whitman. They spent many happy family evenings together. Lear and Symonds were of similar temperament and background; each had been separated from his mother in early childhood, and both were victims of psychosomatic illness. Symonds too was anxious about receiving affection and was easily depressed, and he was also homosexual, though more overtly than Lear.

Just before Christmas Lear wrote "The Owl and the Pussy-cat," a small picture poem, for Symonds's daughter Janet. We know from his diary that as early as the autumn of 1860 he was trying his hand at something larger than the limerick, and there is a hint in a letter to Fortescue which suggests he had been working on some of his later poems for some time before his stay in Cannes. He writes he has "been preparing a little book for some time past, (but which unfortunately cannot be brought out for some months) the originality of which will at least strike those who may not approve of all its contents."[61] His earliest recorded departure from the limerick seems to be the prose nonsense of "The Story of the Seven

Families from Lake Pipple-Popple," written in February 1865, the year *Alice in Wonderland* was published. In August 1866, he wrote "Mr. Lear, the Polly and the Pussybite," and in December 1867, the first version of "The Owl and the Pussy-cat." He wrote most of the longer nonsense poems between 1866 and 1876; and for the first two or three years of this creative decade, he gave up painting almost entirely in favor of sketching, drawing—and nonsense.

At Cannes he heard that Lady Ashburton had bought *The Cedars* for £200. It was less than one-third the price he was asking, but he was nearly penniless, since his tyrants were not selling, and he was more than glad to get it off his hands. He had a good opinion of the buyer, too, and was relieved that the painting would be hung well and properly appreciated. As the New Year came in he began to sell some water colors and once again escaped having to borrow or declare himself bankrupt. He set about finishing his journals of Crete and Egypt, so that by the spring he had eight unpublished journals. He then decided to write a ninth, about Corsica, and he left to explore the island in April. He did 350 sketches in a month, and he wrote the new journal too. He returned to Cannes and then went to London.

The rest of the year was wasted in dealing with publishers. Symonds introduced him to Smith of Smith & Elder, who suggested the Corsican journal should be done in one volume with wood engravings. Lear agreed reluctantly—the engravings would scarcely do his drawings justice. He ran up a £130 bill for them, took them to Smith, and the whole project was rejected. After Lear had recovered from the shock and disappointment, he set out to find a new publisher. By a happy chance that was to prove even happier in the future, he found a man called Robert John Bush who would publish his book so long as it was kept as cheap as possible, with newer, less expensive blocks. Lear ended his lease of Stratford Place, and in December went back to Cannes to finish the journal and to try to find a cheap engraver.

In February 1869, he returned to his painting. He mass-produced sixty new tyrants. Prosper Mérimée, who had become a friend, suggested a firm of Paris engravers. These cuts turned out to be crude, as Lear had secretly expected. He took them to London, nevertheless, and accepted Bush's estimate for the job. He stayed with Lushington, who helped him polish the manuscript. Since Frank had married, their friendship, which the Corfu period had damaged, had improved. Lear was relieved, in fact, that his love had found no response. Through his aristocratic connections he had found Frank a good job as a magistrate, and he was godfather to both his daughters, first Clare, who died, and then Gertrude, for whom he wrote "The Pobble Who Has No Toes." Back in London, with the text of the Corsican journal prepared, he started to collect subscribers by writing hundreds of letters, just as he had done for his book on the Ionian Islands.

He visited the Tennysons at their new home at Aldsworth. Waking on the first morning of his stay: "At 5.30 the vast—for it is really—vast—plain was wondrous to see. Doubtless there is something in SPACE by which the mind (leastways *my* mind,) can work and expand."[62] The next day he and Alfred quarreled, but Emily patched things up. "The Evening was very pleasant in many ways, and he was less violent than often."[63] But Lear and Tennyson never really liked each other. Tennyson was an anxious, melancholy and at times surly man. He was perhaps annoyed by the closeness of Lear's friendship with Emily. He disliked Lear's facetiousness, his fondness for puns and his liberal politics. Lear in turn deplored the poet's "slovenliness, selfishness, and morbid folly."[64] It was really only for Emily's sake that they made up.

Lear went back to town to correct the Corsican proofs. When *Journal of a Landscape Painter in Corsica* came out in time for the Christmas 1869 giftbook season, he had already returned to Cannes for another winter in exile. There he quickly painted two oils of Corsican scenes and sent them, in the spring of 1870, to the Academy, his first entries for fourteen years.

He also paused to reflect.

This time, he decided to stop once and for all—stop the endless, distracting, anxious wandering; stop the aimless, profitless speculation about his nature as an artist; stop the unhappy summers; stop the wretched winters. It was nearly ten years since Ann had died. He had not turned into a painter of any repute. He was completely alone. What did his life amount to? He had to stop.

1870 to 1880

Lear resolved no longer to "hurry on through constantly new and burningly bright scenes."[65] He would buy some land, build a house and settle down. He found a plot that he liked further along the coast at San Remo; he now had £3000 saved. All along, it seems, he had been a prudent saver and borrowed before he broke into capital. By the end of March 1870, contracts for the land and the house were signed, and that summer Lear went to the mountains near Turin. He took lodgings in a hotel which had once been a Carthusian monastery, La Certosa del Pesio. In June, he set to work busily on his nonsense. Three of the long poems of *Nonsense Songs*, his second nonsense book—"The Owl and the Pussy-cat," "The Duck and the Kangaroo" and "The Daddy Long-legs and the Fly"—had been published earlier in the year in an American magazine, *Young Folks*.[66] He worked now on alphabets, botanies, the nonsense stories and a new set of a hundred limericks.

As usual his closest friends were children. Two of them left accounts of him, both from this summer. Daisy Terry describes how he befriended her at the hotel. He "glowed, bubbled and twinkled . . . he seemed happily bathed in kindly effulgence . . . he became my sworn relative and devoted friend." He took her for walks in the forests, and they kicked the chestnut burs before them as they went, calling them "yonghy-bonghy-bòs." He sang her "The Owl and the Pussy-cat" "in a funny little crooning tune," and drew nonsense pictures. Every day he put on the lunch plate for her brother Arthur and herself a new letter of a nonsense alphabet, ending with the title page for the collection, with a portrait of himself as an "Adopty Duncle."[67] Her alphabet was published in *More Nonsense* as "The Absolutely Abstemious Ass."

Another little girl was also adopted by him later in the season. She recalled in her memoirs his "very bright eyes that seemed to be watching a pleasant comedy all the time."[68] The strange dishes and wearisome cutlery at the unmanageable lunch table inspired, she says, such nonsense plants as the "Manyforkia Spoonifolia," and many recipes in the *Nonsense Cookery*. Thereafter Lear usually spent the summers in hotels in the Swiss or Italian mountains, where he could enjoy the temperate climate and find an audience of children for his nonsense.

He wrote to Holman Hunt of his new resolve to settle down and of his plans to take commissions again and paint seriously. He could afford to live on relatively little; he no longer had the expenses of rent and travel. In 1869, the fifteenth Earl of Derby, whom Lear had entertained with the original nonsense when he was a boy, had succeeded to the title, and he commissioned him now to paint a picture of Corfu for £100. So Lear began San Remo life under the same patronage that had set him on his feet in the mid-thirties.

By October 1870, the house was still not ready, and Lear, growing fretful and sad, planned to go to America or wander even further. But he made friends with a family called Congreve, and he was pleased to hear that Fields of Boston had ordered five hundred copies of the new nonsense book. In December he received copies from Bush—who had happily agreed to be his publisher—of his second nonsense book, *Nonsense Songs*, together with the advice to hold over the limericks as a third nonsense book for the 1871 Christmas season. The reviews were not plentiful, but they were mostly favorable. They were a good housewarming present.

On March 25, 1871, he moved in at last and named the house Villa Emily after a niece in New Zealand. He had a large, bright studio with a view south to the sea. Letters arrived from Fortescue and his other English friends, and he delighted in sitting under his olive trees and reading them. He visited the Congreves and sang them his Tennyson airs, as well as his own nonsense songs. They particularly liked "The Cork Legs," probably an early version of "The Quangle Wangle's Hat." He wrote inviting Fortescue to stay, and began work on his illustrations of Tennyson's poems. And he started work on new water colors, despite the saddening news that he had failed to be elected to the Old Water Colour Society.

In the midst of this new contentment he was still restless. In June 1871, he wrote in his diary with his old desperation: "What to do? *What* I say to do? To stay here? or go—*where?*"[69] In the autumn, and then again in the spring of 1872, Thomas Baring, Lord Northbrook, newly appointed Viceroy of India, asked Lear to travel with him to the East. Lear had doubts about a half bohemian like himself traveling in a viceregal retinue. But he had always wanted to see the Himalayas—it was now forty years since he had collaborated with Gould on a book of Himalayan birds. More holy mountains! More birds! The prospect was too tempting to resist. In the summer of 1872 he went to England to gather Indian commissions. He was treated with cruel condescension when he visited Fortescue at Strawberry Hill, and he hurried away at seven on the morning after his arrival. But he found Holman Hunt, who had just returned from the Holy Land, unchanged and affectionate as ever, and he took great pleasure in the endless conversations they had together. In September, Northbrook sent him £50 to do a drawing of Cairo on his way out, and by then he had gathered nearly £1000 in commissions. So much "tin" was not to be turned down.

He fetched Giorgio from Corfu and went to Egypt. But in Suez he quarreled with a customs official over his baggage, and in his distress he suddenly decided to put off his Indian expedition altogether. For a third time he turned back, in Egypt, from a more distant pilgrimage.

He settled in for the winter at San Remo, with Walpole's letters and Thomas Moore's diaries to occupy his mind. By the middle of January 1873, he was making "arrangements for 80 small watercolour drawings,"[70] and these eighty grew at once to "120 new Tyrants."[71] Soon, however, his eyesight was troubling him, and he began to fret. Early in April he heard that a childhood friend had died. "*Fanny Coombe is dead.*"[72] He was greatly shaken. "What is this life becoming to me? utterly blank and desert. . . . It was in the year 1823—just 50 years ago—I first saw Fanny Coombe,—then Fanny Drewitt:—I had walked over to Peppering with Sarah (Street) to breakfast. Indeed indeed. 'The days that are no more'—are going—going—far and farther away."[73]

By April 12, he had finished the tyrants. But later in the month he was bedridden for a few days, a rare and alarming state of affairs, and in May his face swelled up. He wondered whether he should go to India after all—the invitation was still open. In mid-May, after his sixty-first birthday, he wrote "The Pobble Who Has No Toes," and in July he composed an Indian nonsense poem, "The Akond of Swat."

On September 20, he had a crushing letter from Gussie. "What that contained it is useless to write."[74] She told him she was engaged to marry Adamson Parker, an aging invalid. She had chosen a husband far more difficult to live with than Lear would have been: his scruples about the demon and the morbids had been foolish indeed. "There is now no hope of any but a dark and lonely life. I must leave this place." Now he was determined to go to India after all. He confided his sorrows to Hubert Congreve, and "later ran about—mad."[75]

Before he left, he sorted out three chests of letters. He calculated that 444 individuals in all had written to him, and he concluded from such an accumulation of kindnesses that "all my friends must be fools or mad."[76] His surprise reflects the kind of modesty which made him so companionable and such a good correspondent. He was always openly and vulnerably affectionate, and such freely given love was naturally and gratefully answered by the huge number of acquaintances who had been easily transformed by his generosity and attentiveness into fast friends. Even when he was depressed and anxious he was good company, and his loyalty was unquestionable. In his loneliness, he always had the courage of his affections.

On October 25, 1873, he set sail for Bombay. When he arrived a month later he felt nearly driven "mad" by "the sheer beauty and wonder" of the scene. "Anything more overpoweringly amazing cannot be conceived!!!" It was so bright and vivid that it defied description—and painting. "Colours and costumes and myriadisms of impossible pictures. . . ."[77] For the next thirteen months, he traveled all over India, sketching with difficulty a landscape that seemed too sublime for pen or pencil, drinking too much, living now in viceregal palaces and now in railway stations and dak bungalows.

Benares was "startingly radiant."[78] He was particularly taken with a Hanuman temple and with the fakirs on the ghats beside the Ganges.

> The washings and bathings! . . . 2 dead bodies,—one without cover.// Blind Saint of χθes, only now in a hole, with admiring worshippers.// Next, coasted the town Eastwards, and came to other still finer palaces and Temples! Groupes! Very holy bit of Ganges,—saints and sinners; place of burning bodies.// Another big saint, quite naked, and all painted gray, red and yellow, even to his—. So queer a slice of Indian life I never thought to see! . . . Narrow streets—Ghats;—mealy man of meditation.[79]

Lear tried to draw the temples and riverbanks, but something failed him—"nothing is more impossible than to represent them by the pencil."[80] The next day, however, he was back again with his pad, and once more he found himself fascinated by the yogi. "The 'mealy man of meditation' came to the surface, and stood for a time wildly acting, and apparently intending a header,—but he subsided into squatting and lute playing: today he sports a feeble bit of string."[81] In mid-afternoon he drove to the Hanuman temple and drew till after four.

It was all very queer and very wonderful, and, as before in Egypt, Greece and the Holy Land, words and images failed him.

At the beginning of 1874 he went up to Darjeeling to execute his commissions to paint Kinchinjunga. Somehow he felt he was taking a "leap in the dark," and he asked himself, "Is not all life more or less so necessarily?"[82] When he arrived, he was startled by "the enormous and *inimitable* vastness of the mountain."[83] As for the birds he had drawn forty years earlier for Gould, there were few to be found: "How few birds! and such as are,—how absurdly they whistle. No songs."[84] The landscape was "clear and wondrous," but its spirit somehow escaped him, and his art once again failed him. His drawings of the mountain are all foreground and middleground. Something got in the way, just as in the drawings of Athos, from the sea the boats are in the way, and from land the trees are in the way. He decided to blame the mountain: "Kinchinjunga is not a Sympathetic mountain—;—it is so far off—so very God-like and stupendous—and all those dark opal vallies of misty, hardly to be conceived of . . . forms,—and the impossiblity of expressing the whole as a scene—all is rather disgusting and repelling."[85] It was a lonely place, and so cold he could barely hold his pencil. He was awed—he was overawed. He contented himself with sketching the foothills, the stations, and a "little Buddhist shrine—a picture, with Kinchinjunga clear and rosy-heighted beyond."[86]

After six months on the road, he packed five hundred drawings of Bengal, the North-West Provinces and the Punjab into specially made tin trunks, to be shipped home. In Poona, he wrote the final draft of "The

Cummerbund," basing it on his earlier jingle "She sat upon her Bulbul," written on the deck the evening he left Corfu with Evelyn Baring back in 1864. He had it published in the *Bombay Times* in July 1874. He went south to Hyderabad, and read Plato's *Phaedo*, and wrote in his diary what is possibly a confession of his sexual nature. After his death the passage was heavily inked out by Frank. He went further south to Madras and the Coromandel coast. Both he and Giorgio fell ill in Ceylon, and they returned to Bombay to find a letter with the news that Giorgio's wife had died in Corfu. They left India on January 12, 1875. Lear was exhausted, but as the boat left he was already planning to return to see the places he had missed.

He was lonely in the villa but consoled himself with his garden, dazzling in the spring. He had a quiet summer in England, then an ever quieter winter back in San Remo. In the spring of 1876, old friends came at last to visit him. Frank Lushington stayed a fortnight, and Northbrook, who had given up his post in India, dropped in on his way home. More friends followed in the summer. And from time to time he worked on his later nonsense poems. In the autumn he ran off 120 new tyrants to hang in his downstairs gallery, which he opened to the public once a week.

In December, Bush brought out the fourth and last nonsense book, *Laughable Lyrics*. It was well received on the whole, but there were one or two hostile reviews.

All this time Lear was growing very fond of Hubert Congreve, the son of his neighbor Walter Congreve. He taught him drawing and hoped he might become an artist. In February 1877, Giorgio asked leave to return to Corfu. He was ill again, and he said he had not yet recovered from his wife's death. Lear and Hubert accompanied him as far as Brindisi, then made their way back through Naples and Rome. For Lear, it was a little like the Arcadian spring of 1849 all over again. Once home, he was very restless and lonely, and moved into the hotel next door to his house.

He spent the summer in England. He saw Emily Tennyson and also his sister Ellen, who was nearly blind and deaf. She reminisced about their childhood.

Then Lear received another devastating letter, like the one from Gussie four years earlier. Hubert was leaving San Remo to study in London. Lear now recognized how deeply he was in love, and he found the prospect of returning to the villa to find Hubert gone a fearful one. Worse than that, the letter shook to the surface all the sorrow of his unrequited love for Frank. He went to pieces.

> In vain I work for an hour—tears blind me. In vain I play on the Piano,—and I get convulsed: in vain I pace the large room—or try to sleep. True, all these symptoms happened also in 1855—but there was not the finality there is now . . . God help me. I was never nearer to utter and total madness than now. Yet, I don't mean to give way and shall stave off worse things if I can.[87]

But it wasn't easy. A week later, he had his last dinner of the year with "my dear dear F.L.," and wrote in despair before bed that night: "What more?—nothing—"[88] for after all Frank was cold, and married and, if the truth were known, rather dull. Lear tried to keep Hubert out of his diary; the pain was intolerable. "I write little about Hubert—but cannot say I think of him little."[89] If only he had been able to close his heart. "Cutting off heart strings the only serious order of the day."[90] But he was too open.

Back at San Remo, he was kept busy looking after the ailing Giorgio. When his health improved, Lear took him on a sketching tour around Lake Como, and his son Lambi was called to join them at the villa in the late summer of 1878. Lear met a family called Bevan, newly arrived in town, and one day in April 1879, he sat down with the daughter and wrote in tandem with her his autobiographical poem "How Pleasant to Know Mr. Lear!" On another occasion, when he was playing songs on the piano at teatime for the Bevan children, he suddenly burst into tears. He was in the middle of "The Courtship of the Yonghy-Bonghy-Bò."

Fortescue's wife died in the summer of 1879, and Lear invited him out, but he did not come. Samuel Butler visited the villa and found Lear in gloomy spirits. But he seemed very happy when Marianne North, on her way back from India, met him at Lake Como and went with him up to Monza. They had a brief holiday together, and a month later she came to stay with him at San Remo. She saw he was greatly depressed by a new German hotel which had been built between him and the sea. It had been painted a dazzling white, the reflected light in his studio was blinding and his eyes suffered from the glare. But he had promised to entertain Marianne, and with great buoyancy and courage he did. As her train left, he leaned into the carriage and said, "Hasn't someone been good not to mention the Enemy all day."[91] The Enemy was his name for the hotel. In his fury and despair, he wrote—at the urging of Wilkie Collins, who looked like his double—a second part to the story of Mr. and Mrs. Discobbolos. He wanted to blow up the place:

> . . . . beneath it he dug a dreadful trench,
> And filled it with dynamite, gunpowder gench. . . ."[92]

He considered going to live in New Zealand with Sarah's son Charles Street, and he told his American publisher that he might turn up at any time in Boston on his way to San Francisco. Fortunately, his friends rescued him. Realizing he did not have the money to move, Northbrook and Stanley gave him an interest-free loan of £2000 so that he could build again. Aberdare, Fortescue, Clowes and Cross added to the sum.

Fortescue spent two months with him in the winter, and declared when he left that he felt better than at any time since his wife's death. The healing spirit of Lear's company had not weakened either with the advancing years or with the unhappiness they had brought.

Lear had reason to feel cheerful: he had found a new plot of land and was planning a new house to deliver him from the Enemy. In the spring of 1880, he went to London to raise money selling paintings. Lushington lent him rooms in his house in Norfolk Square to use as a sales gallery. When he was unpacking the paintings, Northbrook dropped in and bought fifty for £500. He saw the Tennysons and Holman Hunt, who was working on his *Flight into Egypt*. He made drawings of colored birds for Evelyn Baring's son, who was having difficulty learning his colors. These, some of Lear's most delightful works—half-cartoons, half-formal—were published posthumously as *The Lear Coloured Bird Book for Children* (1912). He visited Gussie and her husband. The three of them sat together on the lawn instead of going to church. Lear was greatly impressed by his fortitude and by her kindness. In June, Bush went bankrupt and told him he had lost all the blocks for the three nonsense books he had published.

Lear left England at the end of August 1880. He had lost count of his homecomings. This turned out to be the last.

He never saw England again.

1880 to 1888

San Remo was too hot, so Lear moved up to Mendrisio for a few weeks. In the winter of 1880, he set to work on a group of three hundred Tennyson drawings. These were to be his *Liber Studiorum*, after Turner, or his *Liber Veritatis*, after Lorrain, his master. But his eyesight had deteriorated—his right eye was nearly useless. He had to start each drawing with heavy outlines to guide him, and he lost thereby his two strongest qualities, delicacy and spontaneity.

The new house was ready by June 1881. He called it the Villa Tennyson, and it was an exact replica of the Villa Emily. He named this second house, and perhaps also the first, after the poet's wife. Emily had received his deepest confidences and comforted him in his worst hours. Now he toiled away at his illustrations of Alfred's poetry. He spent the summer of 1881 in the Swiss mountains, and finished half the drawings. He also planned another huge oil, this one of Enoch Arden's island, with Indian flora and fauna. He was still trying to describe paradise.

He had a bad spell of giddiness once he had settled down to work, and Giorgio warned him, as Fortescue had done when he stayed at Ardee, that he was drinking too much. In fact, he seems to have become more or less addicted to Marsala and water, and some of the diary entries in the last years appear to have been made in a tipsy hand. His gallery, hung with new paintings and drawings, was ready for the public in November. On open days he would answer the door himself so that if any Germans called he could pretend to be ill and send them away. He sold very little, even though his prices were now very modest, about £12 for a drawing and 40 guineas for an oil painting.

He had not given up his nonsense. When Mrs. Stuart Wortley bought a painting, he sent her two drawings for her daughters, with whom he had enjoyed some nonsense conversation. He told them, in the covering letter, that he had done the drawings on the moon "to which I lately went one night, returning next morning on a Moonbeam . . . These journeys are all done by Moonbeams, which, far from being mere portions of light, are in reality living creatures. . . . You have only to whisper to the moonbeam what you wish to see, and you are there in a moment." The first drawing was of the "Jizzdoddle rocks, with 2 of the very remarkable planets which surround the moon rising," and the second was of "the Rumby-tumby ravine, with the crimson planet Buzz and its 5 Satanites on the horizon."[93] Here an element of fantasy seems to soften the nonsense. While Lear had not abandoned the genre he had helped invent, he published no new nonsense in the last fifteen years of his life, and wrote only a few more poems. Why? Perhaps, as this letter shows, he felt the attractions of the vogue for the fantastic which established itself in the eighties. But more than that, the last nonsense poems of *Laughable Lyrics* had fulfilled his artistic and spiritual search. They had also left him—this is the price an artist must pay for self-discovery—more open that he had ever been, both to joy and to pain; and he may have felt that too much was, by this time, enough. The diary entries of the last years reveal a man greatly suffering. Perhaps he felt he had paid too high a price for the openness and understanding which his last poems had brought him, and wished now to close down as best he could. He wrote of himself:

Long ago he was one of the singers,
But now he is one of the dumbs.[94]

The singer of nonsense had persisted long enough in his folly. His nonsense had made him wise. Now, in his wisdom, perhaps he preferred to be a dumb.

By the end of 1882 he had decided to close the gallery. Few people bought his work, and he hated the chatter and inanity of those who did. He arranged for a firm in London to take all his stock, display it, and sell what they could. In January 1883, Lord Derby invited him to Knowsley, but he felt too old to go.

In the spring Gussie passed through with two nieces in tow. She was now widowed, and Lear thought very seriously, even now, of proposing. She put up in a nearby hotel and visited him every day. But, although they agreed that their life was "twofold," Lear could not find the courage to ask for her hand. On the day she left he wrote:

> After Bkft, got as good and large a nosegay as I could for dear Gussie, and 2 others for the nieces:—and, having made them up in parcels,—took them up to the Royal, whence I saw and *took leave* of Gussie. So ends the very last possible chance of a change of life. Many causes occasion this—my age the least among them;—the knowledge of all my misery—physical and psychical—now and of late quite clear to me and unescapable from,—among the greatest.[95]

It was all he could do not to burst into tears "before I left. When I did . . . Gone! gone!" On May 12 he wrote in his diary: "So ends 71 years of my very silly life."[96] On May 22: "Life today happier than this child deserves."[97] At the end of the month Frank came to stay.

Troubles with Giorgio and his three sons, all of whom now lived in the villa, began to plague Lear. Giorgio drank even more heavily than his master. In June 1882 he ran away and was found wandering on the hills above Toulon, half crazy. He had lost his memory. Lear took him up to Monte Generoso, where he recovered both his health and his bad temper. Lear was weary of the constant family quarrels. One of the sons, Lambi, was caught stealing wine and was sent back to Corfu. Then Giorgio fell ill again, and in June 1883 was taken up to Monte Generoso once more. By the time Lear joined him there a month later, he had greatly weakened. On August 5 he died.

Lear was nearly as deeply saddened as he had been by Ann's death. "O my dear George! You are gone!—but oh! be as good a guide and angel to me now as for so many years you have ever been! The good you have done me year by year is what I cannot write, yet know full well—and may I continue to be grateful for it!"[98] He wrote to Emily Tennyson, confiding his sorrow. He recalled all the times he had been angry with Giorgio. Had he treated him well? In later years he had invited him to share a glass and a cigar on Sunday evenings. It was a more generous concession than most Victorian masters would have made. Ten years earlier, in India, Northbrook had scolded him for sticking up for Giorgio's rights. "Your humility," he had said, "is oppressive."[99] Giorgio had been his constant companion, his shadow, for thirty years. Now Lear was crying not because he had been a hard master but because the master had never really been able to express his deep affection for his servant. He had been so lonely, when all the while, he now realized, friendship had been at his side—on the slopes of all those cold, exalting mountains, on the steps of the temples of Isis, Apollo and Hanuman, in the streets of all those holy cities.

At once Lear wanted to be on the move again, to Madeira or Japan or Java. Instead, he made a leisurely walking tour of Tuscany, Umbria, Spezia and Genoa. He was home by autumn, and as he prepared a site for his own grave, he erected next to it a stone in commemoration of Giorgio.

That winter he read more Plato and more St. John. He also sorted his possessions and decided what to leave to each of his friends. He sold the Villa Emily for a third of the price he had been asking, and spent the summer of 1884 in Abetone, where the air helped him recover from a bout of pleurisy. In the autumn, Dimitri, Giorgio's youngest son, was caught stealing and had to be sent home to Corfu. Nicola, the eldest son, remained behind to serve Lear, but it soon became clear that he was dying of consumption. Lear ministered to him with great tenderness until his death on March 4, 1885. Less than two weeks later, Lear's sister Ellen also died, in Leatherhead. He was left now only with nieces and nephews far away in New Zealand and North America.

He worked on seventy new tyrants and on the Tennyson project. Toward the end of the year Fortescue visited him and almost at once fell ill with a fever and chills. After Christmas, Lear came down with bronchitis. He wrote "Incidents in the Life of My Uncle Arly" in bed, a confessional nonsense poem which so pleased him that he sent copies to his close friends. When he read in the *Pall Mall Magazine* in February 1886 that Ruskin considered him his favorite author, he sent him a copy too. Fortescue left in February, Lear stayed in bed till April. It had been a four months' illness and he never really recovered from it. He summered in the mountains as usual. When he came home, he had lost the sight of his right eye, rheumatism made his right side more or less useless, and for the first time he had no work planned.

Lushington came to stay in November. He wrote telling Hallam Tennyson that Lear was greatly enfeebled, scarcely ever went out, and spent his few active hours on the Tennyson project. He was saddened to see the large Mount Athos picture standing unfinished on its easel. He had always said it was his favorite, guessing, perhaps, that the subject meant more to Lear than all the others. The foreground, which, according to the style, should have had two or three people in it, remained empty and incomplete. Lear no longer had the heart to paint the ghosts of his stick-men.

Spring came round and he was bedridden. He wrote to Gussie; she came, took a room in a nearby hotel, and visited him daily. On April 4, 1887, he wondered again, in his diary, if he should ask her to marry him. "Once or twice the crisis nearly came off, yet she went at 5 and nothing occurred beyond her very decidedly showing me how much she cared for me. . . . This I think was the day of the death of all hope."[100]

Now his friends all rallied round him. The Barings came to stay for a few weeks after Gussie had left, and Lushington helped sell some of the paintings back in England. Hallam Tennyson arranged for an American publisher to visit the villa and look over the Tennyson drawings with a view to using them in an edition of the poems. He bought a painting for himself, but nothing came of the project except a small edition of one hundred copies of "The Daisy," "The Princess" and "The Palace of Art," with a few pictures chosen from the two hundred which Lear had finished.

Lear read the New Testament in Greek, and *In Memoriam* and some Shakespeare. He watched his garden bloom. He spent the summer of 1887 in Adorno in the mountains. In the autumn his cat Foss died. On December 5 he made his last full diary entry: "I shall try and get some sleep if possible, but I have no light or life left in me,—And the flies are as horrible as ever!"

He grew weaker. He wrote to Frank on January 6. Then, at half-past midnight on Sunday, January 29, 1888, he spoke his last words—in Italian—to his servant Guiseppe. He asked to be remembered to Lushington, Northbrook and Fortescue, and added, "I did not answer their letters because I could not write, as no sooner did I take a pen in my hand than I felt as if I were dying."[101] He died two hours later.

Afterword

We may look back over the swiftly changing yet monotonous scenes of this bustling, nervous, mysterious life rather as if we had wandered into Lear's winter studio on Corfu and had come upon the first sixty tyrants, each perfectly half-finished, each out of focus in the exact same degree, each missing the same colors. And somehow we feel that there is something right about the suspension, the hanging back, the refusal to give in, the struggle and the muddle. The folly presents itself as a species of truth. We do not see the life whole or clear because its point lay in the bemused seeking, in the painter's "bits and wanderings," and in the pilgrim's dazed stumble along a path he could not see toward an always hidden goal.

It was a search without the clear colors of the Romantic quest: the feeling is often too mean, the ideals lie not just beyond reason, but beyond feeling. Lear groped and fell where Childe Harold was always surefooted, and in the end he had to give up the adventurer's Himalayas for the tourist's Alps. He grew weary of tripping himself up.

Yet, when he settled, the search did not stop. The journey became more inward, until with a little more room for reflection Lear began to gather together his nonsenses in cartoons and poems, and to make more of them; and to find in that most desolate and sublime of all landscapes, the inner, private one, a way to limn out the human figure faithfully and warmly and to edge closer to the knowledge he had formerly sought in holy mountains, ruined temples and ancient cities.

If I have already suggested more than this, and said less, it is out of respect for the spirit of nonsense. Nonsense has to be read openly. It is not, as I said at the beginning, a critical art, and it resists closed interpretations. In the same way, the best reading of the man is an open one, one that respects his bewilderment and sees that there is a fidelity in making nonsense of the kind Blake recommends in his proverb: "If the fool would persist in his folly he would become wise." Where Lear has resisted clarity, perhaps we should too. Where he has turned the world upside down, we should stand on our heads to share his view.

It is best to follow his example and to stand back a little, leaving his life to some degree unquizzed. If we are to understand the poems and the cartoons we have to allow his bemusement its true range. We leave him, then, as unresolved as the half-perfected tyrants in the winter studio, a set of vivid impressions. Lear and his two would-be wives, Helena and Gussie. Lear and the three men he loved—Fortescue, Frank and Hubert. Lear and his two guides—Ann and Giorgio, one always near, one always far, both beyond reach. His kinship with birds—owls, ravens, parrots—the tenement full of parrots in his first years, the Himalayan birds he drew for Gould, and the ones in India, much later, which did not sing. His afflictions—the tyrants and the Enemy, the morbids, the demon, the diary crosses. His reading—Pascal, Plato, St. John. The hundreds of children he befriended, from Eliza to Lionel, Guy, Violet and Slingsby. The places of his pilgrimages—Olympus (1849), Athos (1856), Ida (1864), Kinchinjunga (1874) the Campagna and Arcadia, Ascension, Philae, Petra, Jerusalem, Rome, Benares, Constantinople, Thebes. The places where he hesitated—Egypt and Corfu. His happy times—the Arcadian spring of 1849. His bad times—the London winter of 1854. The times of near madness—the Corfu winter of 1855, the London summer of 1877. The restless wandering for forty years, annual, dreary homecomings, the restless settling, for twenty years. Lastly, some echoes, the words of a few who met him on his muddled way—"could do nothing like other people" . . . "bright eyes that seemed to be watching a pleasant comedy all the time" . . . "bathed in kindly effulgence. . . ."

Chapter Two

The Limericks

Lear first had the idea of writing his limericks when he was at Knowsley drawing the Stanley menagerie. The origins of the form are unknown, though Baring-Gould[1] in *The Lure of the Limerick* suggests that it begins as early as "Sumer is i-cumen in" (c. 1300), and cites examples of its use by Shakespeare, Jonson and Herrick. More fanciful authorities have found it in the work of Aristophanes. These histories are premature. Gershon Legman, for instance, is clearly mistaken in claiming the early seventeenth-century song "Mad Tom" as a limerick:

> From the hagg & hungry Goblin,
> That into raggs would rend yee,
> & the spirit that stands
> by the naked man,
> In the booke of moones defend ye . . .

Lear's limerick is only superficially similar to this. It has a much firmer structure: two amphibrachic trimeters, followed by two anapaestic dimeters (at first written as a single tetrameter with internal rhyme and a regular caesura), and the first line repeated in the last with only minor variations of syntax or vocabulary. Lear has, moreover, a regular set of characters and a geographical setting. His first line nearly always begins with the formula "There was an Old Man [Young Lady, Old Person, Young

Person]" followed by a place-name or, occasionally, a relative clause. The whole verse pivots like a haiku, or seesaws like "Hickory, Dickory, Dock" and other nursery rhymes and cradle songs.[2] It is dramatic in that its characters are involved in a decisive, or vividly indecisive, action; and also lyrical, because of a strong sense of refrain which the variation of the first line in the last evokes. It may well be that "Mad Tom" is a distant ancestor of Lear's limerick, but it hardly deserves to be called by the same name. The word *limerick* itself was not officially admitted to the language until 1898, when the *Oxford English Dictionary* defines it as "an indecent nonsense verse." By then it had lost not only its respectability, but also its final refrain, in favor of the novel and epigrammatic tail-line which it almost invariably has today.

Lear himself never called the verses limericks. He simply adopted the form, unnamed, from three, or possibly more, books published at the beginning of the 1820s: *The Adventures of Fifteen Young Ladies;* its sequel *The History of Sixteen Wonderful Old Women*, published by John Harris in London in 1821; and what appears to be a parody of these two, *Anecdotes and Adventures of Fifteen Gentlemen*, published in 1822 by John Marshall. They were evidently popular books, and the third contained the "sick man of Tobago" limerick mentioned by Dickens in Chapter 2 of *Our Mutual Friend.* In the preface to *More Nonsense*, Lear makes it clear that it was this limerick in particular which inspired his efforts at imitation:

> There was a sick man of Tobago,
> Who liv'd long on rice-gruel and sago;
> But at last, to his bliss,
> The physician said this—
> "To a roast leg of mutton you may go!"

In fact, Lear prefers the form used in the earlier two volumes, with its refrain intact:

> There was an old woman of Leeds
> Who spent all her life in good deeds;
> She worked for the poor
> Till her fingers were sore,
> This pious old woman of Leeds.

We can guess that he likes the third book for its exuberance, for its inconsequentiality and for the way it mocks evangelical propriety.

The limerick seems to have been around in this geographical form, with the refrain, since at least the mid-eighteenth century. In *The Midwife, or Old Woman's Magazine* (c. 1750) there appears this verse:

> There was a jovial butcher
> Who liv'd at Northern-fall-gate,
> He kept a stall
> At Leadenhall
> And got drunk at the Boy at Aldgate . . .

There is also a French limerick in a footnote in Chapter 47 of Boswell's *Life of Johnson;* and there have been speculations that the name may have come from a verse form popular among veterans of the Irish Brigade who served Louis XIV after the surrender of Limerick to King William in 1691, and who on their return home sang limericks at convivial reunions. However, the choruses of these songs, which are all that survive of them, in no way resemble the limerick form as we know it, and the connection of the form with the town remains uncertain. All that is clear is that the limerick was a popular folk form,[3] perhaps a song, and that it acquired its present name and characteristics sometime in the nineteenth century. In unwritten form it had probably been current for centuries. When Lear found it, it had already entered the literary world, in an underground way. He seems to have been the first to prefer the refrain line; he strengthened the pivotal power of the final adjective; and he added to each verse, as an organic part of it, a drawing which reflected the dramatic and lyrical properties of the jingle.

He wrote two series of limericks.[4] The first was published in final form in 1861. It was an expanded version of *A Book of Nonsense* of 1846, which had grown through several editions in the fifties. The second appeared as part of *More Nonsense,* the third nonsense book, in 1872. From the thirties to the seventies, and on into his old age, Lear composed many of these picture poems, principally to amuse children.

It would be helpful to know if he intended the two series to be read in a particular order. Of the first, we may guess that it was the publisher who arranged them[5] in the 1846 edition, and perhaps Lear in the Routledge reissue of 1861; of the second, that they appear in the author's own order, and that he was concerned with the ending but not the beginning or middle. There are two series, then, but they do not flow serially; at best they have only a rough continuity. There are 112 limericks in the first book, and 100 in the second, and he wrote about a dozen that appear elsewhere.[6] The first series was begun when Lear was in his twenties and was completed when he was in his late forties. The second was written in his fifties, in the ten years that also saw the composition of Lewis Carroll's *Alice* books. The first marks the beginning of the Victorian vogue for nonsense books, and the second marks the height of the fashion.

On the surface, the two series are remarkably similar. The casual reader may decide that the form is so static that it allows for little variation of theme, and can hardly express or sustain a development of feelings and thoughts. But a closer look reveals a considerable difference between the two series and an active life within each. Indeed, it is not too strong to say that Lear committed his emotional and spiritual life to this cryptic form, and that an investigation of the two groups provides enough evidence about his inner thoughts and feelings to add significantly to his biographies. More than that, the contrast between the 1861 and the 1872 limericks shows an artistic maturing of the form itself, so that we can glean from an examination of these seemingly slight pieces a crucial account of how Lear the artist grows and finds in the invention of a unique graphic and literary mode a complete and powerful way of expressing himself and his vision of the world.

The Old Man, the Young Lady, the Old Lady, They and The Beasts

Lear saw himself not just as a painter of birds and "dirty" landscapes, but as a poet and singer, too. He was a composer of songs, which he sang to his own piano accompaniment. His settings for Tennyson's poems were well known and caught the popular taste exactly. They were the laureate's own favorites, and Lear often performed them at Farringford. He became a sort of drawing-room Orpheus, provoking tears as well as laughter in his audience when he sang, to a soft vamping on the keyboard, his version of "Sweet and Low" or "The Courtship of the Yonghy-Bonghy-Bò."[7] However comic the words, his music was always grave in manner and sweet—somewhat like a hymn. Perhaps his greatest success was his rendition of "Tears, Idle Tears."

Many of the limericks are about music. Often the Old Man and the Young Lady are musicians. The Old Man of Whitehaven is an accomplished dancer.

There was an Old Man of Whitehaven,
Who danced a quadrille with a Raven;
But they said—"It's absurd, to encourage this bird!"
So they smashed that Old Man of Whitehaven.

The Young Lady of Welling plays the harp.

There was a Young Lady of Welling,
Whose praise all the world was a telling;
She played on the harp, and caught several carp,
That accomplished Young Lady of Welling.

In the first book there are nine music limericks. In five of these an Old Man plays a gong, a flute and a fiddle, dances a hornpipe, jigs and a quadrille, and sings a little. But things do not go well for him. The Old Man with a gong, like the Old Man of Whitehaven, is "smashed" for his pains.

There was an Old Man with a gong,
Who bumped at it all the day long;
But they called out, "O law! you're a horrid old bore!"
So they smashed that Old Man with a gong.

The Old Person of Ischia's face is blackened with frenzy.

There was an Old Person of Ischia,
Whose conduct grew friskier and friskier;
He danced hornpipes and jigs, and ate thousands of figs,
That lively Old Person of Ischia.

And the Old Man with a flute plays for his own safety, to scare off a snake.

There was an Old Man with a flute,
A sarpint ran into his boot;
But he played day and night, till the sarpint took flight,
And avoided that man with a flute.

Here the role of musical enchanter is reversed, and that, of course, is part of the joke. Only once is the Old Man's lot an entirely happy one—when he plays the fiddle.

There was an Old Man of the Isles,
Whose face was pervaded with smiles:
He sung high dum diddle, and played on the fiddle,
That amiable Man of the Isles.

In the other four music limericks the Young Lady is the subject, and she enjoys a much better fortune. She plays the harp twice, and a flute and a lyre. The first Young Lady makes a virtue of what conventional folk might think a misfortune.

There was a Young Lady whose chin
Resembled the point of a pin;
So she had it made sharp, and purchased a harp,
And played several tunes with her chin.

The others are female Pied Pipers.

There was a Young Lady of Bute,
Who played on a silver-gilt flute;
She played several jigs, to her uncle's white pigs,
That amusing Young Lady of Bute.

There was a young Lady of Tyre,
Who swept the loud chords of a lyre;
At the sound of each sweep, she enraptured the deep,
And enchanted the city of Tyre.

The Young Lady of Welling, whom we have seen, is a rather more predatory figure. Her skill as a harpist provides her with a good fish dinner, and she is widely celebrated.

It is not merely the rhyme that has supplied her dinner. Here we have a pattern. The Young Lady—let us suppose that she is one Lady in several guises—is an enchantress: with her music she charms nature. The best the Old Man—and let us suppose he is one Old Man—can hope for is to keep nature at bay. The only time he is in happy command is when he lives in the "Isles," in an earthly paradise. In the real world, only the Young Lady has any success with music.

Ten years later, the situation has changed completely. Of the ten music limericks in the second series, eight are about the Old Man and only two about the Young Lady, despite the fact that in both series there is the same proportion of men to women. Singing and dancing have now taken the place of instrumental music; a whistle, a bell and a nose-trumpet are all that remain for accompaniments. Moreover, the Young Lady, who has never looked very young in the pictures, appears to have aged, and with the years she has lost her power to enchant. The old lady of France is rebuffed.

There was an old lady of France,
Who taught little ducklings to dance;
When she said, "Tick-a-tack!"—they only said, "Quack!"
Which grieved that old lady of France.

And, the old person of Jodd is considered a perplexing outsider.

There was an old person of Jodd,
Whose ways were perplexing and odd;
She purchased a whistle, and sate on a thistle,
And squeaked to the people of Jodd.

Neither the ducklings nor the citizens of Jodd are much impressed.

The roles are not reversed: the Old Man has not become an enchanter in her place. Rather, he has made musical peace with the world around him.

Nature and society no longer threaten his love for a tune. True, he has had to abandon his instruments, and this may represent a small victory for the forces of society; but instead of menacing him, his neighbors are now either solicitous or defensive. The people of Filey, or their representative, actually accompany him with a bell.

There was an old person of Filey,
Of whom his acquaintance spoke highly;
He danced perfectly well, to the sound of a bell,
And delighted the people of Filey.

The people of Fife come to his aid with a song.

There was an old person of Fife,
Who was greatly disgusted with life;
They sang him a ballad, and fed him on salad,
Which cured that old person of Fife.

The people of West Dumpet are astonished, but dare not interrupt.

There was an old man of West Dumpet,
Who possessed a large nose like a trumpet;
When he blew it aloud, it astonished the crowd,
And was heard through the whole of West Dumpet.

Obviously they no longer have the power to "smash" him, and he no longer has any fear of them. They live together in an uneasy accord. And twice the musical Old Man strikes some sort of peace with the natural world. He teaches a frog to sing.

There was an old man in a Marsh,
Whose manners were futile and harsh;
He sat on a log, and sang songs to a frog,
That instructive old man in a Marsh.

And he dances with a giant fly.

There was an old person of Skye,
Who waltz'd with a Bluebottle fly:
They buzz'd a sweet tune, to the light of the moon,
And entranced all the people of Skye.

Here, indeed, he manages to please both nature and society.

What more can the beasts in the limericks tell us of this strange alteration? In the first series, a third of the verses present creatures of one sort or another; in the second, slightly more of them do so. In the first, all of them stand in a wary or hostile relation to the Old Man, while the Lady, as we have seen, succeeds in charming them until, in the last of the series, she is apparently killed by a bear.

There was a Young Lady of Clare,
Who was sadly pursued by a bear;
When she found she was tired, she abruptly expired,
That unfortunate Lady of Clare.

Exit, pursued by a bear. The joke is perhaps based on *The Winter's Tale*, and it is a rather frosty one. Indeed, the casual reader, accustomed to thinking of Lear's nonsense world as benign and reassuring, may find this bit of savagery somewhat chilling. Nature here is "red in tooth and claw," or at least very menacing.

In both series there are more birds than any other creatures. Lear began his career drawing parrots, and he was always fascinated by owls, ducks, geese and ravens. On both his trips up the Nile he was astonished by the number of birds, by their many species and their beauty. One of his most beautiful nonsense books is the neglected *The Lear Coloured Bird Book for Children,*[8] painted for Gussie Bethell's nephew. But here the relationship between the Old Man and the birds is awkward.

There was an Old Man with a beard,
Who said, "It is just as I feared!—
Two Owls and a Hen, four Larks and a Wren,
Have all built their nests in my beard!"

So runs the first limerick of the 1861 series. By the end, matters have not greatly changed.

There was an Old Man on whose nose,
Most birds of the air could repose;
But they all flew away, at the closing of day,
Which relieved that Old Man and his nose.

The birds try to roost but the man looks anxious, and is relieved when they fly off. The Old Man of Dundee is upset by four friendly but importunate crows.

There was an Old Man of Dundee,
Who frequented the top of a tree;
When disturbed by the crows, he abruptly arose,
And exclaimed, "I'll return to Dundee."

And as we have seen, the Old Man of Whitehaven is "smashed" for dancing with a raven. The birds are not hostile. They are more rebuffed than rebuffing. When they settle on the beard and the nose, they have merely mistaken them for nest and branch—a pardonable error. Who can say that their intentions are bad? Yet the Old Man is afraid. At best, he manages a breathless standoff. Frozen with astonishment, he inspects a large bird, which in turn inspects him.

There was an Old Man who said, "Hush!
I perceive a young bird in this bush!"
When they said—"Is it small?" he replied—"Not at all!
It is four times as big as the bush!"

It is an amazed, and still awkward, truce. But the Young Lady, on the one occasion when she encounters the birds, is completely unperturbed.

There was a Young Lady whose bonnet,
Came untied when the birds sat upon it;
But she said, "I don't care! all the birds in the air
Are welcome to sit on my bonnet!"

She is happy to make a home of herself for them.

In the second series, there are nearly twice as many bird limericks. Now the Old Man has conquered his fear and has made his peace with them.

There was an old person of Hove,
Who frequented the depths of a grove;
Where he studied his books, with the wrens and the rooks,
That tranquil old person of Hove.

They share his reading, and he shares their food.

There was an old man of El Hums,
Who lived upon nothing but crumbs,
Which he picked off the ground, with the other birds round,
In the roads and the lanes of El Hums.

Or, out of a kindliness for nature at large, he civilizes them and teaches them how to take tea politely.

There was an old man of Dumbree,
Who taught little owls to drink tea;
For he said, "To eat mice, is not proper or nice,"
That amiable man of Dumbree.

In these last two, the Old Man closely resembles the birds. Once, this is commented upon.

There was an old man of Dumblane,
Who greatly resembled a crane;
But they said,—"Is it wrong, since your legs are so long,
To request you won't stay in Dumblane?"

But they do not try to run him out of town.

Even the timorous and conventional can see that the Old Man and the birds are enjoying an amicable and intimate friendship, a friendship so close that at times the Old Man starts to look like a bird. It is strange, doubtless, but within the bounds of decency. Now, instead of having to flee the attentions of inquisitive crows, the Old Man is happy to ride out to sea on his goose and then to return home with him.

There was an old man of Dunluce,
Who went out to sea on a goose:
When he'd gone out a mile, he observ'd with a smile,
"It is time to return to Dunluce."

Nesting and roosting, which seemed so difficult in the first series, are now accepted calmly by the Old Man. If the verses express some anxiety, the drawings show that all is well.[9]

There was an old man in a tree,
Whose whiskers were lovely to see;
But the birds of the air, pluck'd them perfectly bare,
To make themselves nests in that tree.

When the old person of Nice takes a promenade with a number of geese, they all look like a family out for a walk.

There was an old man of Nice,
Whose associates were usually Geese.
They walked out together, in all sorts of weather,
That affable person of Nice!

Only the old person of Florence, who chokes on a bustard, has an unlucky time with a bird, and he, after all, has been less than friendly.

There was an old person of Florence;
Who held mutton chops in abhorrence;
He purchased a Bustard, and fried him in Mustard,
Which choked that old person of Florence.

His action, considering the concord between man and bird in the other limericks, is tantamount to cannibalism, and he deserves his misfortune.

The Lady appears three times with birds in the second series, each time unhappily. Where the Old Man succeeded in teaching a frog to sing, she fails altogether to teach the ducklings.

There was an old lady of France,
Who taught little ducklings to dance;
When she said, "Tick-a-tack!"—they only said "Quack!"
Which grieved that old lady of France.

The Young Lady in white is depressed by the night owls.

There was a young lady in white,
Who looked out at the depths of the night;
But the birds of the air, filled her heart with despair,
And oppressed that young lady in white.

And the old person in gray seems to get very little pleasure, for all the verse says, out of feeding her parrots.

There was an old person in gray,
Whose feelings were tinged with dismay;
She purchased two parrots, and fed them with carrots,
Which pleased that old person in gray.

She approaches them with the utmost caution, and offers a very long carrot. He who sups with the devil?

It is a strange reversal. The Young Lady is now afraid and the Old Man now has the mastery of the birds. A similar, but less complete, change occurs in the fish limericks. In the first series, with one exception, they involve the Young Lady, and she either charms or captures them. The Young Lady of Welling did both. The Young Lady of Wales catches a huge, magically scaleless fish.

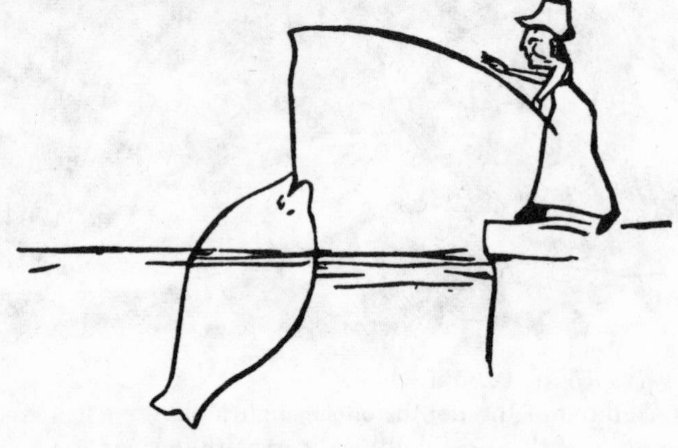

There was a Young Lady of Wales,
Who caught a large fish without scales;
When she lifted her hook, she exclaimed, "Only look!"
That extatic Young Lady of Wales.

In the second series, she retains her powers, but they are both feebler and ambiguous. She nurses the fish, while she washes the dishes.

There was an old person of Bree,
Who frequented the depths of the sea;
She nurs'd the small fishes, and washed all the dishes,
And swam back again into Bree.

Here we cannot be sure whether she is laying a trap for her dinner, or is altogether sincere. The Old Man definitely has an anxious time with fish. The old person of Brill is rebuked, it seems, for resembling a fish.

There was an old person of Brill,
Who purchased a shirt with a frill;
But they said, "Don't you wish, you mayn't look like a fish,
You obsequious old person of Brill?"

He looks startled and unhappily stiff. When he tries to teach fish to walk, he kills them.

There was an old person of Dundalk,
Who tried to teach fishes to walk;
When they tumbled down dead, he grew weary, and said,
"I had better go back to Dundalk!"

Here and in the other limericks, fish are alien creatures, especially for the Old Man, who eats them in the first series and kills them in the second. But he has at least tried to help them, and the Young Lady, too, seems more interested in nurturing them than in casting spells over them, although her intentions are not plain.

Pigs, snakes, cats, rabbits and bears are also troublesome to the Man in the early limericks, but completely friendly in the later ones. In the first, the Young Lady charms the magical white pigs, while the Old Man carries them around in a violent manner, mishandling them.

There was an Old Person of Anerley,
Whose conduct was strange and unmannerly;
He rushed down the Strand, with a Pig in each hand,
But returned in the evening to Anerley.

In the second, she has nothing to do with pigs, while he takes them around in a gig.

There was an old person of Ealing,
Who was wholly devoid of good feeling;
He drove a small gig, with three Owls and a Pig,
Which distressed all the people of Ealing.

Often he sings to them.

There was an old person of Bray,
Who sang through the whole of the day
To his ducks and his pigs, whom he fed upon figs,
That valuable person of Bray.

He even has his daughter ride on the back of one.

There was an old man of Messina,
Whose daughter was named Opsibeena;
She wore a small wig, and rode out on a pig,
To the perfect delight of Messina.

Father and pig are on the best of terms, and their friendship is respectable. It is the same with snakes. In the first series, the Old Man with a flute managed to scare off a serpent; in the second, the snakes follow after him, in a devoted procession.

There was an old person of Shields,
Who frequented the valley and fields;
All the mice and the cats, and the snakes and the rats,
Followed after that person of Shields.

The mice, rats and cats follow, too. In fact, the Old Man of Shields, who is placed near the end of the second series, shows how thoroughly the Man has tamed nature. Gone forever are the days when he could make himself ill by devouring rabbits.

There was an old Person whose habits,
Induced him to feed upon Rabbits;
When he'd eaten eighteen, he turned perfectly green,
Upon which he relinquished those habits.

He really has given up "those habits." Now he turns to the animal world for help and comfort. Riding on the back of a hare partly lifts his depression.

There was an old man whose despair
Induced him to purchase a hare:
Whereon one fine day, he rode wholly away,
Which partly assauged his despair.

In a merrier mood, he rides on a tortoise, a crocodile, a giant fly, a goose and a bear.

There was an old person of Ware,
Who rode on the back of a bear:
When they ask'd,—"Does it trot?"—he said "Certainly not!
He's a Moppsikon Floppsikon bear!"

When he is not riding on a creature, he is on the verge of turning into one. Metamorphoses abound in the second series.[10]

Of the thirty animal limericks in the first series, over twenty are fraught with anxiety or difficulty, and at least a dozen involve violence. Of the nine in which the Lady meets creatures, nearly all enact situations which are happy for her, or in which danger has been averted. The Old Man resembles the creatures in five pictures, the Lady in none. Of thirty-one animal limericks in the second series, over twenty are untroubled, except where the neighbors—"They"—disapprove. Violence is rare. Of the nine involving the Lady, most express anxiety or trouble of some kind; but there is still hardly any violence. The Man frequently resembles the creatures, nearly always happily; the Lady only once, when she fans her fowls. Only insects* and dogs remain wary or hostile in both series—insects, doubtless because it is hard to see them as kin, and dogs, because Lear feared them all his life.

The music and animal limericks have changed together. They are mirrors of the same shift in the poet's view of the world. The Old Man of 1872 finds nature tamer and more manageable, less magical and more sociable, more domestic and less troubled. The Young Lady, having lost much of her power to enchant nature, has nearly vanished, along with the violence and anxiety. The beasts are now more numerous; and mostly of the farmyard or the household—domesticated and tame. The music is less potent and more beneficent. Where there was disaster, there is now a truce, or a real peace.

But not everything has come right, nor has it been an easy struggle. The limericks have a dark side—they are full of frenzy, despair, oppression and threats of punishment or banishment—or death. What of this, the darkest aspect of all? How does Lear present death in the limericks?

In the first series, there is a great deal of drowning, choking, burning and smashing. The Old Man, the Young Lady and many beasts are killed at one time or another. More than a quarter of the limericks deal with death, in fact, and there are, besides, many narrow escapes and near-misses. The Old Man is the main victim. Sometimes, weary of study or out of a pure despair, he kills himself.

*Except for the fly who dances with the Old Person of Skye.

There was an Old Person of Cromer,
Who stood on one leg to read Homer;
When he found he grew stiff, he jumped over the cliff,
Which concluded that Person of Cromer.

There was an Old Man of Cape Horn,
Who wished he had never been born;
So he sat on a chair, till he died of despair,
That dolorous Man of Cape Horn.

Sometimes They kill him.

There was an Old Person of Buda,
Whose conduct grew ruder and ruder;
Till at last, with a hammer, they silenced his clamour,
By smashing that Person of Buda.

There was an Old Man of Leghorn,
The smallest as ever was born;
But quickly snapt up he, was once by a puppy,
Who devoured that Old Man of Leghorn.

There was an Old Man of the Cape,
Who possessed a large Barbary Ape;
Till the Ape one dark night, set the house on a light,
Which burned that Old Man of the Cape.

Sometimes it is the creatures who are killed, nearly always, as we have seen, by the Young Lady in her role as musical enchantress. On one occasion she saves herself from death by having a cat killed in her place.

There was a Young Person of Smyrna,
Whose Grandmother threatened to burn her;
But she seized on the Cat, and said, "Granny, burn that,
You incongruous Old Woman of Smyrna!"

Since Lear loved cats, it is not hard to guess what his feelings toward this Young Lady must have been. Very often gluttony is to blame for the Old Man's death.[11]

There was an Old Man of the South,
Who had an immoderate mouth;
But in swallowing a dish, that was quite full of fish,
He was choked, that Old Man of the South.

There was an Old Man of Berlin,
Whose form was uncommonly thin;
Till he once, by mistake, was mixed up in a cake,
So they baked that Old Man of Berlin.

In all this slaughter—ingenious, domestic, uninhibited—two significant discriminations are made. The Young Lady is killed only once, at the very end, and They are never killed. The Old Man and the beasts are the defensive parties. But it would be wrong to suppose that they are always mistreated. The Young Lady, as we have seen, is kind to birds, and while They kill the Old Man half a dozen times, They actually save him from some dilemma or impending doom on an equal number of occasions. They rescue the Old Man of the West from a perpetual state of agitation.

There was an Old Man of the West,
Who never could get any rest;
So they set him to spin, on his nose and his chin,
Which cured that Old Man of the West.

Then the Old Man of Nepaul breaks in two after falling off his horse, and They mend him with glue.

There was an Old Man of Nepaul,
From his horse had a terrible fall;
But, though split quite in two, by some very strong glue,
They mended that Man of Nepaul.

And, in the form of a cook, They fish him out of a boiling cauldron.

There was an Old Man of the North,
Who fell into a basin of broth;
But a laudable cook, fished him out with a hook,
Which saved that Old Man of the North.

This solicitousness surprises some readers. Usually They are taken for a persistently menacing group that represents the murderous forces of convention and propriety. Although it is true that They are more hostile than friendly, They are not a tribe of ferocious Podsnaps. They feel curiously ambivalent about the Old Man and his strange behavior, and They are gentlemen enough never to harm the Lady.

In the second series, death has all but disappeared. There are only three certain cases, involving the Young Lady, the Old Man and They. The young person of Kew is scalded to death by eating hot paste.

There was a young person of Kew,
Whose virtues and vices were few;
But with blameable haste, she devoured some hot paste,
Which destroyed that young person of Kew.

The old person of Florence, as we have seen, dies because he tries to cook a Bustard. These are both cases of accidental death, caused by a reckless greediness for hot food. There is no instance in which They kill. But They are, for the first and only time, the victims when the old person of Stroud slays and scrunches them.

There was an old person of Stroud;
Who was horribly jammed in a crowd;
Some she slew with a kick, some she scrunched with a stick,
That impulsive old person of Stroud.

For the rest, there are a few close calls and some incidents where death is miraculously defied. The Albanian uncle of the young person of Janina does not seem to have committed manslaughter.

There was a young person of Janina,
Whose uncle was always a fanning her,
When he fanned off her head, she smiled sweetly, and said,
"You propitious old person of Janina!"

Presumably, she can replace her head at will and her life will continue.

Moreover, the creatures neither kill nor are killed. Indeed, the Old Man of Bree instructs his owls to give up their natural prey in favor of tea. As for the neighbors, who are the most hostile group in the first series, They do not kill, either; and in the second series, They have grown even more solicitous. They rescue the old person of Fife from suicide.

There was an old person of Fife,
Who was greatly disgusted with life;
They sang him a ballad, and fed him on salad,
Which cured that old person of Fife.

In most of the other limericks of the second series, They are either on uneasily friendly terms with the Old Man, or They are on the defensive, in a state of resigned bewilderment. They are no longer secure, and the Young Lady has also lost her power. She can kill Them—but that seems mainly to be a sign of their weakness. It is the exception which proves the rule; she has lost command and can neither enchant nor kill creatures any longer. As we shall see, it is only when Lear draws her as still young that she retains some of her old force. She has grown old and pacific, like the Old Man, who has made his peace with both nature and society and has also overcome his dread of death.

The pattern is becoming clearer. The two series express a search, intense and unconscious, for peace of mind, a struggle against the fears of the heart, a reaching out toward the joys of the spirit.

But before we jump to conclusions, let us examine the role They play throughout. They appear in about forty, or a third, of the first limericks. Thirty of these involve Them with the Old Man, and in six They kill or seriously injure him.

There was an old Person of Chester,
Whom several small children did pester;
They threw some large stones, which broke most of his bones,
And displeased that old Person of Chester.

Their behavior can be treacherous. Here, for instance, They appear as the Old Man's children, and their unruliness and greed are such that he perishes of mortification.

There was an Old Man of the East,
Who gave all his children a feast;
But they all ate so much, and their conduct was such,
That it killed the Old Man of the East.

But sometimes he seems quite indifferent. Judging from the posture and expression of the Old Man with a gong, we cannot be sure if "smashing" really means death.

Generally They fall into two groups, offensive and defensive. In half a dozen, They clearly mock the Old Man.[12]

And in another half dozen, They seem distressed by his actions.[13]

In extreme cases, They succeed in killing him. But just as often, he retaliates effectively. The Old Man with a poker knocks them down.

And the Old Man at a casement fills Them with consternation.

There was an Old Man at a casement,
Who held up his hands in amazement;
When they said, "Sir! you'll fall!" he replied, "Not at all!"
That incipient Old Man at a casement.

The relationship is not always antagonistic, of course. On several occasions, They come to the Old Man's rescue.

There was an Old Person of Prague,
Who was suddenly seized with the plague;
But they gave him some butter, which caused him to mutter,
And cured that Old Person of Prague.

When the Old Man of Nepaul falls off his horse, They glue him together again, and They put a stop to the Old Person of Rheims's nightmares.

There was an Old Person of Rheims,
Who was troubled with horrible dreams;
So, to keep him awake, they fed him on cake,
Which amused that Old Person of Rheims.

But somehow this does not seem the kindest cure, and on the whole he is not happy with their ministrations.

There was an Old Man of Columbia,
Who was thirsty, and called out for some beer;
But they brought it quite hot, in a small copper pot,
Which disgusted that man of Columbia.

The Old Man of the Abruzzi rebuffs their counsel.

There was an Old Man of th' Abruzzi,
So blind that he couldn't his foot see;
When they said, "That's your toe," he replied, "Is it so?"
That doubtful old Man of th' Abruzzi.

Their assistance sometimes looks subversive, or at least mistaken.

There was an Old Man with a beard,
Who sat on a horse when he reared;
But they said, "Never mind! you will fall off behind,
You propitious Old Man with a beard!"

In some cases, it is impossible to tell whether their advice is offered genuinely. The Old Man may be right to ignore it.

There was an Old Man of Aôsta,
Who possessed a large Cow but he lost her;
But they said, "Don't you see, she has rushed up a tree?
You invidious Old Man of Aôsta!"

When we note that They are on the offensive in about twenty limericks, while the Old Man has the upper hand in only half a dozen, perhaps we can assume that the Old Man of Aôsta has his reasons for passing Them by. At least this is a particularly unresolved limerick and it leaves the reader on edge.

In the first series, then, the relationship between Them and the Old Man is hostile, ambiguous, uneasy. In the second, the relationship has undergone a profound change. They are now more numerous—appearing in nearly half the limericks, and They are much friendlier. They never kill the Old Man, and on the few occasions when They seem to try, he manages to rebuff them.

There was an old man of Ibreem,
Who suddenly threaten'd to scream:
But they said, "If you do, we will thump you quite blue,
You disgusting old man of Ibreem!"

When They abuse or threaten him, either he seems indifferent or he clearly has control of the situation.

There was an old man of Thermopylae,
Who never did anything properly;
But they said, "If you choose, to boil eggs in your shoes,
You shall never remain in Thermopylae."

There can be no question of Their actually running him out of town this time. Only in two limericks, where he tries to transform himself into one of the creatures, do They seem to have the advantage.

There was an old person of Brill,
Who purchased a shirt with a frill;
But they said, "Don't you wish, you mayn't look like a fish,
You obsequious old person of Brill?"

Even here, They cannot bring themselves actually to expel him.

There was an old man of Dumblane,
Who greatly resembled a crane;
But they said,—"Is it wrong, since your legs are so long,
To request you won't stay in Dumblane?"

Their questions are taunting but indirect, and the confrontation, both times, is something of a standoff. In nearly half the limericks of the second series in which They figure, They are on the defensive—rebuffed, perplexed, astonished, or in flight.[14]

In about half a dozen, They again offer advice or help. This time it seems more sincere, and is accepted more openly. But we can see from the drawings that while They no longer seem subversive, They are still nervous or distressed.[15]

In one exceedingly strange limerick, They punish him, and at the same time, to his masochistic glee, provide him with a salve for the pains They inflict.

There was an old man who screamed out
Whenever they knocked him about;
So they took off his boots, and fed him with fruits,
And continued to knock him about.

The Old Man of Dee-side makes a more wholesome peace, one in which, moreover, his dominance is clearly illustrated.

There was an old man of Dee-side
Whose hat was exceedingly wide,
But he said "Do not fail, if it happen to hail
To come under my hat at Dee-side!"

Here the tables are turned. Cowering and nervous, it is They who are in need of help. They accept his invitation in stunned submission. It is as if their former professions of concern have been unmasked. They were never really able to help him, perhaps They wanted only to harm him, or at least to exercise their misguided mastery. Now he has command, and he shows himself to be a more generous protector than They would have been. It is not an equal relationship, of course, but he is not at all vindictive. He wants a warm and generous peace. If we put all of Them together we see Them for what They now are—a gallery of defeated rogues, subdued, bewildered, fearful, pacified.[16]

These aside, there is another large group of limericks where neither the Old Man nor They have the better of the other. The relationship remains tense, but it is not clearly antagonistic. Both parties are more or less inscrutable.

There was an old man of Toulouse
Who purchased a new pair of shoes;
When they asked, "Are they pleasant?"—he said, "Not at present!"
That turbid old man of Toulouse.

There was an Old Man at a junction
Whose feelings were wrung with compunction;
When they said, "The Train's gone!" he exclaimed "How forlorn!"
But remained on the rails of the junction.

There was an old person of Barnes,
Whose garments were covered with darns;
But they said, "Without doubt, you will soon wear them out,
You luminous person of Barnes!"

There was an old person of Deal
Who in walking, used only his heel;
When they said, "Tell us why?"—he made no reply;
That mysterious old person of Deal.

There was an old person of Ware,
Who rode on the back of a bear:
When they ask'd,—"Does it trot?"—he said "Certainly not!
He's a Moppsikon Floppsikon bear!"

They seem neutral, noncommittal, up in the air or simply inexpressive. We shall return to these, and limericks like them, later on. For all their placidity, they are among the most vivid, revealing and nonsensical of all the picture poems.

In a way, everything in the relationship between the Old Man and Them tends toward this state of congenial nonplus. As the Old Man gains control and exorcises his fear of Them, he arranges a benign state of coexistence in which he will not lord it over Them, on condition that They give up their threatening and censorious behavior toward him. He is happy, and They nervously contrive somehow to endure his folly and get along with him. They are still an impersonal horde, but no longer the menacing invaders conjured up by an alienated imagination. What remains is not paranoia but an understandable fear of conformism and unnatural proprieties. If the Old Man is still an outsider, his condition is ours too, and we are grateful to him for what he has shown us of ourselves, and for demonstrating with clarity and courage that our foes, wherever we find them out, whoever they may be, can all be vanquished.

Meanwhile, how has the Young Lady fared with Them? In the first series, she appears in about a quarter of Their limericks. She has far less to do with Them than the Old Man does. She is always clearly in charge. She astonishes and repels them.

There was a Young Lady whose eyes,
Were unique as to colour and size;
When she opened them wide, people all turned aside,
And started away in surprise.

When she curtseys she wrings from five of Them five distinct kinds of amazement.

There was an Old Lady of Chertsey,
Who made a remarkable curtsey;
She twirled round and round, till she sunk underground,
Which distressed all the people of Chertsey.

Sometimes she uses noisy persistence.

There was a Young Lady of Russia,
Who screamed so that no one could hush her;
Her screams were extreme, no one heard such a scream,
As was screamed by that Lady of Russia.

Or she shows imperturbable taciturnity.

There was a Young Lady of Parma,
Whose conduct grew calmer and calmer;
When they said, "Are you dumb?" she merely said, "Hum!"
That provoking Young Lady of Parma.

Ten years later, in the second series, the Young Lady has all but disappeared in favor of an Old Lady or Person; or rather, she has grown old with the years. Now she appears in only a fifth of Their limericks. She has even less to do with Them, a natural development, perhaps, of her earlier indifference. Moreover, she has an even greater power over Them. On one occasion she actually kills Them, the only time They die in either series.

There was an old person of Stroud,
Who was horribly jammed in a crowd;
Some she slew with a kick, some she scrunched with a stick,
That impulsive old person of Stroud.

Her taciturnity has grown more abrupt.

There was a young lady in blue,
Who said, "Is it you? Is it you?"
When they said, "Yes, it is,"—She replied only, "Whizz!"
That ungracious young lady in blue.

When They try to rebuff her, she stands her ground.

There was an old person of Loo,
Who said, "What on earth shall I do?"
When they said, "Go away!"—she continued to stay,
That vexatious old person of Loo.

She does not heed Their wishes.

There was an old person of Jodd,
Whose ways were perplexing and odd;
She purchased a whistle, and sat on a thistle,
And squeaked to the people of Jodd.

Nor does she respect Their advice.

There was an old person of Rimini,
Who said, "Gracious! Goodness! O Gimini!"
When they said, "Please be still!" she ran down a hill,
And was never more heard of at Rimini.

Her lack of propriety, as we can tell from this drawing, astounds and dismays Them.

There is a young lady, whose nose,
Continually prospers and grows;
When it grew out of sight, she exclaimed in a fright,
"Oh! Farewell to the end of my nose!"

There is nothing They can do. She appears to be all-powerful. In her dealings with Them she appears, in the picture at least, as the Young Lady still; the Old Lady has only one encounter with Them, when she kills Them, and in this cartoon her face is too well hidden for us to tell whether she is really old. Lear seems to be vindicating her youthful powers, and at the same time acknowledging that her influence, with age, has mostly come to an end. He allows her a last fling.

So, in the second series, the Old Man learns how to master Them, and he imposes a peaceful rule; and the Young Lady, who has never feared Them, helps him subdue Them, and then vanishes. The Old Lady chooses to have nothing to do with Them, wisely enough. Under the new dispensation, They grow more tolerant and genial, though They are still greatly discomforted. They have had their comeuppance. But we do not have to feel sorry for Them. The fears They represent—of conformity, censorship, isolation, alienation—are quelled. In this broader, fresher world there is less room for the bullies of convention and more for friends and good company. Or, if the individual chooses, he may keep his own company, unmolested. Perhaps it is this, the freedom to be alone without being lonely, which has been at the heart of the poet-cartoonist's struggle.

But there is no point in rushing to assign particular motives. The work is sufficiently ambiguous to foil special guesses. The general pattern, now that an overall view has revealed it, is more than enough to satisfy our curiosity and help our investigation. Just as nature has become tamer and the beasts are more sociable, the music has grown more beneficent and death is a rare event, so also human relations have been transformed from the disastrous to the pacific. Everywhere there is a joyful truce—the heart unclenches, and the spirit is released.

But the Lady remains an enigmatic figure. If we look more closely at the first series, we may observe that her age seems to be something of a pretense. The verses say she is young, but in only a quarter of the pictures of her is her age clearly confirmed. In the rest, the drawings are discrepant; she appears older, and the verses seem to be flattering her age. The Young Lady of Portugal looks decidedly matronly.

There was a Young Lady of Portugal,
Whose ideas were excessively nautical:
She climbed up a tree, to examine the sea,
But declared she would never leave Portugal.

The Young Lady of Russia looks dowdy.

There was a Young Lady of Russia,
Who screamed so that no one could hush her;
Her screams were extreme, no one heard such a scream,
As was screamed by that Lady of Russia.

Of course, the drawings are so broad that there is always room for doubt. But there are three limericks which show plainly that Lear, perhaps unconsciously, was playing with this discrepancy. The Old Lady of Prague, for instance, has a lined face, but her waist is slender and her bust is firm, whereas the young lady who attends her is plain and dumpy.

Lear is allowing the properties of age to blur and overlap. It is much the same with the Young Girl of Majorca[17] and her aunt. The girl has lost her figure and looks almost middle-aged; her aunt is sprightly, and still thin.

There was a Young Girl of Majorca,
Whose aunt was a very fast walker;
She walked seventy miles, and leaped fifteen stiles,
Which astonished that Girl of Majorca.

There can be no doubt about the Young Lady of Parma. She is either middle-aged or older, a stiff spinster many years the senior of the woman who questions her.

There was a Young Lady of Parma,
Whose conduct grew calmer and calmer;
When they said, "Are you dumb!" she merely said, "Hum!"
That provoking Young Lady of Parma.

Is Lear merely enjoying the joke that ladies lie about their age? Perhaps—but there is surely something more. The discrepancy is only half-conscious; he draws her old out of some deeper compulsion.

Her power and her age are her two main attributes, after her sex. In the first book, Lear puts her age in doubt. In the second, when she has grown older, he undoes her potency. She becomes more moderate in the 1872 volume. At times she is still strong. She slays Them and is able to flaunt her peculiarities in the face of the whole world.

There was a young lady of Firle,
Whose hair was addicted to curl;
It curled up a tree, and all over the sea,
That expansive young lady of Firle.

But it is really only in her few dealings with Them that she has her old strength, and in the drawings of these limericks she is pictured as young. In the others in which she appears, as she ages she becomes much more oppressed, confined or disturbed. Our first impressions were not thorough enough, and overlooked this. Some limericks depict her in a state of physical imprisonment, or she is immersed in a restricting element. In the first series she seems always to have chosen this for herself, and she looks happy.

There was a Young Person of Crete,
Whose toilette was far from complete;
She dressed in a sack, spickle-speckled with black,
That ombliferous person of Crete.

When her husband tries to nail her up in a box—a coffin perhaps—she is in no danger, and it is he who is worried.

There was an Old Man on some rocks,
Who shut his wife up in a box;
When she said, "Let me out," he exclaimed, "Without doubt,
You will pass all your life in that box."

In the second series, her feelings about confinement are more negative. The lady in green looks withdrawn or depressed.

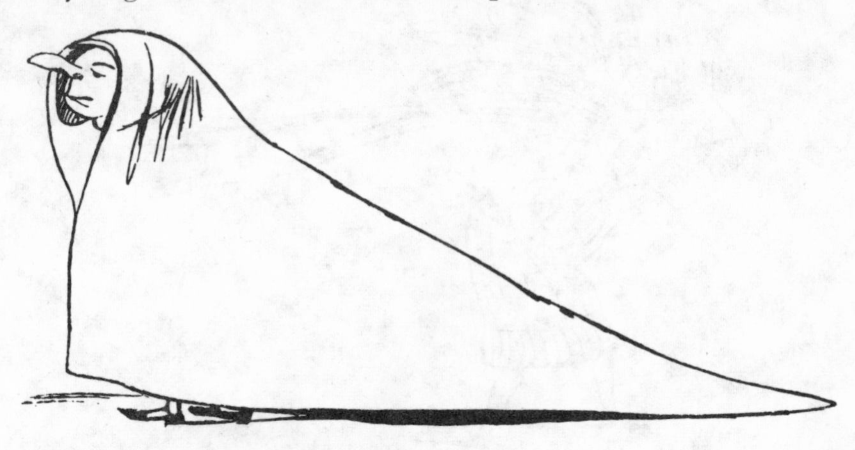

There was a young person in green,
Who seldom was fit to be seen;
She wore a long shawl, over bonnet and all,
Which enveloped that person in green.

The young lady in white, afloat in the depths of the dark night, is in despair.

There was a young lady in white,
Who looked out at the depths of the night;
But the birds of the air, filled her heart with despair,
And oppressed that young lady in white.

The Young Lady in a bonnet in the first series seems a great deal happier than her successor in the second, though neither seems to find the right balance between shyness and exhibitionism.

There was a young person in red,
Who carefully covered her head,
With a bonnet of leather, and three lines of feather,
Besides some long ribands of red.

There was a Young Lady of Dorking,
Who bought a large bonnet for walking;
But its colour and size, so bedazzled her eyes,
That she very soon went back to Dorking.

The old person kills Them, it is now evident, not because she is on top of things, but because she is "horribly jammed in a crowd" and has to fight her way out. The Lady of Bar is the only confined figure who feels happy with her lot.

There was an old person of Bar,
Who passed all her life in a jar,
Which she painted pea-green, to appear more serene,
That placid old person of Bar.

But why does she wish to "appear more serene"? Is she fooling herself? If she is genuinely happy in her jar, she is the exception who proves the rule: elsewhere in the second series, the Young Lady often feels imprisoned, and this makes her desperate and afraid.

We have observed already how she has lost her mastery over the beasts. The ducklings reject her instruction and the owls of the night depress her. She can ride on a pig, it is true, but is she comfortable?

There was an old man of Messina,
Whose daughter was named Opsibeena;
She wore a small wig, and rode out on a pig,
To the perfect delight of Messina.

A spotted calf eats her shawl, and she is powerless to prevent this event.

There was a young lady of Greenwich
Whose garments were border'd with Spinach;
But a large spotty Calf, bit her shawl quite in half,
Which alarmed that young lady of Greenwich.

Can this be the same shawl under which she was taking cover? In most of her encounters with beasts, there is a strong feeling of dismay or perturbation. We have seen how warily she goes about feeding her two parrots, and how her nursing of the fish may have predatory motives. Her relation with the creatures nearly always involves food or eating, but there is no oral gratification for her. Rather, the association of animals and eating gives her anxiety. She has a strange demonic dog which she must appease.

There was a young lady of Corsica,
Who purchased a little brown saucy-cur;
Which she fed upon ham, and hot raspberry jam,
That expensive young lady of Corsica.

When she sleeps in the pantry she has to keep the mice at bay.

There was a young person of Bantry,
Who frequently slept in the pantry;
When disturbed by the mice, she appeased them with rice,
That judicious young person of Bantry.

This is one of the few occasions when she reaches some kind of understanding with the animal world, but it is still a restless peace.

If we look again at her dealings with her neighbors, we may find reason to revise our original impressions once more. The Lady in the bonnet is not fit to be seen, and she hides her head in shame or fear. The lady in blue is awkward and ungracious in a way that happy or peaceful people can never be. And the old person of Loo is angry and unyielding.

There was an old person of Loo,
Who said, "What on earth shall I do?"
When they said, "Go away!"—she continued to stay,
That vexatious old person of Loo.

Society does not succeed either in condemning the Lady or in punishing her, but she is considered beyond the pale, not merely because of her eccentricity, but also because of her ungraciousness. She has withdrawn into a state of anxious depression or nervous and rigid indifference.

She is rarely joyful or self-possessed. Throughout, she looks agitated or cowed, aggressive and retiring by turns, impulsive and withdrawn, ill-mannered and hemmed in by bad opinion and her own distress. She does not like her family.

There was an old person of Pisa,
Whose daughters did nothing to please her;
She dressed them in gray, and banged them all day
Round the walls of the city of Pisa.

Nor does she like the farmyard, nor the wild, nor the drawing room. No wonder she cries out, in her dismay, "What shall I do?"

The second series ends with two mysterious limericks in which she reappears in her most youthful form. The penultimate shows her in a state of vexation once more. She calls out for something to drink, and when an older woman, perhaps her mother, tells her there is only water and brings her a large jug of it, she faints dead away. It is as if she is brought face to face with the facts that she has grown into another, older person, and that she can no longer rely on the refreshments of youth for her powers. What, indeed, can she do, except collapse?

There was a young person in pink,
Who called out for something to drink;
But they said, "O my daughter, there's nothing but water!"
Which vexed that young person in pink.

But in the final limerick Lear allows her a silent yet emphatic last word.

There was a young person whose history,
Was always considered a mystery;
She sat in a ditch, although no one knew which,
And composed a small treatise on history.

Here she makes a quiet last-ditch stand and exhibits a mystifying independence and inviolability. She is well—even fashionably—dressed in her late Regency manner, and she has chosen a comfortable place in the setting sun, with her feet propped up and her hair neatly fixed. She smiles enigmatically and composes a small treatise on history—her own, perhaps. Her youth and her power have, for the moment, been restored to her. But it is only for a moment: this limerick is placed at the end, the sun is setting, and she is looking back over her life, a brief one since she is still young and her treatise is small. Soon she will dab her quill pen in her ink bottle for the last time; then it will all have been written. It is as if Lear were saying goodbye here to the tutelary and enigmatic spirit who has ruled his first "nonsenses." Now that she has helped him conquer his fears and has herself grown old and frail, she may burn brightly for an instant and then vanish.

She may, on the other hand, represent a malignant force in Lear's life; and one might construct an interpretation with this as the basic observation. The limericks are sufficiently open-ended and consistent enough for us to invent many arguments concerning their meaning. And Lear's life invites us to enquire further. For instance, to what extent does the Lady represent the character and circumstances of his sister Ann? She was a Young Lady—his sister; and, since she was twenty years older than he, a middle-aged lady—a surrogate mother. Lear felt guilty about leaving her after she had devoted her youth to his upbringing. When he left for the Continent he must have realized that his departure spelled the end of her youth and that she had nothing to look forward to but a lonely old age.

Or to what extent might the Young Lady represent the female aspect of the artist's own personality, the anima? He had several relationships of a homosexual character and suffered a general confusion of sexual identity. Perhaps he felt the more feminine part of him as the more potent, and a threat to his happiness and sanity. He found peace only when he could do away with it—when in middle age the prospect of love faded for him, or when he had managed to root out his love for Lushington once and for all. The Old Man feels less intimidated and finds his awkward peace only when, in the second series, the enchantress-woman has lost her power, grown old, or gone away.

Although some of these speculations look promising, there is too little information about Lear's early life to take them much further. Besides, the limericks have already yielded biographical information of a fresh and certain kind. It is clear that in his forties, when his nonsense was maturing and his life was growing more agitated, Lear succeeded in making peace with himself. He had exorcised his fears of man and nature, he had found quiet counsel where formerly there were only terror and disarray, he had discovered a place where he could be his eccentric self as well as a happy participant. He no longer suffered so intensely, as he had suffered at Millais' party, the feeling of being on the outside, "woundily like a spectator."[18] He realized that there was now no point in hurrying on "thru constantly new and burningly bright scenes,"[19] and that the peace of mind he sought was to be found rather by pausing and reflecting on the moment, and by ruminating—in his nonsense picture poems—on the hidden movements of the heart and the secret flights of the spirit. So he settled at San Remo, and though he felt as lonely as before, he at least opened himself to his own feelings and began to understand something of the mysteries around and inside him. Out of this honesty and clarity emerged the best of the limericks and the longer, mature nonsense poems.

Not that he had turned into a happy man. Rather, he saw his misery more lucidly. The main troubles remained, and he never found a way of either giving or receiving intimate love. He was still shy with women; the Lady is still, to the end, a baffling mystery. Her enigma, and the other mysteries which bewilder or bring joy, kept their secrets.

His peculiar gift was to be able to express the undisclosed, and we should be wrong to approach the remaining puzzles of the limericks as if the author knew any better than we what lies behind them. We should accept them in their unsolved state. What we have discovered is not a clear narrative characterization or a fully disclosed psychological portrait, but instead a dynamic set of dramatic situations which express a wide range of feelings and ideas and then leave them suspended for the reader to mull over. The limericks do not present their characters for us to come to understand, as a psychological novel might, nor do they develop situations, in the manner of detective fiction, for us to puzzle out. There is puzzlement, but it is left up in the air. There is characterization, but it is not fully manifest. We are left, quite properly, nonplused and with the feeling not just that there is more here than meets the eye, but that there is more than the eye can ever hope to discern. The Young Lady's mystery is secure, and we should be wrong to pester her for an answer, since this mystery is a kind of joke, and to explain a joke is, of course, to explain it away.

Picture and Poem Discrepancy

But if there is no solving the enigma, there is still much more to be said about how the limericks work and what they say. We have already explained something of the Young Lady's character by dwelling on the difference between what the verse told us about her and what the cartoon depicted. A glance through both series will quickly satisfy the reader that in nearly every picture poem there is a discrepancy; and when we look closely, we see that, in each, this discrepancy is the key which unlocks not the whole secret but as much of it as we are allowed to know. Even more significantly, by observing what the discrepancies have in common, we come to understand the principal motive and point behind the strange drama which the limericks enact.

Frenzy

A large number of the limericks are concerned with states of agitation or frenzy. Lear suffered terribly from epilepsy and continually suppressed his feelings; he lived a life of quiet desperation. It is hardly surprising, then, to find in well over half the limericks a combustible situation or a frantic mood. But for nearly every frenzied verse, there is a cartoon which defuses or mollifies, indicating that the agitation is not what it seems. Consider this verse, for instance.

> There was an Old Man in a boat,
> Who said, "I'm afloat! I'm afloat!"
> When they said, "No! you ain't!" he was ready to faint,
> That unhappy Old Man in a boat.

It is accompanied by this picture.

Obviously the verse and the drawing differ. The Old Man throws his hands and legs in the air, but it is not clear from his expression whether he is overjoyed because he thinks he is afloat or on the point of fainting with dismay because he thinks he has learned that he is still beached. They leap on tiptoe and demonstrate with extended arms the truth of what They are saying. But while one of Them smiles sweetly, the other looks anxiously at his companion and seems rather uncertain. This small gesture is the pivot of the whole picture poem. Is there really cause for alarm? Perhaps the Old Man is having fun. Is he really upset or unhappy? The verse describes the drama in very certain terms: the Old Man shouts out that he is afloat, and They flatly contradict him. But the drawing renders it all very uncertain: even They do not have their feet on the ground, and it is hard to tell where land ends and the water begins. Perhaps they are all three afloat.

Again, we might compare two occasions when the Old Man screams.

There was an old man of Ibreem,
Who suddenly threaten'd to scream:
But they said, "If you do, we will thump you quite blue,
You disgusting old man of Ibreem!"

There was an old man who screamed out
Whenever they knocked him about;
So they took off his boots, and fed him with fruits,
And continued to knock him about.

When They threaten to thump the Old Man of Ibreem, They certainly look angry and censorious. But the Old Man looks extremely savage and more than their match. Are They about to bring down their canes? Or is he roaring at Them to put them aside? They look stern but also puzzled, and Their canes hesitate. The result is more of a standoff then the verse might indicate. In the second limerick, the ambivalence is even more marked. The drawing damps down the frenzy of the verse by suggesting that Their cruelty may also be kindness—an odd but not unacceptable paradox.

In all three picture poems the agitation of the verse is quietened in the cartoon, which presents a more ambivalent state of affairs. By what seems an unconscious strategy of discrepancy, the cartoon disagrees in part with the verse, in order to soften the blows of life. The explosion is baffled. Once or twice the verse banks down the high feelings of the cartoon. The Old Man of Ischia, for instance, is black in the face in the drawing.

But in the verse, with nice English understatement, he is described as merely "lively."

> There was an Old Person of Ischia,
> Whose conduct grew friskier and friskier;
> He danced hornpipes and jigs, and ate thousands of figs,
> That lively Old Person of Ischia.

But the general rule is: the image calms the word.

This is especially clear in a group of frenzied limericks in which the Old Man is described in the verse as rushing up and down, and in the drawing he appears striding widely leftward with outflung arms. If we gather them together, we see how compulsive a pattern they form.

There was an Old Man on a hill,
Who seldom, if ever, stood still;
He ran up and down, in his Grandmother's gown,
Which adorned that Old Man on a hill.

There was an old person of Dover,
Who rushed through a field of blue Clover;
But some very large bees, stung his nose and his knees,
So he very soon went back to Dover.

There was an old person of Bude,
Whose deportment was vicious and crude;
He wore a large ruff, of pale straw-coloured stuff,
Which perplexed all the people of Bude.

There was an Old Man of Corfu,
Who never knew what he should do;
So he rushed up and down, till the sun made him brown,
That bewildered Old Man of Corfu.

There was an Old Person of Anerley,
Whose conduct was strange and unmannerly;
He rushed down the Strand, with a Pig in each hand,
But returned in the evening to Anerley.

There was an Old Man of Coblenz,
The length of whose legs was immense;
He went with one prance, from Turkey to France,
That surprising Old Man of Coblenz.

There was an old person of Wilts,
Who constantly walked upon stilts;
He wreathed them with lillies, and daffy-down-dillies,
That elegant person of Wilts.

The picture gives a fair representation of the text in only two cases: the Old Person of Anerley is agitated in both picture and verse, and no essential elements of the last limerick are omitted from the cartoon of the old person of Wilts. All the others exit stage right as if they were part of a tableau. The pose is struck and held. The old person of Dover looks almost statuesque and placid. Corfu is still smoking his pipe and carrying his walking stick. His indecision leads to frenzy in the verse, but the cartoon transforms this into a sort of frozen hesitation. In five of the picture poems, the cartoon quiets the agitation. But it does not altogether cancel it. Rather, by depicting the poem's action in terms of repose which contradict its principal emotion of alarm, the drawing makes a nonsense paradox of the whole. One illusion—the Old Man is frantic—has been dispelled in favor of another, more ambivalent one—the Old Man is both alarmed and hushed. We gain the sense of calm without losing the sense of alarm.

This relationship between image and word is more obvious still in the most frantic limericks of all—the ones about death.

There was an Old Person of Tartary,
Who divided his jugular artery;
But he screeched to his wife, and she said, "Oh, my life!
Your death will be felt by all Tartary!"

He calls out to his wife, but it is too late. The whole country will feel the loss, she exclaims. But will Tartary indeed have cause to feel sorry? She advances toward him as the knife falls from his hand, her arms outstretched, her expression one of eager surprise. Here Lear is not merely indulging the easy joke that the wife really welcomes his death while pretending to be shocked. Her smile seems to say, without malice or pretense, that nothing really alarming has occurred. She smiles away the disaster. The verse pivots on "Oh, my life! / Your death. . . ." and the cartoon decides the issue in favor of life. And what fun there is in acting as if violence or death cannot touch us! This has become one of the staple conventions of the modern comic.

The paradox—of death-in-life, frenzy-in-calm—is clearer still in the second series; for example, in the limerick concerning the young person of Janina, who has her head lopped off by an uncle.

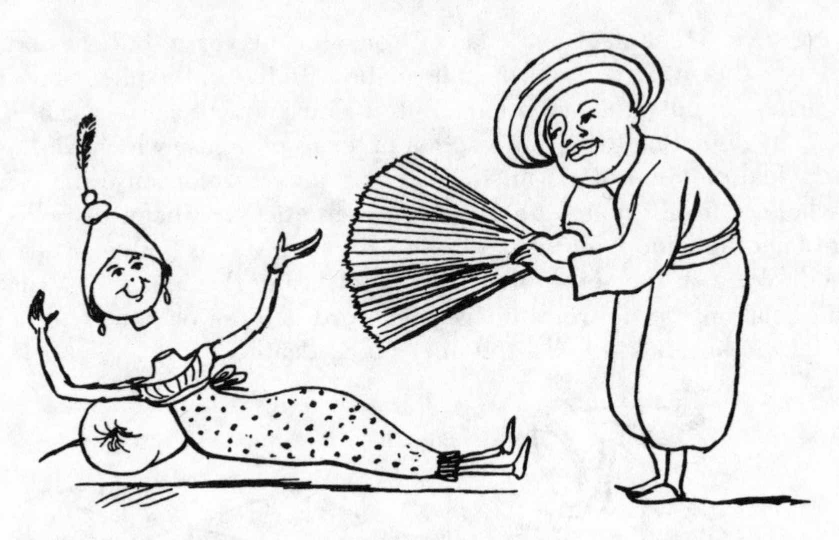

There was a young person of Janina,
Whose uncle was always a fanning her;
When he fanned off her head, she smiled sweetly, and said,
"You propitious old person of Janina!"

Here the cartoon continues and completes a paradox set up in the verse. The smile of defiance on the face of the wife of the Old Man of Tartary enters the poem here, and it is even broader in the drawing. Both picture and poem overwhelm the catastrophe by denying it. The smile and the expansive gesture of the arms assure us that life goes on.

In the ten limericks where the cartoon damps down the agitation, the drawing, in creating a more ambivalent situation, also creates a more positive one. The paradox is expansive and moves us away from a state of intelligible unhappiness (fuss, agitation, frenzy, death) toward a state of mysterious pleasure (calm, hope, life).

Indifference

There is another large group of limericks which is concerned with the opposite of agitation—indifference. In them we see more clearly both the relationship of cartoon and verse and Lear's deeper meanings. In the verse, the hero (or heroine) is involved in a situation which could spell discomfort or even disaster: but instead of expressing alarm, he declares his indifference. The cartoon justifies this attitude, so that it stands in a contradictory relation to the "objective" situation of the verse and in a complementary relation to the "subjective" situation. The cartoon, to put it another way, now allies itself with one aspect of the verse against another—as it did in the last "death" limerick. It is both discrepant and consonant, and by confirming the hero's courage and enforcing the peace, it is also expansive. The contradiction is still felt as a paradox, since in gaining a sense of calm, we do not altogether lose the sense of alarm. But with both image and word warring against the commonsense, objective disaster, the weaker term of the paradox grows weaker still, so that an attitude of mysterious calm threatens to overwhelm both commonsense and the paradox itself. Nonsense here is a vindication of the less sensible term of a paradox, threatening even the revised and ambivalent sense which the paradox itself has made. Life is not the disaster it seems; life is not the mixture of success and disaster which a happier view takes; life is a mysterious success, all round. This is the progress described by the nonsense moral.

The Old Man of th' Abruzzi, for example, makes a rude gesture of indifference when They point out his foot to him.

There was an old Man of th' Abruzzi,
So blind that he couldn't his foot see;
When they said, "That's your toe," he replied, "Is it so?"
That doubtful old Man of th' Abruzzi.

Without the cartoon, we should not know how to take either his response or the adjective "doubtful". When, however, we see him cock-a-snook at Them, we can be sure that he does not care for Their commonsensical assistance. "Doubtful" is a euphemism for "defiant." It is unkind and meddling of Them to remind him, quite unnecessarily, of his shortsightedness (Lear was very myopic). The cartoon allies itself with the attitude of the Old Man and opposes the situation which They contrive. The Old Man may be very blind, but why make an emergency of it? The jeweler's glass in Their eye suggests that objectively, technically, They are right. But there is a higher sense than common sense. The cartoon complements the subjective view of the verse and contradicts the objective view; and while the situation remains paradoxical or "doubtful," word and image appear to be moving to a common focus which will show life in a clear and happy aspect. The less sensible term of the paradox is the stronger; the paradox itself is on the verge of a resolution which will undo it.

The limerick about the Young Lady of Norway works in the same way. Indifferent to physical pain, she shrugs off her misfortune with a wonderfully rhetorical question.

There was a Young Lady of Norway,
Who casually sat in a doorway;
When the door squeezed her flat, she exclaimed "What of that?"
This courageous Young Lady of Norway.

In the drawing Lear plays with the idea of flatness. At first sight, this seems the scratchiest and most awkward of all the cartoons. But on closer scrutiny, it is seen to be exact and to possess a powerful sense of decorum. The door seems to be off its hinges, floating in the air without force; and the Young Lady and her chair seem to be on exactly the same plane with it, despite the fact that the part of the floor below the door is at some distance from the part on which the Lady stands. But then the Lady is not exactly standing on the floor—like the door and the chair, she is suspended just above it. She appears also to be tripping daintily forward. The cartoon depicts the flatness—that is, the result of the mishap—but by depriving the scene of all force or violence, it contradicts the alarm and justifies the Lady's attitude. What, indeed, of that? The image all but annuls the harm of the word, leaving us with a Lady who is paradoxically squashed flat but unhurt, her courageous indifference vindicated.

The Young Lady of Hull parries at a charging bull with a spade.

There was a Young Lady of Hull,
Who was chased by a virulent Bull;
But she seized on a spade, and called out—"Who's afraid?"
Which distracted that virulent Bull.

The cartoon and the verse disagree. The Bull chases the Lady, and she distracts it. But the Bull does not look "virulent"—in fact, he looks much more like a cow.† The image justifies her nonchalance. She is shown flinging up her left arm in delight, or for balance as if the spade were a sword, and she is smiling widely. Even the Bull is smiling. So the cartoon sides with the Lady's part in the verse and opposes the ferocity of the Bull. Here, indeed, the sensible term of the paradox (the Bull is dangerous) is about as weak as it can be without the paradox dissolving. The mysterious triumph of the Lady, in verse and picture, is nearly complete.

Other limericks of indifference have the same relation between cartoon and verse: the Old Man at a casement who denies he will fall; the Old Man of Hurst who, when told that drink is fattening, replies "What matter?"; the Young Lady of Parma, asked whether she is dumb, who says only "Hum!"; the Young Lady in blue who exclaims "Whizz!" when she learns who They are; the Old Person of Wick who says "Tick-a-Tick, Tick-a-Tick"; the Young Lady of Lucca who runs up a tree when her lover deserts her,

†Compare this limerick with the preceding one in the Dover edition, in which a cow chases the Old Man; the cow looks like a bull in the cartoon.

and says "Fish-fiddle-de-dee!"; or the old person of Ware who denies that his "Moppsikon Floppsikon bear" can trot.

It would be a mistake, however, to think that every limerick works this way. In some, the paradox is absent, and there is no discrepancy between the cartoon and the verse. They may together declare the hero's indifference.

There was an old person of Deal
Who in walking, used only his heel;
When they said, "Tell us why?"—he made no reply;
That mysterious old person of Deal

Withdrawn into his own world, the hero is not in the slightest degree concerned with their opinion. Their question reverberates—"Tell us why?" Is walking on your heels the opposite of walking on tiptoe? If so, is it also a matter of stealth, or delicacy, or a fine consideration for the feelings of others? Or is it the opposite of these? Considering the character of the Pobble who has no toes, perhaps the Old Man of Deal has no toes to tiptoe on—so he has to walk on his heels. Their question goes unanswered, and there is no helpful disagreement of verse and picture to provide a clue. Everything has been rendered so purely a matter of indifference that only the mystery remains, and this is Lear's basic point. When the paradox is dissolved, we are left not with a grand answer, but with the continuing mystery of an unexplained triumph.

In the limericks both of frenzy and of indifference, the cartoonist supports only the positive, joyful, calming attitudes of the poet. In the limericks of frenzy, he is more or less at odds with the poet until the stronger and less sensible terms of the paradox, which are his, overwhelm the words. In the limericks of indifference, the poet is already partly on the cartoonist's side, and his task of imposing a happier, if more mysterious, order is easier. The second group is, as we might expect, larger in the second limerick series, when the tensions of Lear's life have slackened and he has made some sort of peace with the world. It is interesting to note that the sense of affirmation is first expressed by the graphic, rather than the poetic, imagination. The image and not the word was, after all, Lear's real love. Through it, he finds the magical potency he needs to drive distress into the verbal corners of the limerick, and then, with the paradox dissolving under our eyes, to vanquish it altogether. Later on we shall see what happens when this dispersal of the moral categories of the drama takes place.

Metamorphosis

But first it is worthwhile taking a third group of limericks to see how many variations Lear was able to work upon the essential word-image relationship. A large number have as their subject—though it is an unstated one—the metamorphosis of man and nature.

There was an Old Man in a tree,
Who was horribly bored by a Bee;
When they said, "Does it buzz?" he replied, "Yes, it does,
It's a regular brute of a Bee!"

Cartoon and verse are very discrepant here. The drawing shows the Bee, the Man, Them and the boredom. But They are not questioning the Old

Man, nor is there any sign of the buzzing. Instead, They are depicted jumping in the air with surprise—and it is easy to see why. The giant Bee seems to be about to turn into the Man and vice versa. A wonderful transformation is at hand, or has just happened. The main joke here is that the Old Man and the Bee react in exactly the wrong way. They should be amazed, but, instead, they are bored. The Man's boredom disguises not irritation (a merely social joke) but wonder (a metaphysical joke). All the surprise is displaced and shows itself only incidentally in the behavior of Them in the corner. The cartoon agrees with the verse by depicting the boredom. It disagrees, however, by showing us an event—the metamorphosis—which renders the apathy of the verse comically inappropriate, and by sketching in the astonishment of Them. It begins by complementing the verse; but it ends by subverting its general theme, with the result that we feel an understated astonishment more intensely than the boredom which occupies almost the entire surface of both poem and picture. The cartoon complements, then transforms and overrides the meaning of the verse. We are left with the paradox—apathy-in-amazement—and we feel that when our laughter subsides, only astonishment will remain, rippling outward in ever-widening circles.

Again, there is the Young Lady in white.

There was a young lady in white,
Who looked out at the depths of the night;
But the birds of the air, filled her heart with despair,
And oppressed that young lady in white.

Only the inky blackness of the drawing expresses the despair of the verse. The Young Lady balances on her hands on the window sill and looks as if she is about to float out into the night air, entranced. She stares at two owls (the birds Lear felt closest to), and they stare back. The inspection is close and mutual, and the two parties seem to recognize each other. A stern, alert owl is winging his way into the picture. Will he, too, fall under the spell that so clearly binds the Lady and the two other birds? Is she about to fly off with them, or have they come to roost with her? Her owl-like face shows little emotion, but she is certainly not in despair. Inexpressive, she seems rather to have withdrawn into a state of complete contentment. The paradox—despair-in-enchantment—is sustained, but its sensible term, though forcefully stated in the verse, is enfeebled by the magical dimension which the cartoon adds.

There are happier, and less discrepant, variations. The Old Person of Tring, for instance, is blessed in both the poem and picture.

There was an Old Person of Tring,
Who embellished his nose with a ring;
He gazed at the moon, every evening in June,
That ecstatic Old Person of Tring.

The words tell us he is ecstatic, and the picture confirms this. The verse, however, is oddly quiet about certain essential matters. The cartoon is not of the moon, but of a sun-moon: it has radiant spikes like the sun and the face of the Old Man in the Moon. Moreover, the sun-moon face is about the same size as the ring in the Old Man's nose; so that, if the Old Man's face—especially his nose and his smiling mouth—are put inside the ring, the sun-moon and the Old Man become one and the same. The verse speaks only of embellishment, moon-gazing and ecstasy—he recognizes himself in the heavens, and the heavens see themselves in him. Some discrepancy is felt in how little the verse tells. The cartoon does not enforce a paradox, but works rather as an expansive complement to the verse, illustrating the mystery of his ecstasy in terms that are even more mysterious and enchanted.

The Old Man of Dunluce sets sail on a goose, and after a brief but happy voyage, returns home.

There was an old man of Dunluce,
Who went out to sea on a goose:
When he'd gone out a mile, he observ'd with a smile,
"It is time to return to Dunluce."

The strategy here is much like the strategy in the Tring limerick; there is no paradox, and the cartoon works by expanding wonderfully the sense of the verse. But the verse is almost purely neutral—only the smile indicates the Old Man's feelings. The amplification of this slight joy is astonishing in the picture: the Old Man's eyebrows are raised in delighted surprise as he stares intently and with a look of loving recognition into the upturned eyes of the goose. The cartoon discloses what the verse does not indicate—a radiant affinity between man and nature. The small, unexceptional happiness of the verse expands into the strange and self-assured bliss of the cartoon.

Lastly, we find complement, contradiction and expansion in this, one of the most mesmerizing of all the limericks.

There was an Old Man who said, "Hush!
I perceive a young bird in this bush!"
When they said—"Is it small?" he replied—"Not at all!
It is four times as big as the bush!"

The bird is not merely four times as big as the bush—it is as big as the Man, and yet it seems to be a baby bird. Moreover, the Man—his nose like a beak, his arms thrust back like wings—looks exactly like the bird. He stands on tiptoe, drops his stick in amazement and stares intently at the giant fledgling, which stares back. "What on earth!" is his real feeling, not "Not at all!" The verse is purely neutral, reporting an abstract zoological inspection and ending with a slight note of surprise that the bird should be so much larger than the bush. The cartoon and verse are not altogether discrepant: the cartoon completes the idea of inspection begun in the poem and amplifies the hint of surprise into a state of amazement. The man's avian eyes are popping out. But the drawing omits Them altogether and exchanges for a wholly detached inspection a totally engaged one. So once more there is a paradox, this time a detachment-in-engagement. The mysterious term nearly extinguishes the sensible term. We are left with the spectacle of a splendid recognition of identity between man and nature.

In all three groups of the frenzy, indifference, and metamorphosis limericks, the sense of nonsense comes partly from a discrepancy between cartoon and verse. Probably this discrepancy was not always fully intended by the artist, though he must have been aware of it in, for instance, the metamorphosis limericks; and by and large it is felt only unconsciously by the reader. The gap between cartoon and verse varies greatly from limerick to limerick, and although it commonly involves a paradox, this is not always so. The cartoon may complement or contradict the verse in different degrees and in various ways. But the discrepancy has one governing principle: the cartoon expands the sense in the direction of a mysterious happiness at the expense of an intelligibly sensible, and often sensibly glum, view of life. The motive of the discrepancies is to make life look strange and more joyful.

A Minor Sublime

Lear is engaged in the propagation of an idea of mystery. His gift is for expressing the undisclosed, for suspending feelings and thoughts in mid-air, so that we should have our curiosity strenuously exercised and yet feel content that the mystery remain intact. If there is a general theme to the drama, it seems to be strangeness itself. To this idea of strangeness, we have also been able to give a vivid emotional character—of joyfulness. What more are we to make of this joyful strangeness?

Although the distance between the surface of the limericks and their depths is bewilderingly great, Lear's central concern is clear: his picture poems—these small intense mysteries—express a state of wonder. He uses discrepancies to uncover the differences which bewilder, sadden and separate man, so that they may be dispelled. These petty secrets once demystified, he transports us happily to a height from which we are able to see and enjoy, if not a greater harmony, at least a grander and all-enveloping mystery. It is to the unfolding of the miraculous, the exalted, the transcendent that each limerick has been working. Each expresses a kind of minor sublime.[20]

Many of Lear's characters rise on tiptoe. The Old Man of Melrose, though he is perhaps portly, rises with the grace of a ballet dancer.

There was an Old Man of Melrose,
Who walked on the tips of his toes;
But they said, "It ain't pleasant, to see you at present,
You stupid Old Man of Melrose."

We see at once his indifference and Their agitation. We are left baffled by the mystery of his unconcern. Or are we? His pose expresses so much more than nonchalance. His eyes are downcast or closed, his smile is comtemplative or blissful. His composure contains surprise as much as indifference. His shrug is not dismissive, it is beatific, and his arms are outflung in a manner which welcomes rather than rebuffs—a gesture repeated as often as the ecstatic precision of standing on tiptoe throughout the limericks. He proclaims or completes. He expresses a mysterious sense of wonder—total, private, and baffling to his would-be antagonists.

Such gestures impart a sense of wonder and hush all the questions that might arise from our sense of bafflement. The Young Lady of Lucca may rout her neighbors by her unconventional fortitude when she is jilted.

There was a Young Lady of Lucca,
Whose lovers completely forsook her;
She ran up a tree, and said, "Fiddle-de-dee!"
Which embarrassed the people of Lucca.

But that is not the central meaning. She is really expressing a sensation of wonder, as if she is amazed by her own freedom and courage; and this is reflected as a kind of jagged astonishment in the attitudes which They, severally, strike. The Young Lady of Hull disarms the Bull not by bewildering it, but by making it share her entrancement.

There was a Young Lady of Hull,
Who was chased by a virulent Bull;
But she seized on a spade, and called out—"Who's afraid!"
Which distracted that virulent Bull.

The old person of Dutton[21] appears agitated in the verse but calm in the drawing because of some secret happiness which he feels. His smile and the outflung arms proclaim it.

There was an old person of Dutton,
Whose head was as small as a button:
So to make it look big, he purchased a wig,
And rapidly rushed about Dutton.

All the rushing-up-and-down limericks declare the same all-comforting joy and amazement. The Old Man is not concerned to explain the source of his happiness or to engage in its consequences: he simply manifests it in the here and now. He is caught in an act of bliss. The same gestures unite the Old Man of Whitehaven, whose music brings him misfortune, with the Old Man of the Isles, who is utterly happy, in a common state from which the troubles of the world are remote. They have both found a contentment beyond everyday understanding.

They both smile, they have flung out their arms and dance lightly on the ground. The Young Lady in a bonnet is overjoyed that all the birds of the air roost on her head; but that is not the cause of her bliss. Rather, her joy has attracted their roosting.

They flock to her as if to share her secret ecstasy. With outflung arms and downcast eyes and a serene smile, she dances in wonder.

In the second series, when Lear is altogether happier, these gestures are more abundant. Moreover, now that the secret is at some private level fully understood, it can be kept more securely, so that although nearly every limerick expresses a sense of wonder, it does so more quietly. Nearly every surface is unruffled, indifferent; beneath it lies a vast and strange joy; and the complete work—picture and poem together—inspires us with a minor sense of the sublime.

Wonder makes the old person of Wick gibber and throw his arms back.

There was an old person of Wick,
Who said, "Tick-a-Tick, Tick-a-Tick;
Chickabee, Chickabaw," and he said nothing more,
That laconic old person of Wick.

Wonder makes Them uncertain. They know he is making no sense, and yet when They remonstrate, They come face to face with an understanding which They can see the Old Man possesses and They lack. It is the same, though quieter, with the Young Lady in blue. When They assure her that

They know who They are, she replies "Whizz!" and throws her arms back and stares at Them.

There was a young lady in blue,
Who said, "Is it you? Is it you?"
When they said, "Yes, it is,"—she replied only, "Whizz!"
That ungracious young lady in blue.

The confidence is about to drain from the face of the other lady. She is about to realize that her sense of identity is nonsense, compared with the superior wisdom which the lady in blue possesses. At the same time, her arms are flung outward in a gesture which promises that she will share the secret, if only the Young Lady will relent and tell her. Both situations bring us back to the here and now; the before and after of cause and effect have been carefully pared away. There is only a hint of what has led up to, and what might follow, each confrontation. All speculation is hushed by a sense of something providentially joyful and grand beyond comprehension.

The same wonder commands the old person of China, the Old Man who teaches a frog to sing, the old person of Bree who nurses the fish and washes the dishes, and the old man in a barge who carries a lamp on his nose so he can fish by night. It is declared by the old man of Blackheath with his inexplicably strange headdress.

There was an old man of Blackheath,
Whose head was adorned with a wreath,
Of lobsters and spice, pickled onions and mice,
That uncommon old man of Blackheath.

The young lady of Firle shows it.

There was a young lady of Firle,
Whose hair was addicted to curl;
It curled up a tree, and all over the sea,
That expansive young lady of Firle.

Her eyes, this time, are wide open. She stares ecstatically out of the picture, her hands are open, her arms outflung, and her hair embraces the world. The eyes of the old man in a tree are also wide open, and although his bliss is quieter, it is none the less assured.

There was an old man in a tree,
Whose whiskers were lovely to see;
But the birds of the air, pluck'd them perfectly bare
To make themselves nests in that tree.

His happiness attracts the roosting, not the other way round. The wonder felt by the old man of Grange is fiercer.

There was an old person of Grange,
Whose manners were scroobious and strange;
He sailed to St. Blubb, in a waterproof tub,
That aquatic old person of Grange.

He is perhaps too astonished to smile, and his eyes are heavy and blank with amazement. But if he is overawed, he nevertheless contemplates the same mysteries; and though what has been revealed to him is not revealed to us, we still feel his wonder with him. The eyes of the old person of Bude are glazed with yet another version of astonishment, and he too is frantic. He rushes around his hometown, his arms extended in a gesture which says "Surprise! Surprise!" He has been startled by the recognition of some effortless joy or peace. Yet there is a repose about him that transcends his alarm. What else does his ruff—a magical circle—proclaim, if not the completeness of his exaltation?

There was an old person of Bude,
Whose deportment was vicious and crude;
He wore a large ruff, of pale straw-coloured stuff,
Which perplexed all the people of Bude.

Neither we nor the people of Bude may understand the nature of his transport. But we at least need not be perplexed to the point of wanting to damn him. Rather, we can receive his silent benediction with some part of the joyful spirit in which it has been given. We can feel elevated without having to understand.

The gesture of blessing once noticed, we find it everywhere in the cartoons. The Old Man of Spithead may not make much sense in the verse, but it is plain from the drawing what he means.

There was an old man of Spithead,
Who opened the window, and said,—
"Fil-jomble, fil-jumble, fil-rumble-come-tumble!"
That doubtful old man of Spithead.

He has thrown open the window, and his arms extend in a gesture which dispells the "doubt" of the refrain. The old person of Sheen lives in an unnatural element and drinks too much.

There was an old person of Sheen,
Whose expression was calm and serene;
He sat in the water, and drank bottled porter,
That placid old person of Sheen.

But beyond the infectious confidence he has in his own eccentric condition, he transmits a feeling of grace. The same blessing is expressed more covertly in the mock-explanatory gesture of the old person of Ware.

There was an old person of Ware,
Who rode on the back of a bear:
When they ask'd,—"Does it trot?"—he said "Certainly not!
He's a Moppsikon Floppsikon bear!"

Even They express it when the Old man has withdrawn in upon himself.

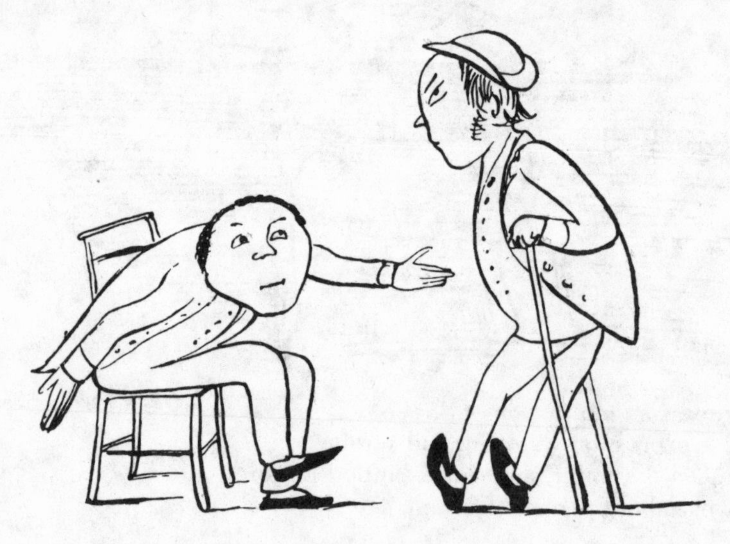

There was an old person of Deal
Who in walking, used only his heel;
When they said, "Tell us why?"—he made no reply;
That mysterious old person of Deal.

Their gesture is both enquiring and explanatory; and beyond that, it acknowledges a sense of revelation. Lastly, with the same gesture of embrace and completion, the Old Man of Dee-side, standing ecstatically on one foot, welcomes under the protective circle of his huge hat the dumbfounded and awestruck crowd of neighbors. He smiles broadly, his eyes are downcast or closed. Neither we nor They can understand, but it is abundantly clear that he does.

There was an old man of Dee-side
Whose hat was exceedingly wide,
But he said "Do not fail, if it happen to hail
To come under my hat at Dee-side!"

Throughout, there is a strong sense of awe, illumination or epiphany. The hero and often the heroine, and sometimes even They, experience a kind of transport; and the reader is stirred, however faintly, by their elevation. The limericks are nonsensical not because they flirt with meaninglessness, but because they conduct us with a hidden decorum to the edge of what is intelligible in our lives, and then point outward with a bold and happy gesture into the darkness beyond. Of all Lear's contemporaries, perhaps only Tennyson and Emily Dickinson can in so short a measure lift us so swiftly to a contemplation of final mysteries. It should come as no surprise that Lear's favorite poem was "Tears, Idle Tears," nor that he read Whitman with great enthusiasm. The heart of nonsense was wonder, both for Lear and for Carroll, who, in searching for a title for his nonsense, discarded *Alice's Adventures in Elf-Land* and *Alice's Adventures Under Ground* in favor of *Alice in Wonderland.*

Lear's transcendentalism—if that is the right word—is gentle and simple. It is only in an overall view that we recognize it. Each limerick by itself seems inconsequential, and the generally ludicrous character of the surfaces—the food, the odd beasts, the eccentric behavior, the absurdly provincial or strangely outlandish places—hardly encourages the feeling that these slight picture poems speak of matters as large as life itself. Indeed, they seem at first to scale life down to nursery size. They look like warm miniatures of adult life, designed to reassure the child or to flatter his sense of the strangeness and grossness of the grown-up world. All this they do, of course. But the experiences which they reduce, with such bold dispatch, to absurdity are central to the human condition, at least as Victorians felt it—alienation, social and spiritual dislocation, loss of trust and belief; and the purpose behind the reduction is not to belittle life, but to pare away the waste matter so that we are no longer distracted by trouble and pain and can feel with honesty and reverence what we cannot see—the beauty and the power of the life that directs life. And we are buoyed up by our knowledge that we *can* apprehend, although perhaps not with our intelligence, a life within us that is grander than our own understanding of it. What else brings a secret smile to the face of the Young Lady historian of mysteries or provokes the astonished gaze of the Old Man who said "Hush!"

The spiritual yearning which at every step marks Lear's life is expressed in these slight but intense picture poems with an arrested urgency, an indirect radiance. We are aroused from our customary indifference, and our curiosity is excited to the point where we too stand on tiptoe, next to the Old Man, the Lady and Them, and look over the lip of the intelligible world into the wonderful night beyond.

Chapter Three

The Long Poems

In the Christmas season of 1870, nonsense books became a vogue in England. *A Book of Nonsense* and *Alice in Wonderland* were reissued, and imitations of Lear and Carroll started to appear as giftbooks for the young. Instead of descending at teatime to meet the children belowstairs (where Lear had discovered his first nonsense audience at Knowsley), parents—and uncles, too—now climbed up to the nursery to read nonsense to their families before bed. The grown-ups stopped condescending. Here at last was common, and exalted, ground.

In the spring of 1871, when Lear was nearly sixty, he settled at San Remo, his wandering almost over. He was still to go on travels, both short and long—to India in 1873–1874, for instance. But his eyes had become weaker, and his energy was sapped. He determined to rest, tend his garden, draw and paint, and from time to time write his nonsense. He revised some old and some recent poems, and collected them, together with a botany, some prose and three alphabets, into a new volume, *Nonsense Songs, Stories, Botany and Alphabets* (1871), his second book of nonsense. Five years later, he brought out his fourth and last nonsense book, *Laughable Lyrics* (1877).

In these two volumes, we find most of the longer, mature work. Between the first and third books, *A Book of Nonsense* and *More Nonsense*, there were startling changes. Between the second and fourth, there is rather a quiet progression, a deepening of skill and vision; and the subject matter, instead of shifting, has an almost obsessive consistency. There are three main subjects. Ten poems are about courtship and voyages, three about families, and three about paradise and bliss. There are, as well, two poems about cloth or clothes, three autobiographical pieces, and lastly, an unfinished nonsense sonnet.

* * *

But first, Lear's juvenilia is worth a brief glance. It is hardly of the quality of the adolescent Carroll's *Useful & Instructive Poetry*, but it foreshadows some of the qualities of the mature work. "Ode to a China-man"[1] was written for Eliza Drewitt, one of the daughters of a family he had met when visiting Sarah in Sussex:

What art thou—sweet little China Man?—
Your name I want to know,
With your lovely face so pale and wan—
With a high diddle diddledy do.

Your high cheek bones:—your screwed up mouth,
How beautiful they be!
And your eyes that ogle from north to south,
With a high diddle diddledy dee!

"Good folks"—(& he shook his noodle-ding-dong)—
"It's enough for you to know—
That in spite of my eyebrows—two feet long—
I'm Miss Eliza's beau!!"

This rather crude China Man is doubtless an ancestor of the old person of China—

as well as of the Old Man of the East, and if he is to be known by his high cheekbones, long eyebrows and a jingle, also of the Old Man of the Isles.

Lear presents himself to Miss Eliza as a ludicrous and outlandish suitor. It is the same avuncular role he so often plays in the limericks and in later poems like "The Yonghy-Bonghy-Bò."

"Miss Maniac,"[2] an unfinished juvenile piece, is somewhat grimmer. A young girl has an illegitimate child; her lover, a young buck, deserts her, and her father throws her out of her home. Grieving over her lost happiness, she wanders like the Dong till eventually she goes mad. Each couplet has a cartoon, and the rhymes are bathetic. The poem shows that Lear was interested in mixing grief and fun right from the start.

"Peppering Roads"[3] celebrates in jolting anapaests the bone-shaking coach trip to the village of Peppering where the Drewitts lived:

> If you wish to see roads in perfection,
> A climax of cart ruts and stones;
> Or if you have the least predilection
> For breaking your neck or your bones;
> If descents and ascents are inviting,
> If your ankles are strangers to sprains,
> If you'd cure a penchant for sliding,
> Then to Peppering go by all means.

This is reminiscent of the spirit, if not the style, of Cowper's "John Gilpin," and is in the tradition of eighteenth-century light versifying. Except for its anapaests and its exuberance, it has little to do with the later nonsense. Like "Miss Maniac," it resembles the grotesque and facetious virtuoso pieces of Thomas Hood and William Gilbert. Lear was to discover a deeper and more expressive way of commingling sadness and joy.

Early in the winter of 1829, when he was seventeen, Lear tried writing some serious verse.[4] Three pieces survive, and they tell us more about him than the comic pieces do. They all show clearly the influence of Byron, whose death in 1824 had moved him to tears. "The Ruins of the Temple of Jupiter, Aegina, Greece" is fervid, gawky, but not unmelodious:

> Type of thy parent clime!
> In ages past away,
> Greece was like thee sublime—
>   Like thee was bright and gay;
> And on thy mount wert thou,
>   Shrined in her orient sky,—
> A gem upon her brow
>   Of her fair liberty!
> But Greece has fallen like thee!
>   Desolate—wildly lone;—
> Her sons, the brave and free,
>   Forgotten and unknown.
> The echo of her fountains
>   Seems her lost children's sigh,
> And on her loveliest mountains
>   Sits dark captivity!—
> Aegina!—Greece!—the dead,
> And ye have perishéd!

Here is the clumsy nostalgia for a lost sublime which might be expected of a schoolboy devotee of Byron. Its banality is charming, and also a measure of Lear's infatuation. The verses ring—or perhaps jingle—even more tellingly true when we realize that he never outgrew the feelings behind them. Lear imitated Byron not just in the art, feeding upon a Romantic sublime, but also in the life—as exile and bohemian, an artist wandering in lost and splendidly ruined worlds. His history, in fact, looks like a comical negative of Byron's: more vacillating, with the same commitment to a life of passions; antibourgeois but without the aristocrat's detachment; the same agony but more drawn out. In the end, it is Byron who is perhaps the less heroic figure. Lear was above the squalor of gossip and lechery, and he had to endure his pain; he lived on into an age where a Romantic defiance of the world could only be a laughable pose. He could not afford the luxury of a patriot's death. A more timorous man would have turned to the dulling comforts of home. Lear chose to face, with his other favorite poet, Tennyson, the more difficult conditions of alienation and exhaustion. Of course, he would not have preferred his own courage to Byron's. Nor did he dare imitate him consciously. He kept a respectful distance, a trailing camp follower. But for all the modesty of his emulation he was still remarkably faithful to his hero's themes and to his voice—exalted, nostalgic, humorous, ebullient.

The second surviving piece is entitled "Bury Hill,"[5] after one of the Sussex downs near his sister Sarah's home. Here again his theme is a ruined sublime and the mood is sickly-sweet nostalgia. The lyrical anapaests and the elegaic tone are typical of Byron's shorter poems, "Stanzas for Music," for instance:

> When the light dies away in a calm summer's eve
> And the sunbeams grow faint and more faint in the west
> How we love to look on till the last trace they leave
> Glows alone like a blush upon modesty's breast!
> Lonely streak! dearer far than the glories of day
> Seems thy beauty, 'mid silence and shadow enshrined,
> More bright as its loneliness passes away—
> And leaves twilight in desolate grandeur behind!
> So when grief has made lonely and blighted our lot,
> And her icy cold chain o'er her spirits has cast,
> Will not memory oft turn to some thrice hallowed spot,
> That shines out like a star among years that are past?
> Some dream that will wake in a desolate heart,
> Every chord into music that long has been hushed,
> Mournful echo!—soon still—for it tolls with a smart,
> That the joys which first woke it, are long ago crushed.

The poetry of "desolate grandeur" is clearly in his blood, and there are echoes of it in all the major nonsense poems, especially in *Laughable Lyrics*. But it does not work as a direct influence. Lear was fascinated by a genuine Byronic voice, but he was repelled by the parlor versions of it which, in the twenties and thirties, were smothering real Romanticism with safe, sweet emotion and respectable, genteel thought. Byron did not write for the parlor, but he was read there, and his anapaests were only too comfortably suited to the gentle vamping of the family piano. In the mature nonsense, Lear is not so much imitating Byron's desolate grandeur as spoofing the domesticity of late Romanticism; he is guying Thomas Moore in a covert protest against the decadence which had wasted the favorite poetry of his childhood and youth. It is rather as if "The Pobble Who Has No Toes" and "The Dong with a Luminous Nose" were composed in order to rescue Romanticism from the decadence of the parlor by transporting it into the nursery and disguising it in a comic mode. Since it can flourish only in exile or underground, Lear finds it a home away from home in the only underground available to high-minded Victorians—the world of children. But in finding a new setting for the Byronic sublime, Lear discovered also a new sense for it. His was not merely a saving operation. He transformed what he rescued.

His third juvenile piece, "From the pale and the deep," written at the same time as his lines on Bury Hill, illustrates how much of his lyrical gift, too, he owes to Byron:

From the pale and the deep—
  From the dark and bright—
From the violets that sleep
  Away from the light:
From the lily that flashes
  At morn's glad call—
The bee gathers honey
  And sweets from all.

It is a debt he shares with his friend Tennyson. Of course, by the seventies neither poet could safely allow a lily to "flash." Tennyson wished to conserve the old diction and often sounded silly. Lear tried, instead, to express in his mature verse how far such figures had been compromised. The world had grown too disturbed, and the fine lyric voice was too faint to be heard over the din. Only Walter Landor could still write with such a thin purity, and he had outlived his audience. Lear knew that if he tried to sing in this vein, They would laugh and smash him. So he tricked Them with a laughter of his own, sympathetic and absurd; and by seeming to mock Romantic softness, succeeded in conserving a Byronic purity. His pumpkins "blow" on the coast of Coromandel, and on the Groomboolian plain a strange nose "flashes."

The grown-up Lear is in some ways a merely childish figure. But he is also the conserver of a child's vision—of a world where sadness and joy are bewilderingly commingled—as well as the champion of adolescent regrets that the Romantic ways of childhood should fade, and the high sentiment and clear, sweet sounds become laughable. Lear's three serious pieces are especially instructive; they adumbrate most of his complicated feelings about Romantic poetry and suggest how exactly, in his case, the child was father to the man.

Love and Roving

Lear wrote "The Owl and the Pussy-cat"[6] for Janet, the daughter of John Addington Symonds, while he was staying with the family at Cannes in 1867. It has become his most famous nonsense song, and it was one of his own favorites. He set it to music and often played it after dinner in the great country houses he visited. It is a musical piece in the style of the post-Romantic ballads which filled the songbooks of Victorian England. These were attenuated versions of traditional and early Romantic ballads. As a plain harmonium is to a concertina, so Bishop Percy's and Coleridge's stanzas are to the stanzas of the Victorian song, the refrains of which are longer and more frequent, the line and rhyme schemes more languidly intricate. To an impersonal narrative mode, there has been grafted a gentle lyricism capable of expressing the homelier sentiments of parlor and drawing room. Where the notes of the *Lyrical Ballads* sounded hard and clear, the Victorian ballad has *rubato* and *vibrato*. The ballad has moved indoors.

Lear adopts the form with a devious wholeheartedness, as if he approved of it. He plays two tricks upon it. First, he turns it into a sort of literary nursery rhyme. He leads it underground into the nursery, where adult sentimentality cannot spoil it. Second, he writes it with a flawless ear. A masterful prosodist, he never slips. While he was composing "The Owl and the Pussy-cat," he and Symonds and his wife sat up late at night reading Shelley, Byron and Swinburne; and their voices are heard, in a general but sure way, in the musical precision of this first nonsense ballad, and in all the rest. Lear pays the form a compliment it scarcely deserves, but of course he does so for a higher purpose. His aim, both radical and conservative, is to restore to the Romantic ballad, if not its original form and theme, at least more honest and more vigorous versions of them than are found among the soft and silly productions of the Victorian drawing room.

Here, wound simply together, are two quatrains of rhyming iambic tetrameters and trimeters, with familiar anapaestic variations and a tail refrain. Lear uses the same technique of ballad collage for all his later poems, a simple patchwork in *Nonsense Songs*, a highly complicated and expressive nonsense ode in *Laughable Lyrics*. From this later viewpoint, "The Owl and the Pussy-cat" looks like apprentice work; certainly his practice makes the sophistication of the late work possible. Yet the form is already curiously perfected. Probably his long exercises with the limerick, which contains in compressed form a quatrain and a refrain as well as a literary relation with folk and nursery conventions, have helped him to an early maturity. When one reflects how narrow a path he has chosen to tread between sentimentality and coldness, between adult sophistication and childish delight, it seems that the limerick was indeed a good place to develop the sort of lyrical-dramatic poetry which combines innocence and experience, exuberance and restraint, and is light enough to please the casual reader and resonant enough to enchant the serious one.

The skill of "The Owl and the Pussy-cat" lies in the pivoting between these qualities, and in the discrepancy between the surface of the song and its depths. It is "nonsense" not merely because the surface is daft and whimsical—after all, the narrative, however inconsequential, makes perfectly good sense. It is "nonsense" also because of the strange distance, the empty space, between what is said and what is meant. The Victorian reader must have recognized the gap, however dimly; the gap makes the poem seem unintelligible, and both provokes and justifies the description "nonsense."

What is concealed in this song? Is it not just a simple and joyous account of the elopement of two lovers, their safe voyage to a sort of paradisiacal land, their nuptials, and a party at the end to celebrate?

> The Owl and the Pussy-cat went to sea
> In a beautiful pea-green boat,
> They took some honey, and plenty of money,
> Wrapped up in a five-pound note.
> The Owl looked up to the stars above,
> And sang to a small guitar,
> "O lovely Pussy! O Pussy, my love,
> What a beautiful Pussy you are,
> You are,
> You are!
> What a beautiful Pussy you are!"
>
> Pussy said to the Owl, "You elegant fowl!
> How charmingly sweet you sing!
> O let us be married! too long we have tarried:
> But what shall we do for a ring?"
> They sailed away for a year and a day,
> To the land where the Bong-tree grows,
> And there in a wood a Piggy-wig stood,
> With a ring at the end of his nose,
> His nose,
> His nose,
> With a ring at the end of his nose.
>
> "Dear Pig, you are willing to sell for one shilling
> Your ring?" Said the Piggy, "I will."

So they took it away, and were married next day
  By the Turkey who lives on the hill.
They dined on mince, and slices of quince,
  Which they ate with a runcible spoon;
And hand in hand, on the edge of the sand,
  They danced by the light of the moon,
    The moon,
    The moon,
They danced by the light of the moon.

The landscape is familiar Romantic stock: the sea, the wood, the shore, illuminated by starlight and moonlight. Nursery rhymes, ballads, the literature of quest, all have made such a tale and its setting unsurprising. Of course, we may feel somewhat startled by a "pea-green" boat, and wonder what exactly a "Bong-tree" and a "runcible spoon" are. Perhaps, too, we pause to consider why mince and quinces are plied together at a wedding feast, and why it is necessary to ask a pig for his nose-ring as a wedding band. Owls do not mate with cats, and beasts are said not to marry. But these oddities would disturb only the most literal and unread soul, the sort of literary Podsnap who will not tolerate beast fables and has forgotten his nursery jingles.

The surface oddities are so familiar and comforting, in fact, that they distract attention from the real oddities underneath. The reader has only to ask himself who is the man and who is the woman to realize that the song conceals at least part of its essential meaning. Obviously, the Owl should be the suitor and the Cat his lady. She steers the boat and he serenades her. She is "lovely," he is "elegant." But, contrary to the code, it is she who proposes, and in the picture in which the Owl gets the ring from the Pig, the Owl looks very timid, bashful even, while the Cat towers over him and looks down with a severe, even predatory glare.

We recall at once that cats eat birds, and while a cat may not get the better of an owl, this particular Cat looks more like the Panther of Carroll's " 'Tis the voice of the lobster." There are at least two jokes here: a timid gentleman is being pressed into marriage by an overdominant lady, and courtship is about to end, not in consummation, but in death, after the manner of "The Spider and the Fly" (a joke familiar enough to the Victorian reader). We may leave to Freudians the extra significance, if they choose to find it there, of a timid man buying a pig's nose-ring for a wedding band; to allegorists, the possibility that the Cat stands for Sensuality and the Owl for Wisdom; and to medievalists, the improbable suspicion that Lear had for a model the early thirteenth-century debate poem, "The Owl and the Nightingale."

Lear may indeed be expressing a fear that the life of the senses can overwhelm a man's better judgment. The enigmatic smile of the Pig and the fact that his eyes are closed only confirm the sense of trouble, and of pleasure in saying covertly what cannot be said openly. The verse does not dispel the anxiety or the secret pleasure, since the poet has not made it clear which of the two creatures asks the crucial question:

> "Dear pig, are you willing to sell for one shilling
> Your ring?" Said the Piggy, "I will."

This is too brief to make comforting sense. Everything is not as it seems. Wooing may lead to death, elopement to deception; marriage is something to be feared, and sexual passion inspires dread. All these darker readings are possible, and once recognized, they make the voyage itself seem not so much a happy adventure or a gay elopement as an escape or an evasion, a running away from life. The quest ends not in joyful physical union in an earthly paradise, but in a general condition of alienation for which the queer and dislocated landscape is only too striking a metaphor.

No doubt other readings are possible. Certainly no single reading is the right one. The point, as in the limericks, is in the suspense or seesaw: the enigmatic smile and closed eyes of the pig, and the hurried question which begins the last verse, are all pivotal. The song is happy and sad at once, both a celebration and a defeat. Yet the final feeling, again as in so many of the limericks, is one of completion and wonder. The entranced ending makes sure of this. The partners dance by the sea in the moonlight, and the fantail of the Turkey spreads out in benediction over the wedding ceremony.

There is distress and blessing, but the sense of grace prevails, transforming any curiosity about the darker side of the poem into a feeling of illumination.

The poem works roughly like a limerick—it proceeds from strangeness through joyfulness to wonder. But there is a crucial difference in the relation of picture to verse. We can see this clearly if we examine the stages of our response. First, we enjoy the whimsical narrative surface. Then we notice the discrepancies, partly in the words and partly in the drawings. We register dismay at the darker meanings these reveal. But finally the paradox—defeat-in-celebration—seems to be decided, by the last verse and its tail-piece picture, in favor of celebration, the joyful term of the paradox. The joyfulness does not come primarily from the cartoons, and this breaks the limerick rule that the picture extend the strangeness in the direction of joy. We recall the few limericks—exceptions to the rule—where the cartoon restricts the movement of happy and mysterious expansion.

Clearly the drawings are no longer organic parts of the whole. With the longer ballad form, Lear entrusts his meaning to the words and allows the cartoons only an incidental force. They may help explain the darker and more ambiguous aspects of the verse, but only by spelling them out for us. They neither deepen the mystery nor display the joy. It seems unlikely that Lear would have noticed this shift in cartoon-word relations: he worked too instinctively and too casually. But it hardly matters that his art is not, to this degree, a conscious one. This early exercise in a new vein bodes well for his success. The essential strategy of his nonsense still works well. He has lost something of the intensity, perhaps, but he has gained delicacy. There is less of the buffo, but in his place a more engaging fool has our attention.

"The Duck and the Kangaroo"[7] also has a courtship and a voyage. The stanza is elegantly constructed, one ballad quatrain stitched to another, with bounding anapaests for the Kangaroo, and a regular pattern of three- and four-foot lines:

> Said the Duck to the Kangaroo,
> "Good gracious! how you hop!
> Over the fields and the water too,
> As if you never would stop!
> My life is a bore in this nasty pond,
> And I long to go out in the world beyond!
> I wish I could hop like you!"
> Said the Duck to the Kangaroo.

It is a dramatic lyric of the tidiest and most mellifluous kind. The landscape is now a little barer. The Duck has rather more homely tastes than the Owl and the Pussy-cat: she wants to visit the Dee, a real river, as well as the Jelly Bo Lee, and in the end she is content merely to circle the world three times, an exuberant but practical tourist:

> Said the Kangaroo, "I'm ready!
> All in the moonlight pale,
> But to balance me well, dear Duck, sit steady!
> And quite at the end of my tail!"
> So away they went with a hop and a bound,
> And they hopped the whole world three times round:
> And who so happy—O who,
> As the Duck and the Kangaroo?

The question in the refrain is not altogether rhetorical. Their happiness is partly a good bluff. Once again, the sexual roles of the two creatures are confused. The lady does the proposing:

> "Please give me a ride on your back!"
> Said the Duck to the Kangaroo.

The man is bashful and demure in the drawings.

In the verse, he is scrupulous, dainty, hypochondriacal:

> Said the Kangaroo to the Duck,
> "This requires some little reflection;
> Perhaps on the whole it might bring me luck,
> And there seems but one objection,
> Which is, if you'll let me speak so bold,
> Your feet are unpleasantly wet and cold,
> And would probably give me the roo-
> Matiz!" said the Kangaroo.

He expects only good luck, certainly not passion, from their partnership. The Duck overrules his effeminate reservations with a masculine decisiveness:

> Said the Duck, "As I sate on the rocks,
> I have thought over that completely,
> And I bought four pairs of worsted socks
> Which fit my web-feet neatly.
> And to keep out the cold I've bought a cloak,
> And every day a cigar I'll smoke,
> All to follow my own dear true
> Love of a Kangaroo!"

In the second drawing of the autograph copy reproduced at the end of the Dover edition,

we see her puffing away on her cigar.

On the surface the joke is: how funny to have a timid kangaroo and a bossy duck. But Lear also gives away his fears of sexuality and his anxiety about the difficulties of love. The creatures are more radically mismatched than they seem, and their voyage is not so much a honeymoon trip as a misguided escape. They circle the globe three times—but frantically. What consummation or liberty is to be enjoyed in so giddy and barren a relationship? Lear expresses here his dread of the *penates* of England and of the lonely exile to which he has resigned himself—a loneliness made even more wretched by the absence of love. The poem is in these respects more desperate than "The Owl and the Pussy-cat," which at least ended with a wedding. Here the Kangaroo is left chasing his tail round the globe, hopping away from love, and the Duck looks more like a stowaway or a Jonah than a companion or paramour. The bounding anapaests are at once lyrical and mechanical, joyful and desperate, liberating and confining. We are left feeling both the sadness of entrapment and the happiness of release. The situation contradicts itself, and the paradox is held in a simple suspense; the happier term is not winning. There is a sort of dazed astonishment, perhaps, but certainly not wonder. For the first significant time, Lear has stopped short of his minor sublime. He seems to be using the new ballad form to examine rather than celebrate. He is plotting his ground more cautiously now that he has room for more scrupulous reflections.

The elegiac notes of the first ballad are drowned out by the whirring and the buzzing of the second. But the tender and sweetly sad voice returns in "The Daddy Long-legs and the Fly,"[8] a third variation of the courtship voyage theme. The elopers here are not lovers, but two male companions. The stanzas are fashioned from three quatrains, the last of which has iambic tetrameter couplets:

> Once Mr. Daddy Long-legs,
> Dressed in brown and gray,
> Walked about upon the sands
> Upon a summer's day;

And there among the pebbles,
    When the wind was rather cold,
He met with Mr. Floppy Fly,
    All dressed in blue and gold.
And as it was too soon to dine,
They drank some Periwinkle-wine,
And played an hour or two, or more,
At battlecock and shuttledore.

The trimeters help make the scene bleak, the measure is briskly plaintive. The insects meet on the desolate seashore. The Fly tells the Daddy Long-legs that he cannot go to court because his legs are too short; the Daddy Long-legs tells the Fly that he can no longer sing because his legs have grown too long. They commiserate:

So Mr. Daddy Long-legs
    And Mr. Floppy Fly
Sat down in silence by the sea,
    And gazed upon the sky.
They said, "This is a dreadful thing!
    The world has all gone wrong,
Since one has legs too short by half,
    The other much too long!
One never more can go to court,
Because his legs have grown too short;
The other cannot sing a song,
Because his legs have grown too long."

Their deformities are cruelly complementary, and they are both beyond the pale. There is no course for them but to leave:

Then Mr. Daddy Long-legs
    And Mr. Floppy Fly
Rushed downward to the foamy sea
    With one sponge-taneous cry;
And there they found a little boat,
    Whose sails were pink and gray;
And off they sailed among the waves,
    Far, and far away.
They sailed across the silent main,
And reached the great Gromboolian plain;
And there they play for evermore
At battlecock and shuttledore.

Their nonsense games are made up of mixed properties, fulfilling their wish that if they could only share their features, their deformities would vanish. Or perhaps, since Lear does not say they are happy, the nonsense games are as maladroit compared with the real games as the deformed insects are compared with their conventional, normal fellows. A dark and more difficult meaning underlies the jolly oddity of the surface. The lament expresses the poet's sense of his own deformity and of the alienated condition which his ugliness aggravated in him. Lear may also be recalling an awkward period of adolescence, when legs grow too long and the voice changes; the growing boy is still awkward in polite society ("at court") and he can no longer sing sweetly. Or he may be expressing a more general sense of artistic failure and social distress.

Can we doubt, as we hear about the misshapen bodies and games of this the third poem in the book, that the first two issue from the same ugly predicament? Once the love element has gone, the essential alienation is revealed only too clearly. The voyage is no longer of lovers to an earthly paradise, but of wretched companions to a gloomy Elysium, where their only comfort is in playing crippled and genteel games. It is useless that the Fly is blue and gold: his legs are too short for him to call on his red and green rulers with propriety. So he has to sail away in a boat with sails that are merely pink and gray, and with a comrade drably dressed in brown and gray. For these Victorian seafarers the world is colorless indeed, and the elegiac note is as bleak as it is sweet.

In the second and third poems, Lear's interest has turned from the voyage to the state preceding it—a sort of loveless courtship. The movement is both evasive and honest: evasive because he appears to suppress romance, and honest because he faces up to his own lovelessness. Perhaps sadness has goaded him into self-analysis. But there is courage here too. That he has grown strong enough to quarrel with his own cozy sublime is evident not just from these new, bleaker views, but also from the way he uses the ballad form. He gives himself room for keener and bolder reflection, and he displays on a now-spacious word surface the paradoxes which in the first limerick series he confined almost entirely to the cartoons.

Lear's frankness has a lot to do with the gradual decline of his own roving. As he begins to settle down, naturally he becomes interested in the condition of the land-bound and in the emotional and spiritual states which precede and motivate exile and adventure. With retirement, he feels little personal risk ahead, and no fear to obscure his view. He pauses and looks inward, and sees alienation coexisting with comradeship, deformity with right proportion, and desolation with comfort. What possible sense can be made of such contradictions? Life is bewildering, and there can be no reveling in the grand or exalted—so he now seems to feel—until he discovers what feelings the "spongetaneous" cry expresses, or what the deformed games and the overseas flight lead to, or why the "main" is "silent" as the freakish sailors pass over it.

The essential strategy of the limerick is here skirted or forestalled. Instead of leading from strangeness through joy to wonder, the nonsense now stops short of wonder and examines, in a new and dingier daylight, the bizarre and estranging reality in which the poet finds himself.

Lear works three more variations on the courtship and voyage theme in *Nonsense Songs*. The heroes, already reduced from animals and birds to insects, are now only household utensils, and the landscape also contracts; the scene becomes domestic. "The Nutcrackers and the Sugar-Tongs"[9] is the most joyful of the three, but its ebullience has a violent edge. Confined to the table, like the Duck to the pond, the two heroes wish to escape:

The Nutcrackers sat by a plate on the table,
    The Sugar-tongs sat by a plate at his side;
And the Nutcrackers said, "Don't you wish we were able
    Along the blue hills and green meadows to ride?
Must we drag on this stupid existence for ever,
    So idle and weary, so full of remorse,—
While every one else takes his pleasure, and never
    Seems happy unless he is riding a horse?"

It occurs to them that their legs are ideally constructed for riding, and they resolve to escape on horseback. In leaping and bounding anapaests, they rush to the stables, leap on two ponies,* and, to the consternation of all the other household objects, they flee:

The whole of the household was filled with amazement,
    The Cups and the Saucers danced madly about,
The Plates and the Dishes looked out of the casement,
    The Saltcellar stood on his head with a shout,
The Spoons with a clatter looked out of the lattice,
    The Mustard-pot climbed up the Gooseberry Pies,
The Soup-ladle peeped through a heap of Veal Patties,
    And squeaked with a ladle-like scream of surprise.

*Cream-colored ponies with speckles—cf. the Old Man of Madras who rode a cream-colored Ass, and died of fright because its ears were so long [see Jackson's *The Complete Nonsense of Edward Lear* (Dover, 1951), p. 11]. Note also that the anapaestic meter here is very like the amphibrachic meter of the limericks.

The Frying-pan said, "It's an awful delusion!"
    The Tea-kettle hissed and grew black in the face;
And they all rushed downstairs in the wildest confusion,
    To see the great Nutcracker-Sugar-tong race.
And out of the stable, with screamings and laughter,
    (Their ponies were cream-coloured, speckled with brown,)
The Nutcrackers first, the Sugar-tongs after,
    Rode all round the yard, and then all round the town.

This is no elegy, but a boisterous ballad in which fierce spirits, dulled by the stale and melancholy world of domestic conventionalism, escape with a ferocious abandon:

They rode through the street, and they rode by the station,
    They galloped away to the beautiful shore;
In silence they rode, and made no observation,
    Save this: "We will never go back anymore!"
And still you might hear, till they rode out of hearing,
    The Sugar-tongs snap, and the Crackers say "crack!"
Till far in the distance their forms disappearing,
    They faded away.—And they never came back!

They scream and laugh with joy and hysteria till at last they are out in the open.

In its cantering vigor this poem resembles "The Duck and the Kangaroo," and both describe the horrors of pond or home life. It resembles as well "The Daddy Long-legs and the Fly," which also lacks an overt love relationship. The poet's attention is more firmly fixed, as the series unfolds, on his dread of domestic England; and now that he has examined in two poems the condition of entrapment, he writes here mostly about the business of escaping. "The Owl and the Pussy-cat" expressed the whole theme; each subsequent poem has taken an element of the whole and examined it. Three of the six stanzas of "The Nutcrackers and the Sugar-tongs" are busy describing the fuss and uproar caused by the getaway. Lear's impatience with domesticity, its loneliness and gloominess, is nowhere so vividly expressed. So the Crackers say "Crack!" and the Tongs "Snap!"

Where they are headed seems not to matter. They wish at the beginning to ride "on the blue hills" and "green meadows." But we are not told whether they reach them, and we last see them cantering away to the "beautiful shore." The landscape is the familiar one, but it has been reduced to its essentials. There is in the last verse a strong feeling of contraction that throws the reader back on the three preceding stanzas and the sensation of escape. The poem closes down very suddenly. Where a moment before they had been screaming and laughing hysterically, the Crackers and Tongs now ride "in silence" and they "made no observation." The same phrase is a cue in the limerick about the Young Lady of Sweden for a swift rejection of local England:

> There was a Young Lady of Sweden,
> Who went by the slow train to Weedon:
> When they cried, "Weedon Station!" she made no observation,
> But she thought she should go back to Sweden.

At the end of "The Yonghy-Bonghy-Bò" the hero crosses a "silent-roaring" ocean, and the Fly and the Daddy Long-legs also cross the "silent main." The fleeing heroes pass, without speaking or looking, over a hushed and perhaps desolate landscape, and the silence, especially after the noisiness of "The Nutcrackers and the Sugar-tongs," is deafening.

There is little discrepancy here between surface and depths, and little feeling of wonder, except perhaps in the magically abrupt last stanza: "They faded away. —And they never came back!" But there is enough paradox, both simple and concealed, for us to feel that the poem is nonsensical. When the ladylike Soup-ladle is surprised by their escape, she "squeaks" with a "scream" (albeit a "ladle-like" one). When the Tongs and the Crackers ride out into the yard, they are screaming and at the same time laughing. And the hysterical animation of household utensils and the uproar of the escape are described in six strict stanzas, each with two tetrametrical, regularly rhyming quatrains—the most severely unvaried of all Lear's nonsense ballad forms. Nowhere else does he write with such wildness and such restraint. Indeed, the main paradox of the poem might be described as wildness-in-restraint, and Lear's purpose is to inspect and express the hysteria which the confinements of home life provoke. But while he releases and relieves himself of a frenzy which closely resembles the agitation found in many of the limericks, he does not reach the point of calm from which a feeling of wonder unfolds. The poem remains something of a whirring toy, mechanical and tightly wound up.

As if to assuage the hysteria, the next poem in the series, "The Broom, the Shovel, the Poker and the Tongs,"[10] restores the love element. Mr. Poker and Miss Shovel accompany Mr. Tongs and Mrs. Broom on a coach drive round the park:

The Broom and the Shovel, the Poker and the Tongs,
They all took a drive in the Park,
And they each sang a song, Ding-a-dong, Ding-a-dong,
Before they went back in the dark.
Mr. Poker he sat quite upright in the coach,
Mr. Tongs made a clatter and clash,
Miss Shovel was dressed all in black (with a brooch),
Mrs. Broom was in blue (with a sash).
Ding-a-dong! Ding-a-dong!
And they all sang a song!

In the second verse Mr. Poker serenades Miss Shovel. He compliments her on the delicate sound she makes when she scrapes up the coals. In the third verse, Mr. Tongs asks Mrs. Broom why she will not requite his love:

"Alas! Mrs. Broom!" sighed the Tongs in his song,
"O is it because I'm so thin,
And my legs are so long—Ding-a-dong! Ding-a-dong!
That you don't care about me a pin?
Ah! fairest of creatures, when sweeping the room,
Ah! why don't you heed my complaint!
Must you needs be so cruel, you beautiful Broom,
Because you are covered with paint?
Ding-a-dong! Ding-a-dong!
You are certainly wrong!"

Physical deformity gets in the way of love again. In the last verse, the ladies deliver a smarting rebuff, the singing is abandoned, and they drive home:

Mrs. Broom and Miss Shovel together they sang,
"What nonsense you're singing to-day!"
Said the Shovel, "I'll certainly hit you a bang!"
Said the Broom, "And I'll sweep you away!"
So the Coachman drove homeward as fast as he could,
Perceiving their anger with pain;
But they put on the kettle, and little by little,
They all became happy again.
Ding-a-dong! Ding-a-dong!
There's an end of my song!

The poet adds a drawing of the pot steaming on the stove and the uneasy lovers sitting down to a nice tea in domestic harmony.

If escape does not seem necessary here, neither is real happiness possible. Domestic contentment is all that can be won, and the refrain, "Ding-a-dong," encourages as it mocks the kind of compromise which, so the other poems tell us, is exactly what Lear most dreads. It is the coward's way out, a false peace; it spells the loss of the sublime. There is nothing within the poem to tell us this, neither a discrepancy between the surface and the inner meaning, nor traces of muffled emotion, nor a sense of mystery. Even the paradoxes have disappeared. Joy, fear and bewilderment have all been too thoroughly concealed. A modern reader may see nothing more nonsensical in the poem than anthropomorphism, inconsequentiality and a conventional battling of the sexes. But if he recalls the limericks where the hero and heroine are rebuffed and have to return home, he will find it hard to accept the poem's contentment at face value. Indeed, in the picture of the tea,

he may prefer to see the lovers not as household utensils which have been given a miraculous life, but as real people who have been so stripped of their vitality and warmth that they can only scrape and rattle like worn kitchenware. Like "The Nutcrackers and the Sugar-tongs," this poem is severe and reductive, for all its zest. The kettle sits peacefully on the hob, but the hysteria is not, after all, assuaged.

We do not know if Lear arranged the poems in a deliberate order. But the pattern of gradual reduction, to this point, suggests that he may have. He has painted himself into a domestic corner, and in the final courtship voyage poem in the book, "The Table and the Chair,"[11] he strips his characters of even the oddity that kitchen utensils have. He is content with a surrealistically spare Table and Chair for his heroes. There is no room for further stripping. He turns and faces his fiercely reduced world, and, almost experimentally, he reintroduces the sublime and tests it.

Like the Cracker and the Tongs and the Duck, the Table and Chair are weary of home life, but they doubt their ability to get away. Their legs, like those of the Fly and the Daddy Long-legs, seem to disqualify them:

Said the Table to the Chair,
"You can hardly be aware,
How I suffer from the heat,
And from chilblains on my feet!
If we took a little walk,
We might have a little talk!
Pray let us take the air!"
Said the Table to the Chair.

Said the Chair unto the Table,
"Now you *know* we are not able!
How foolishly you talk,
When you know we *cannot* walk!"
Said the Table, with a sigh,
"It can do no harm to try,
I've as many legs as you,
Why can't we walk on two?"

They try, and succeed, and stroll safely round town, to everyone's amazement. But the promenade turns into a misadventure:

But in going down an alley,
To a castle in a valley,
They completely lost their way,
And wandered all the day,
Till, to see them safely back,
They paid a Ducky-quack,
And a Beetle, and a Mouse,
Who took them to their house.

They have tried to escape to a Romantic world, to leap from the domestic to the sublime, but without the courage which, as we shall see, the Jumblies have. They are really strays and belong at home. When the animals rescue them, they congratulate each other like tourists who have been badly frightened but do not care to admit it to each other:

Then they whispered to each other,
"O delightful little brother!
What a lovely walk we've taken!
Let us dine on Beans and Bacon!"

So the Ducky, and the leetle
Browny-Mousy and the Beetle
Dined, and danced upon their heads
Till they toddled to their beds.

While they celebrate, like the Owl and the Pussy-cat, with a feast and a dance, they are celebrating not a wedding but a retreat, and the lesson is a stern one: stay within bounds—if you do not have the courage, or experience, or faith, release is impossible, and you will never reach the castle at the end of the valley. Is this what lies behind the "Ding-a-dong" chime of the "The Broom, the Shovel, the Poker and the Tongs"? It is a warning bell, and when the adventure becomes misadventure, a coachman or the animals are on hand to lead the household heroes and heroines safely home. In the strict order of this retreat, there is a sense of despair and of mental confinement. The regularity of the trimeter couplets, with iambic feet occasionally breaking into anapaests, only to be curbed, is so severe that the brief glimpse of the sublime seems especially brief. Lear has, with great hesitancy, placed his hand once more in the fire of the sublime—and has withdrawn it with a child's cry of distress.

In returning, however shyly, to his sublime, Lear has come nearly full circle. Not quite, since "The Owl and the Pussy-cat" embraces the marvelous much more boldly; but firmly enough, because the poems in between increasingly forgo the wonder in order to investigate the sense of estrangement. The pattern is clear. Lear describes the whole predicament in "The Owl and the Pussy-cat," and then he isolates this element and that until he understands more fully the feelings which keep him indoors and alone. He moves the paradoxes and discrepancies from the drawings into the poetry, where they soon reveal themselves in their perplexing and unresolved state—the wildness-in-restraint of "The Nutcrackers and the Sugar-Tongs," the entrapment-in-release of "The Duck and the Kangaroo." By the time he reaches "The Broom, the Shovel, the Poker and the Tongs," he has reduced life to a mere surface, and he discards the paradoxes together with the feelings they express. Once he finishes this work of stripping, he returns in "The Table and the Chair" to hints of that exaltation which, in many of the limericks and in the first ballad, had taken him beyond paradox and confusion. Of course, this progress is hypothetical since we do not know if the present order is Lear's, or his publisher's, or the printer's. But even if random, the pattern still stands: now the poet dares to peep at the sublime, now he examines the paradox in which he is stuck, now ("The Broom") he reduces life fiercely to a rattling absurdity.

"The Table and the Chair" makes a good conclusion, whether or not

Lear intended it for one, because it allows us a slight lift of the kind we feel at the end of a Shakespearean tragedy. The lift does not amount to elevation, let alone transport, nor can Lear recover his minor sublime. But he leaves us with a paradox which, like that of the first ballad, is loaded with the possibility of happiness—wonder-in-confinement. Which is the stronger term? We cannot say—but where wonder is in doubt, at least there is clarity. In telling how he has to be rescued from his view of the castle in the valley, he gives the best figure we may have of his bewildering predicament. How, he asks, am I to escape the confinements of this domesticated empire, how can I let go of my attachment to household safety, and "carry out the views and feelings of landscape I know to exist within me?"[12] How can I undo the blindfold which keeps me from a clear view of the marvelous?

Five years passed. Lear settled in at San Remo, but he was still restless enough to travel to India in the winter of 1873–1874 after two false starts. When he returned in February 1875, he settled for good. He published *Laughable Lyrics, a Fourth Book of Nonsense Poems, Songs, Botany, Music, etc.* two years later, at the end of 1876. Among these poems are four which develop the courtship voyage theme further—"The Dong with a Luminous Nose," "The Courtship of the Yonghy-Bonghy-Bò," "The Pobble Who Has No Toes" and "The Pelican Chorus."

The new ballads begin where the old ended. The poet seems to have put home firmly behind him. Now he can investigate the sublime—without confinements. Lear places his hero from the outset in a paradise, abroad, and he allows the love element to return. As soon as the poet-hero looks around, however, he finds the situation has not really changed very much. He may have settled in a soft climate, at San Remo or Coromandel, but he is not exactly in paradise. He soon sees that a home away from home is still a home, and that it seems even more cruel to be at home abroad than it was to feel, as he did when a child, all abroad at home. Home and abroad, England and paradise, the familiar and the strange, the domestic and the sublime, identity and alienation—the confining paradoxes are still with him, an oppressive crowd, and he can only make more nonsense of them. The new hero starts in a paradise, isolated, only to end up in a paradise, doubly deserted.

While this new tack is not so new after all, at least the poet is able to extend the clarity found in "The Table and the Chair": we do learn more about the nonsense sublime. Now that he has withdrawn from life and its delusive contracts, he writes more frankly of the concerns of his heart. Perhaps India helped. It was such a final disappointment. After *Nonsense*

Songs and Stories, Lear seems to have felt so freshly intoxicated by the sublime that he threw down his pen and rushed off to Coromandel and the Himalayas. When he returned to his garden exile, he must have realized that the voyage was over for good, and that he had only made a fool of himself by pretending otherwise. So he started *Laughable Lyrics* with all the resignation and clarity that we expect of a last work. Perhaps he would find in verse what he had missed in life.

This new predicament demanded a new form, and he developed one swiftly. There is a remarkable difference between the early and the later ballads. The simple patchwork has gone, and in its place there is an intricate kind of lyric, still dramatic and narrative, but resembling an ode more than a ballad and at a further remove from the nursery rhyme. The dramatic exchanges are now more intense and moving, and the imaginary landscapes more vivid. The new form is much more sophisticated and expressive. "The Dong with a Luminous Nose"[13] begins *in medias res:*

When awful darkness and silence reign
Over the great Gromboolian plain,
  Through the long, long wintry nights;—
When the angry breakers roar
As they beat on the rocky shore;—
  When storm-clouds brood on the towering heights
Of the Hills of the Chankly Bore:—

Then, through the vast and gloomy dark,
There moves what seems a fiery spark,
  A lonely spark with silvery rays
  Piercing the coal black night,—
  A Meteor strange and bright:—
Hither and thither the vision strays,
  A single lurid light.

Slowly it wanders,—pauses,—creeps,—
Anon, it sparkles,—flashes and leaps;
And ever as onward it gleaming goes
A light on the Bong-tree stems it throws.
And those who watch at that midnight hour
From Hall or Terrace, or lofty Tower,
Cry, as the wild light passes along,—
    "The Dong!—the Dong!
  The wandering Dong through the forest goes!
    The Dong! the Dong!
  The Dong with a luminous Nose!"

It is interesting that the Gromboolian plain, to which the Fly and the Daddy Long-legs fled, is a gloomy place, a darkened Elysium; and that the Hills of the Chankly Bore, which the brave Jumblies visit, are towering and awful. The landscape, with its cliffs, lofty tower, hall and terrace, darkening clouds and fitful light, is comical-Gothic, an absurdly somber sublime.

The middle two stanzas tell us, in a flashback, the cause of the Dong's mournful search. Long ago the Jumblies landed in Gromboolia (as we know from "The Jumblies"). The Dong fell in love with a Jumbly girl, and he danced and sang with her people. But when they went home, she went with them, leaving the Dong alone on the shore, singing the Jumbly chorus by himself. All this we are told in two irregularly rhymed stanzas, one of ten lines, the other of sixteen, each concluding with the Jumbly refrain:

> "Far and few, far and few,
> Are the lands where the Jumblies live;
> Their heads are green, and their hands are blue;
> And they went to sea in a sieve."

Lear carries the flashback over into the sixth verse:

> But when the sun was low in the West,
> The Dong arose and said:—
> —"What little sense I once possessed
> Has quite gone out of my head!"—
> And since that day he wanders still
> By lake and forest, marsh and hill,
> Singing—"O somewhere, in valley or plain
> Might I find my Jumbly Girl again!
> For ever I'll seek by lake and shore
> Till I find my Jumbly Girl once more!"

Since the Dong knows she has left, the faith that sustains his search is a faith in the absurd. The seventh stanza tells us, in a second flashback, the origin of the mysterious luminous nose:

> . . . because by night he could not see,
> He gathered the bark of the Twangum Tree
> On the flowering plain that grows.
> And he wove him a wondrous Nose,—
> A Nose as strange as a Nose could be!

The last verse, in plangent couplets with a long, drawn-out refrain, describes his continual, fruitless wandering in the dreary night of his predicament:

> And now each night, and all night long,
> Over those plains still roams the Dong;
> And above the wail of the Chimp and Snipe
> You may hear the squeak of his plaintive pipe
> While ever he seeks, but seeks in vain
> To meet with his Jumbly Girl again;
> Lonely and wild—all night he goes,—
> The Dong with a luminous Nose!
> And all who watch at the midnight hour,
> From Hall or Terrace, or lofty Tower,
> Cry, as they trace the Meteor bright,
> Moving along through the dreary night,—
>   "This is the hour when forth he goes,
>   The Dong with a luminous Nose!
>   Yonder—over the plain he goes;
>   He goes!
>   He goes;
>   The Dong with a luminous Nose!"

This is the most desperate of Lear's longer nonsense poems. In the paradise where the Jumblies find all their answers, the Dong is cruelly forsaken and trapped in a useless quest. Gromboolia is a barren, Gothic purgatory for lost and aimless souls. The sublime has turned out to be a cruel joke, no fun at all, "laughable." After "The Table and the Chair," where the sublime seemed to be unreachable, we may ask which is worse—to be confined, loveless, in domestic comfort, or to be trapped, loveless, in a ruined paradise. Yet the alien has at least known the delights of love. If he now wallows in the depths, it is because he has floundered comically for a short while on the heights: "Happily, happily, passed those days!"

The grief and its origin are so clearly explained that we may ask how the poem is nonsensical. The displacement of sexual fear is obvious. Any poet writing after the publication of Freud's *Interpretation of Dreams* would have dispensed with the Nose as too obvious. Vast, red, with a rounded end, luminous—"A Nose as strange as a Nose could be!"—this is the phallic make-believe of a man who, disappointed in love, has only a squeaking, plaintive pipe to play on. The fear of sexuality, and of sexual inadequacy in particular, has floated to the surface.

Deeper fears *are* concealed. Lear is afraid that his art has failed. The plaintive pipe in the desolate pastoral reminds us of the failed shepherd of the music limericks, the Old Man who is unable to tame nature, where the Young Lady succeeds; and of the Old Man of the Isles, whose joyful fiddling expresses Lear's feeling of artistic fulfillment. The nonsense poetry itself is both a second-best, to make up for his failure to master the human figure or the craft of oil painting, and a real artistic success, original and perfected in a way the painting could never be. It would be wrong to underestimate the tension produced in Lear by these two contradictory self-estimates; and we shall see it again, though happily expressed, in "The Quangle Wangle's Hat."

There is another, subtler concealment. Just as the surface oddities in "The Owl and the Pussy-cat" distract us from the real nonsense underneath, so here the blatant though unconscious sexual displacement perhaps conceals a deeper difficulty. For, by playing, however unwittingly, with sexual metaphors, Lear is hiding his fear of love from himself. In real life he tended perhaps too easily to blame his loneliness on his sexual nature, in order to cover the real fear—that of giving his heart freely and deeply. It may be that what the Dong fears in his Jumbly girl friend is her love rather than her sex, and the gleaming light in the end of this strange Dong-like nose blinds him—and the reader—to the real truth.

The sense of nonsense lies partly in these concealments. They disturb the general meaning in much the same way that paradoxes and discrepancies make nonsense of the earlier work. There is nonsense, too, in the theme—in the failure of the conventionally wonderful to make sense. The poem is an honest account of Lear's failure to find in love or nature the wonderful assurances which Romantic tradition had promised. The pastoral is deserted, the paradise is purgatorial, love is ruined, the sublime is bathetic. But the best and most intense nonsense is in the admirable, recreative courage of the Dong, who pursues his quest beyond all reason, believing by virtue of the absurd, where he cannot see or fairly hope.

"The Courtship of the Yonghy-Bonghy-Bò" is sadder but less desperate. Again Lear places his hero in a desolate paradise, and again he is spurned. But this time the wooing is in the present, it is the central action of the drama, and at the end the Bò is allowed the release of a sudden, comical-epical flight. His love is not merely a thing of the past, and he does not end up imprisoned. Furthermore, this is the only poem in the series where the wooing is done by the male and the female is unequivocally kind, soft and feminine. The poem is frankly autobiographical and direct.

The verse is measured and intricate, and perhaps represents Lear's craft at its best:

On the Coast of Coromandel
Where the early pumpkins blow,
In the middle of the woods
Lived the Yonghy-Bonghy-Bò.
Two old chairs, and half a candle,—
One old jug without a handle,—
These were all his worldly goods:
In the middle of the woods,
These were all the worldly goods,
Of the Yonghy-Bonghy-Bò,
Of the Yonghy-Bonghy-Bò.

Once, among the Bong-trees walking
Where the early pumpkins blow,
To a little heap of stones
Came the Yonghy-Bonghy-Bò.
There he heard a Lady talking,
To some milk-white Hens of Dorking,—
" 'Tis the Lady Jingly Jones!
On that little heap of stones
Sits the Lady Jingly Jones!"
Said the Yonghy-Bonghy-Bò,
Said the Yonghy-Bonghy-Bò.

"Lady Jingly! Lady Jingly!
Sitting where the pumpkins blow,
Will you come and be my wife?"
Said the Yonghy-Bonghy-Bò.
"I am tired of living singly,—
On this coast so wild and shingly,—
I'm a-weary of my life:
If you'll come and be my wife,
Quite serene would be my life!"—
Said the Yonghy-Bonghy-Bò,
Said the Yonghy-Bonghy-Bò.

"On this Coast of Coromandel,
Shrimps and watercresses grow,
Prawns are plentiful and cheap,"
Said the Yonghy-Bonghy-Bò.
"You shall have my Chairs and candle,
And my jug without a handle!—
Gaze upon the rolling deep
(Fish is plentiful and cheap)
As the sea, my love is deep!"

Said the Yonghy-Bonghy-Bò,
Said the Yonghy-Bonghy-Bò.

Lady Jingly answered sadly,
And her tears began to flow,—
"Your proposal comes too late,
   Mr. Yonghy-Bonghy-Bò.
I would be your wife most gladly!"
(Here she twirled her fingers madly,)
   "But in England I've a mate!
   Yes! you've asked me far too late,
   For in England I've a mate,
Mr. Yonghy-Bonghy-Bò!
Mr. Yonghy-Bonghy-Bò.

"Mr. Jones—(his name is Handel,—
Handel Jones, Esquire, & Co.)
Dorking fowls delights to send,
   Mr. Yonghy-Bonghy-Bò!
Keep, oh! keep your chairs and candle,
And your jug without a handle,—
   I can merely be your friend!
   —Should my Jones more Dorkings send,
   I will give you three, my friend!
Mr. Yonghy-Bonghy-Bò!
Mr. Yonghy-Bonghy-Bò!

"Though you've such a tiny body,
And your head so large doth grow,—
Though your hat may blow away,
   Mr. Yonghy-Bonghy-Bò!
Though you're such a Hoddy Doddy—
Yet I wish that I could modi-
   fy the words I needs must say!
   Will you please to go away?
   That is all I have to say—
Mr. Yonghy-Bonghy-Bò!
Mr. Yonghy-Bonghy-Bò!"

Down the slippery slopes of Myrtle,
Where the early pumpkins blow,
To the calm and silent sea
   Fled the Yonghy-Bonghy-Bò.
There, beyond the Bay of Gurtle,
Lay a large and lively Turtle;—

"You're the Cove," he said, "for me,
On your back beyond the sea,
Turtle, you shall carry me!"
Said the Yonghy-Bonghy-Bò,
Said the Yonghy-Bonghy-Bò.

Through the silent-roaring ocean
Did the Turtle swiftly go;
Holding fast upon his shell
Rode the Yonghy-Bonghy-Bò.
With a sad primaeval motion
Towards the sunset isles of Boshen
Still the Turtle bore him well.
Holding fast upon his shell,
"Lady Jingly Jones, farewell!"
Sang the Yonghy-Bonghy-Bò,
Sang the Yonghy-Bonghy-Bò.

From the Coast of Coromandel,
Did that Lady never go;
On that heap of stones she mourns
For the Yonghy-Bonghy-Bò.
On that Coast of Coromandel,
In his jug without a handle
Still she weeps, and daily moans;
On that little heap of stones
To her Dorking Hens she moans,
For the Yonghy-Bonghy-Bò,
For the Yonghy-Bonghy-Bò.

It has been suggested that Lear takes his meter from Tennyson's verses on Catullus—"Row us out from Desenzano, to your Sirmione row!"[14] If he does, he uses it only as a comical point of departure. Tennyson's attempt to write hexameters has little to do with these traditional measures which Lear stitches together out of ballad and nursery-rhyme forms—quatrain, couplet, triplet, and two-line refrain repeating the fourth line. An intricate rhyming scheme binds each stanza. It is possible to read the first quatrain as trochaic, but a glance at Lear's piano setting, which was written down for him by his friend Professor Pomè, shows that he intended anapaests: two semiquavers precede the quaver G-sharp of "Coast." The piano accompaniment reminds us that the poem's principal tone, for all its dramatic skill (the rejection of the Bò's proposal, his flight), is lyrical, and that while there are mock-classical touches (the imitation of hexameters and the nonsense epithet "silent-roaring") as well as literary echoes of the parlor-ballad style of Moore, the strength of the poem lies in its closeness to simple folk song.

The lyricism has a very personal intensity. Lear has put himself directly into the poem. It is the only one in the series where the man and his lady are fully human. The Pobble resembles a merman, and the Jumbly Girl has odd hands and hair; the Dong is badly deformed in his own poem, and in the illustration of "The Quangle Wangle's Hat" he is depicted as a quadruped, while in one version of "The Dong with a Luminous Nose" he marries the daughter of a Jampoodle. But the Bò and the Lady Jingly are flesh-and-blood people, dressed in quiet, late Regency fashion, like the man and woman in the limericks. If the Bò is Lear himself, the Lady is Gussie Bethell and Mr. Handel Jones is perhaps her crippled husband, Adamson Parker. The poet brings the romantic episode of "The Dong" out of the past into the present and allows himself to confront his own predicament much more frankly.

Not that the art is entirely true to the life. There are still some pretenses. Perhaps the most curious aspect of the whole ode is the way the poet represents Gussie's feelings, since he does so more honestly than he was able to in real life, and also more deceivingly. He is startlingly honest when he has the Lady declare her love for the Bò even as she rejects him: he admits here that he really knows Gussie's true feelings for him, and we may guess that it was not doubt about these which inhibited him from proposing to her. The Bò's proposal is, of course, wish-fulfillment; but her response is a sizable part of the truth.

He is deceiving when he ends the poem with a poignant picture of her grief. Gussie may indeed have felt sad that her love for Lear was not requited. But in the poem she has rejected him, and this is a strange way of representing the real-life situation, in which he never had the courage to propose to her in the first place. Since it is he who has been rejected, it is he who should be left desolate and grieving. Instead, the poet places the whole burden of sadness on the Lady, and allows the Bò a bold and decisive escape. While this is a kind of deception, it is not in the end dishonest. It has two cleansing effects. First, it dispels self-pity. The poet cannot pity himself if he is busy making a bold escape. Second, because the real grief has been displaced, it can be safely recognized and expressed. So an evasion of shallow feeling (self-pity) allows for an expression of real and deep feeling (grief).

The reader need not know about Lear's life to see a discrepancy; he has only to ask why the Lady, who rejects, ends up in the situation of the rejected. He will soon see why the ode is nonsensical. It is not because there is a gap between surface and depths, but because the central feeling has been shifted to a periphery. The deep feelings lie much closer to the surface than in the earlier ballads, where the effort at concealment was more severe and the inhibition stricter. Here, the personal predicament is faced more squarely, and the result is an emotional frankness rare in the earlier nonsense.

What of the Bò's flight? He is helped by an animal. A Turkey presided over the nuptials of the Owl and the Pussy-cat, a Coachman drove home the Broom, the Shovel, the Poker and the Tongs, and a Mouse, a Beetle, and a Duck rescued the Table and the Chair. Here there is neither fulfillment, nor retreat, nor rescue. The Turtle helps the Bò make an escape that looks something like a tactical withdrawal or a flight that amounts to a Pyrrhic victory for a wounded heart still strong enough to reject the heart that has rejected it. Sour grapes, or courage? The flight seems to leave open the question of consummation and denial: and if we place the Bò's resolution beside the dejection, we might feel safe in concluding that he is an absurd version of Tennyson's Ulysses, a man who abandons a world in which he feels himself to be a misfit and sets out for the western sea, perhaps to a nonsense Hesperides, perhaps just to fall off the end of the world. The Bò's last dash is comical-epical. He rushes to the shore and commandeers the Turtle. Is he not taking the same risk as the Jumblies, or making the same commitment of faith that the Dong makes, determining, like Ulysses, to believe in an action for the sake of believing, in the hope that what lies unintelligibly beyond will outshine the exhausting terrors and wasteful comforts of ordinary existence? The Lady Jingly might have real cause to weep, since she has been abandoned in a place where the sublime is out of reach.

The pattern of courtship and voyage is the same for the Bo as it was for the Dong. Love has failed, and the roving, though it too looks hopeless, must continue. The sense of nonsense is the same, too. There is concealment, evasion and displacement. There is the criticism of the conventional sublime—from a Romantic viewpoint, it is nonsense to suppose that love cannot be transporting. Lastly, there is the nonsense of the final gesture—the absurd courage of the hero, ready to follow knowledge or nonsense "like a sinking star / Beyond the utmost bound of human thought." The Bò's resolve is grand and funny, and we may feel that he has a better chance than Ulysses of reaching the Happy Isles, not because he is a better sailor, but because there is more risk in being silly than in being severe. It is the Bò, not Ulysses, who really makes a virtue of foolhardiness.

"The Pobble Who Has No Toes,"[15] which was written for Gertrude, Frank Lushington's daughter and Lear's own goddaughter, survives in two versions. One version is hard nonsense, and moving; and one is soft nonsense, pretty but shallow.

In six fairly simple stanzas, each composed of two quatrains in the familiar ballad collage style, Lear spins out in the hard version a tale which explains the title, in the manner of "The Dong."

The Pobble who has no toes
    Had once as many as we;
When they said, "Some day you may lose them all;"—
    He replied,—"Fish fiddle de-dee!"
And his Aunt Jobiska made him drink
Lavender water tinged with pink,
For she said, "The World in general knows,
There's nothing so good for a Pobble's toes!"

The third and fourth lines recall the formulas of the limericks, especially those of the Young Lady of Lucca and the young person in pink. The Pobble sets out from his house, which is somewhere in Wales, to cross the Bristol Channel:

The Pobble who has no toes,
    Swam across the Bristol Channel;
But before he set out he wrapped his nose
    In a piece of scarlet flannel.
For his Aunt Jobiska said, "No harm
Can come to his toes if his nose is warm;
And it's perfectly known that a Pobble's toes
Are safe,—provided he minds his nose!"

The Pobble swam fast and well,
    And when boats or ships came near him,
He tinkledy-binkledy-winkled a bell,
    So that all the world could hear him.
And all the Sailors and Admirals cried,
When they saw him nearing the further side,—
"He has gone to fish for his Aunt Jobiska's
Runcible Cat with crimson whiskers!"

But then there is a disaster:

But before he touched the shore,
    The shore of the Bristol Channel,
A sea-green Porpoise carried away
    His wrapper of scarlet flannel,

And when he came to observe his feet,
Formerly garnished with toes so neat,
His face at once became forlorn
On perceiving that all his toes were gone!

The calamity remains a mystery:

And nobody ever knew
  From that dark day to the present,
Whoso had taken the Pobble's toes,
  In a manner so far from pleasant.
Whether the shrimps or crawfish gray,
Or crafty Mermaids stole them away—
Nobody knew; and nobody knows
How the Pobble was robbed of his twice five toes!

In the last verse, They reappear, and fetch him home:

The Pobble who has no toes
  Was placed in a friendly Bark,
And they rowed him back, and carried him up
  To his Aunt Jobiska's Park.
And she made him a feast at his earnest wish
Of eggs and buttercups fried with fish;—
And she said,—"It's a fact the whole world knows
That Pobbles are happier without their toes."

The other version is softer and longer. In place of stanzas 4, 5, and 6, there are seven others, which tell a love story.* The Pobble, in this version, reaches England and meets Princess Bink, the daughter of King Jampoodle. He falls in love with her, and because his aunt has told him that life is worthless without a wife, he proposes. She accepts, on condition that he give her his flannel and all his toes for her father's museum collection and as proof of his affection. She throws off her beetroot cap and weaves his flannel around her head, while he unscrews his toes, one by one. They exchange vows, and without telling her father, they leave at once, swimming back across the Channel. When the sailors see them returning, they cry out that there are no more fish for the "Runcible Cat with crimson whiskers." The Pobble and the Princess dance all over Wales, and Aunt Jobiska feeds them on "Mice and Buttercups fried with

*See Appendix, section 1.

fish" and declares that Pobbles are happier without their toes. This is straightforward and happy. The only hint of deeper trouble is in the unscrewing of the toes; yet the Pobble is surrendering them to his wife out of affection, and there is no certainty that they are given to her father. Since the lovers leave without telling him, it is likelier that she takes the toes with her and that the unscrewing is a figure for sexual consummation, rather than castration. The aunt seems to be a thoroughly benign influence; she urges the Pobble to marry, and then presides over the nuptial feast and dancing.

The fears of sexuality and of love in this romantic version are so successfully ducked that there is little nonsense of the kind that can move us. Real emotion has been erased by wish-fulfillment. By concealing the love element in the hard version, Lear is able to face up to some of his feelings of fear and give them more open expression. He placed an epigraphic drawing of his hero over the title.

The Pobble is depicted swimming the Channel, with a bell in one hand (the clapper just showing) and a flannel round his nose. The flannel is completely flat; it is plain enough that underneath it he has no nose and the wrapping is really a bandage. We recall with a shiver that the Dong also bandaged his nose. In the verse, the flannel is scarlet, the water pink, the Cat has crimson whiskers; in the romantic version, the Princess has a cap made of a "root of Beetroot red / With a hole cut out to insert her head." The poem is swimming in blood! The Pobble's mission is predatory—he has been sent by his aunt to catch fish for her cat with blood-stained whiskers. Instead, a porpoise steals the Pobble's flannel, and either shrimps, crawfish or Mermaids rob him of his toes. The aunt is the villain of the piece. She pretends to be looking after his best interests, but sends him on a dangerous and murderous expedition. When he returns, horribly mutilated, sexually incapacitated, she declares he is happier as he is—toeless and (though she does not admit this) noseless. The disastrous fish-ing expedition is a ghastly metaphor for the failure of love. In real life, there was no Princess Bink to woo and win. Instead of wooing, there is impotence, and instead of a successful voyage, the hero has to be brought home in a "friendly Bark" by Them. It is the most complete and humiliating of all Lear's retreats. If only there had been a Turtle, or a Coachman, or a Duck, Mouse and Beetle to rescue him!

The soft version, by spinning out a happy adventure and a joyful ending, disguises the real fears of sex and love so they no longer disturb the poem's surface; consequently, though pretty, it is neither moving nor very nonsensical. The hard version manages to condense, displace and dislocate the fears so that they are given fuller, not fainter, expression. In this way, a fib tells the whole truth while seeming to duck it; and the longer version, with its fanciful romance, is like the man who talks with the kind of frank and open garrulousness designed to hide the real facts. The hard version says nothing and everything about the poet's attitude toward love; the soft version says something about love, and nothing.

But if the shorter hard version is better nonsense, it is also regressive. Lear's real concern in *Laughable Lyrics* has been to investigate the nature of the sublime. What does love in a pastoral paradise come to? He has given some painfully honest answers in "The Dong" and "The Bò." But here he removes the courtship altogether, just as he did after the second poem in *Nonsense Songs and Stories*. For the moment, he reverts to his interest in the mysterious condition of confinement, a regression made clearer if we note that the voyage, as in the earlier ballads, occupies the center of the poem, and that Wales and England are really home—in the thinnest paradisal disguise. No wonder "The Pobble" is so fierce and cryptic! Lear has been forced back into a position he thought he had left behind him. The household gods have not been appeased, and this is a late, and savage, sacrifice to them.

We sense something of the horror of this regression in the epigraphic drawing.

This is a butchered version of the gestures of blessing we found throughout the limericks—the smile, the outspread arms. The eyes are especially strange: the right one is half-closed, the left hangs blankly beneath a highly arched and crooked eyebrow. The man should be expressing wonder, but, instead, he looks as though he is in pain. The bandage-flannel binds his mutilated face, and in his left hand he holds up the bell, as if it were his amputated nose, or worse.

While it is a throwback, "The Pobble" differs from the earlier ballads. Lear has not succeeded in precipitating a paradox. We might expect something like impotence-love, or confinement-escape; but instead, both the light and dark terms have moved beyond the frame of the poem, and we are able to guess what they are only because we know the overall pattern and understand, by now, Lear's methods. In the same way, the fib reveals everything only because we have enough outside information from Lear's life, the other poems and especially the longer version. The casual reader may understand the darker point of the Pobble's noselessness, but without the larger knowledge that we have, he will not be able to see the full extent of Lear's condensation, displacement and dislocation. Perhaps fortunately, the nightmare will be beyond him.

So, to speak strictly, the poem works only on its own surface. Like "The Broom, the Shovel, the Poker and the Tongs," it so far suppresses the feelings which have motivated it that all we are left with is a whimsical, happily grotesque, inconsequential jingle. But that is absurd—we *do* know enough to see the truth behind the fib. The other poems provide enough information to unriddle the Pobble's misadventure. We see both the glittering surface and the depths—depths too horrible, this time at least, for the poet to make intelligible nonsense. We see the surface, and the paradox which failed to take shape beneath it.

In the last and happiest poem of the series, "The Pelican Chorus,"[16] Lear writes a sort of nonsense epithalamium. Like the other three in *Laughable Lyrics*, the poem starts in one paradise and moves, at the end, toward another; unlike the others, the courtship is swift and happy, and the voyage is no longer a quest (for love, or truth, or a natural sublime), but a honeymoon, a celebration and a consummation. The courtship is, for the only time, distinguished clearly from the voyage. At the end, the married couple fly off to the Gromboolian Plain, leaving the King and Queen Pelican alone—but this is all according to nature, and the old couple at least have each other. In its action, the poem resembles the first in the series, "The Owl and the Pussy-cat," most closely of all, but without the concealed terror or confusion. By now the poet has managed to take the vicarious viewpoint of the parents, and this detachment helps him accept the natural order of courtship, marriage and leaving home.

Choric and elegiac, brisk and languid, sad and jolly, the poem is also very like "The Courtship of the Yonghy-Bonghy-Bò." There is the same mixture of lyrical sweetness and vigor. It is hard to say which is the more beautiful. Certainly, Lear is at his best:

> King and Queen of the Pelicans we;
> No other Birds so grand we see!
> None but we have feet like fins!
> With lovely leathery throats and chins!
>   Ploffskin, Pluffskin, Pelican jee!
>   We think no Birds so happy as we!
>   Plumpskin, Ploshkin, Pelican jill!
>   We think so then, and we thought so still!
>
> We live on the Nile. The Nile we love.
> By night we sleep on the cliffs above;
> By day we fish, and at eve we stand
> On long bare islands of yellow sand.
> And when the sun sinks slowly down,
> And the great rock walls grow dark and brown,
> Where the purple river rolls fast and dim
> And the Ivory Ibis starlike skim,
> Wing to wing we dance around,—
> Stamping our feet with a flumpy sound,—
> Opening our mouths as Pelicans ought,
> And this is the song we nightly snort,—
>   Ploffskin, Pluffskin, Pelican jee!
>   We think no Birds so happy as we!
>   Plumpskin, Ploshkin, Pelican jill!
>   We think so then, and we thought so still!

The chorus itself is in the refrain of each verse, where the paradox—then, but now—presented by the jumbled tenses mocks the sentimentality of parents who live vicariously in the happiness of the past. At the same time, it allows us to relive the Pelicans' pleasure with them, and to feel gently nostalgic, too. Perhaps Lear confuses the tenses not just to suspend but also to mark time: the Pelicans are trapped between now and then, and their chorus is really an hysterical lament. Dark readings are possible. Yet the overall feeling is happy, especially in the middle which, like the middle of "The Dong," relates the history of the courtship in a long flashback. The

Dong was stuck in the past. Here the outcome is joyful. The Princess Dell is married and leaves home with her parents' blessing.

Last year came out our Daughter, Dell;
And all the Birds received her well.
To do her honour, a feast we made
For every bird that can swim or wade.
Herons and Gulls, and Cormorants black,
Cranes and Flamingoes with scarlet back,
Plovers and Storks, and Geese in clouds,
Swans and Dilberry Ducks in crowds.
Thousands of Birds in wondrous flight!
They ate and drank and danced all night,
And echoing back from the rocks you heard
Multitude-echoes from Bird and Bird,—
Ploffskin, Pluffskin, Pelican jee,
We think no Birds so happy as we!
Plumpskin, Ploshkin, Pelican jill,
We think so then, and we thought so still!

Yes, they came; and among the rest,
The King of the Cranes all grandly dressed.
Such a lovely tail! Its feathers float
Between the ends of his blue dress-coat;
With pea-green trowsers all so neat,
And a delicate frill to hide his feet,—
(For though no one speaks of it, every one knows,
He has got no webs between his toes!)

As soon as he saw our Daughter Dell,
In violent love that Crane King fell,—
On seeing her waddling form so fair,
With a wreath of shrimps in her short white hair.
And before the end of the next long day,
Our Dell had given her heart away;
For the King of the Cranes had won that heart,
With a Crocodile's egg and a large fish-tart.
She vowed to marry the King of the Cranes,
Leaving the Nile for stranger plains,
And away they flew in a gathering crowd
Of endless birds in a lengthening cloud.
Ploffskin, Pluffskin, Pelican jee,
We think no Birds so happy as we!
Plumpskin, Ploshkin, Pelican jill,
We think so then, and we thought so still!

In the final verse, Lear is more openly and comically melancholy. But by ending on a forlorn note, as he does in "The Yonghy-Bonghy-Bò," he is really reinforcing the joy:

> And far away in the twilight sky,
> We heard them sing a lessening cry,—
> Farther and farther till out of sight,
> And we stood alone in the silent night!
> Often since, in the nights of June,
> We sit on the sand and watch the moon;—
> She has gone to the great Gromboolian Plain,
> And we probably never shall meet again!
> Oft, in the long still nights of June,
> We sit on the rocks and watch the moon;—
> —She dwells by the streams of the Chankly Bore,
> And we probably never shall see her more.
> Ploffskin, Pluffskin, Pelican jee!
> We think no Birds so happy as we!
> Plumpskin, Ploshkin, Pelican jill!
> We think so then, and we thought so still!

They will not see her again, but the knowledge that she is happy overwhelms their feelings of absence and desertion, so they sing and dance in celebration.

The dark readings are improbable. There is a slight disturbance at the end of the fourth stanza, when in a parenthetical aside the peculiarity of King Crane's feet is mentioned:

> With pea-green trowsers all so neat,
> And a delicate frill to hide his feet—
> (For though no one speaks of it, every one knows,
> He has got no webs between his toes!)

The joke is on the Pelicans of course, since their web feet are far less natural from the human point of view. Lear is once more laughing at the cruel and petty standards of normality, so many of which cast him beyond the pale. There is, as well, a certain amount of social satire at the expense of the Pelicans, who claim to be uniquely great among birds by virtue of their fishlike feet:

> King and Queen of the Pelicans we;
> No other Birds so grand we see!
> None but we have feet like fins!
> With lovely leathery throats and chins!

Presumably their voices, like their throats, are leathery and their chorus is both sweet and hoarse. When they dance, they are clumsy—"Stamping our feet with a flumpy sound." But Lear is not really mocking them. By sharing first their idiosyncrasies, he shares later in their beauty. We think of him sitting in the cages of the Regent's Park Zoo, sketching the parrots while people look in, or painting his delightful *Coloured Bird Book for Children;* and of his lifelong kinship with owls and ravens and parrots. Once he has identified himself with the birds, he can feel their sociability and beauty, and experience what other, more normal human beings seem to find naturally in one another's company. In other poems, there is sometimes a sad feeling that Lear is closer to birds than to people. But here the anthropomorphism, while it reflects his feeling of alienation, closes the distance between him and his fellow man.

"The Pelican Chorus" is infused with a joy which is at first melancholy, and then, once it has sunk in, purely and wonderfully happy. Nowhere else is Lear's poetry so non-nonsensical. It has a Tennysonian loveliness. The feeling is that of calm splendor, especially in the second verse. The first line has the delicacy of chiasmus and reminds us of the seesawing of the limericks. Then the sense unfolds in an extraordinarily fluent manner, with night, day, eve and dusk for a frame, and long spondaic measures. The heavy alliteration has gone—a sure sign that the main intention here is not comic. Lear breaks in at the tenth line with a ludicrous—"Stamping our feet with a flumpy sound," and saves the verse from insipidness or gloom.

Like "The Pobble," "The Pelican Chorus" does not carry forward the investigation of wonder found in the first two courtship voyage ballads of *Laughable Lyrics.* It is in one sense a positive of "The Pobble's" negative, a happy version of courtship and domestic confinement instead of a troubled one. The wonder and joy are simple and unvexed. Lear is writing not from the obscure corners of his imagination, but in the wholly conscious speculation that married life, were it possible, would probably make him happy enough. Though he supplies a landscape for this devoutly wish-fulfilling consummation directly from his experience of the natural sublime of his Nile journeys, he does not pretend it is anything more than stage scenery. These flats do not disclose the real "views" which he has seen on his way to the castle in the valley, nor do they evoke the true "feelings of landscape" which he knows in his heart and has tried to find in his verse.

The poem is nonsense in manner only. It does not offer the hope that by trusting in the absurdity of life, we may discover wonders, nor does it criticize the old, Romantic ways of seeking them; and where there is no concern for new wonders there is no nonsense. Lear is not trying here to look out into the dark, so the displacement, disturbance and paradox are merely playful. Married love is too intelligible and commonplace, and it is not what bewilders the poet any more than it is what he is seeking. He wanted the truth, not comfort: this is the secret strength of his work, and perhaps the real reason he did not marry.

"The Pelican Chorus" is for Lear a happy holiday poem, a respite from the real work of the nonsense, where he presses his search for the enchantments hidden deep in his heart.

Looking back over the ten poems of the courtship voyage series, we can see that in ringing the changes on the *motifs* of wooing and of quest, Lear has made sense of the strange confinements of home and has gone some way toward understanding the nature of his exiled adventuring. He experiments with and exhausts different stylistic strategies—discrepancy, paradox, displacement—and he develops and perfects a sophisticated ode form. His effort is always to make sense of the absurd by making poetry of absurdity. These ballads reveal his main trouble—alienation. When all those fearful paradoxes which crowd and oppress him are spelled out, alienation is the condition they describe. Home and abroad, England and paradise, the familiar and the strange, the domestic and the sublime, the confined and the free—these are the terms of Lear's estrangement. He is distracted by a sense of otherness, and in his life and his art he tries to find an end to the distraction in the transporting recognition of wholeness which alone can mend his spirit.

Since this was his condition, it is not surprising that the solution of "The Pelican Chorus" was not enough. Everyday love was not the answer, though Lear must have wasted many of his hopes thinking it might be. Nor was nature enough: the years of roving revealed nothing. The answer was deeper and farther off, the search was over more distant territory, his alienation was not an ordinary humdrum human alienation. His trouble was really a spiritual trouble. Love's sublime, or nature's, might have satisfied a run-of-the-mill Romantic. But Lear was not an everyday seeker, nor could he be content with even the most exalted things the world had to offer. His exile was spent in pilgrimages not just to ruins, mountains and towns; he was more than a tourist. They were the ruins of temples, and holy mountains and cities. And he spent a great part of his retirement at San Remo learning Greek in order to read Plato and St. John in the original.

In rescuing the Byronic sublime, Lear also transformed it. Had he been satisfied with the old sublime, he might have been content to write mature versions of his juvenile imitations of Byron. But his dilemma was new, his trouble was Tennyson's—a spiritual alienation. Byron's figures—love and roving—were comically insufficient, so Lear used them comically, nonsensically, carrying the Romantic quest of his boyhood on into the Victorian search of his manhood until the figures failed altogether and the seeker had to look beyond them. The nonsense is a way of ensuring cultural continuity, so that the spiritual tendencies of the child are sustained and rewarded in the spiritual life of the grown man—and the early values are conserved; it is a way, too, of shaking off the old values, with a real clarity and firmness. Lear is true to Byron, and also outstrips him.

We shall see, when we look at the paradise group of poems, how well he expresses this soul-searching. Of the courtship voyage poems we can say that they have succeeded in a work of spiritual investigation. Their extraordinary intelligence has helped the poet to see his path a little more clearly. If he has not fully understood that his sense of alienation is basically a sense of his separation from God, at least he has illuminated some of his more worldly troubles. If the sublime, the paradisal, the strange, the free and the exalted still bewilder him, at least he now sees the full extent of his personal, social and artistic estrangement. In exploring the failure of love and the reluctance of nature to reveal to him the "views and feelings of landscape" which he knows are his real guides, he has begun to make sense of his failure to master the human figure. Persisting in his folly, he has become at least a little wiser.

Family and Cloth

More Nonsense and *Laughable Lyrics* each have two smaller groups, the family poems and the cloth poems. In these, Lear shakes his rattle once more at the silliness of domestic confinement and spiritual timidity. There is a new note, too, of social criticism. The poet scolds not just himself but the pompous and cowering crowd, the bourgeois conformists who torment the Old Man of the limericks.

The family poems have none of the guileless languor of "The Pelican Chorus," nor any of its comfort. Instead, the parents encounter danger, and they retreat, or they are destroyed, along with their children. The first in the group is the least vexed. "Mr. and Mrs. Spikky Sparrow"[17] is a bright, flinty poem, made of tough trochaic tetrameter couplets:

> On a little piece of wood,
> Mr. Spikky Sparrow stood;
> Mrs. Sparrow sat close by,
> A-making of an insect pie,
> For her little children five,
> In the nest and all alive,

Singing with a cheerful smile
To amuse them all the while,
  Twikky wikky wikky wee,
  Wikky bikky twikky tee,
    Spikky bikky bee!

Mrs. Spikky Sparrow said,
"Spikky, Darling! in my head
Many thoughts of trouble come,
Like to flies upon a plum!
All last night, among the trees,
I heard you cough, I heard you sneeze;
And, thought I, it's come to that
Because he does not wear a hat!"
  Chippy wippy sikky tee!
  Bikky wikky tikky mee!
    Spikky chippy wee!

"Not that you are growing old,
But the nights are growing cold.
No one stays out all night long
Without a hat: I'm sure it's wrong!"
Mr. Spikky said, "How kind,
Dear! you are, to speak your mind!
All your life I wish you luck!
You are! you are! a lovely duck!"
  Witchy witchy witchy wee!
  Twitchy witchy witchy bee!
    Tikky tikky tee!

"I was also sad, and thinking,
When one day I saw you winking,
And I heard you sniffle-snuffle,
And I saw your feathers ruffle;
To myself I sadly said,
She's neuralgia in her head!
That dear head has nothing on it!
Ought she not to wear a bonnet!"
  Witchy kitchy kitchy wee?
  Spikky wikky mikky bee?
    Chippy wippy chee?

In the next two stanzas, they fly up to town and buy a hat for Mr. Sparrow, and for Mrs. Sparrow a spotted gown with a satin sash of Cloxam blue, and for both some slippers to protect them from the cold:

Then when so completely drest,
Back they flew, and reached their nest.
Their children cried, "O Ma and Pa!
How truly beautiful you are!"
Said they, "We trust that cold or pain
We shall never feel again!
While, perched on tree, or house, or steeple,
We now shall look like other people."
  Witchy witchy witchy wee,
  Twikky mikky bikky bee,
    Zikky sikky tee.

The poem ends with a spluttering, chirpy name-refrain and a cartoon of the Sparrows in their new clothes, bending fondly over the nest.

Underneath the brilliant and snappy surface, with its tongue-twisting bird-talk and smart trochees, there are hidden anxieties. The refrain in verses 2, 3 and 4 sounds more than a little hysterical. We are perhaps reminded here of Lear's hypochondria and of what it concealed—his real illness, epilepsy. Some of the limericks were very obviously about his fear of fits and of making himself a public spectacle, and one in particular seems also to use hypochondria as a cover:

> There was an Old Person of Mold,
> Who shrank from sensations of cold;
> So he purchased some muffs, some furs and some fluffs,
> And wrapped himself from the cold.

Are They having fits here? Is Mr. Sparrow an epileptic? Perhaps Lear is only talking about the weather after all.

The poet's anxiety about social conformity is not so covert. The Sparrow's last words suggest that they too are shrinking from sensations of social rather than climatic cold:

> Said they, "We trust that cold or pain
> We shall never feel again!
> While perched on tree, or house, or steeple,
> We now shall look like other people."

The Old Man of Mold defies society's standards and dresses in outrageous clothes. The Sparrows, with a show of happiness, put on safe and public clothes. But having made themselves fit for society, they return home and wear their new going-out clothes indoors. Are they making fun of polite society? Or are they anxious to conform, without really understanding how to? Certainly the cold seems just an excuse, as it is with the Old Man of Mold. When Mrs. Sparrow observes that "No one stays out all night long / Without a hat: I'm sure it's wrong," she is more worried about the bohemian Mr. Sparrow's reputation than his health. The displacement of head cold / social cold is intended; that of head and social cold / epilepsy is not.

Lear has fun dressing his birds up. That is the first joke. Then he makes more fun of the idea that, like people, they can catch cold. He also seems to take a light jab at the affectations of fashion. But underneath all this play, he expresses dismay at the strictness of convention and the way people are forced, for the sake of social conformity, to bow to it. The moral buried deep within the jingle seems to be that respectable family life, of the kind the Sparrows return from their shopping expedition to enjoy, is won at the expense of individual freedom. This deeper theme conducts us back to the surface joke, since it is against the nature of birds to wear clothes. Like the courtship voyage poems of *Nonsense Songs and Stories*, "Mr. and Mrs. Spikky Sparrow" examines the feeling of social and domestic confinement. We might have guessed as much from the strict regularity of the verse—always a sign in Lear of mental constriction.

And yet it is sparkling and snappy, and we may be allowed the hope that Mr. Sparrow continues to stay out at night, a bohemian who can enjoy home life without having to sacrifice all his freedom. We hope he neither catches cold nor stays out in the cold, beyond the pale. The issue is left in a proper nonsense state of suspense. On the surface the poem is simply a bright retreat, spirited but mechanical. Underneath, there are darker matters which, because of their honesty, allow us to hope for a true release from confinement. Again a fib tells the whole truth, or as much of it as the poet knows.

The other two family poems, in the fourth nonsense book, are blacker and better. "Mr. and Mrs. Discobbolos"[18] takes the Sparrows' regressiveness to desperate lengths, and the "Second Part" ends in the slaughter of the whole family. The form is typical of the late poems: ballad stanzas strung together so the verse resembles a Pindaric ode—attenuated, irregular, exclamatory, musical, dramatic. In the first poem, the couple, as yet without children, climb a wall and watch the sunset:

> Mr. and Mrs. Discobbolos
> Climbed to the top of a wall.
> And they sat to watch the sunset sky
> And to hear the Nupiter Piffkin cry
> And the Biscuit Buffalo call.
> They took up a roll and some Camomile tea,
> And both were as happy as happy could be—
> Till Mrs. Discobbolos said,—
> "Oh! W! X! Y! Z!
> It has just come into my head—
> "Suppose we should happen to fall!!!!!
> Darling Mr. Discobbolos!"

Like Mrs. Sparrow, she has doubts just as everything is going well at home on their perch:

> "Suppose we should fall down flumpetty
> Just like pieces of stone!
> On to the thorns,—or into the moat!
> What would become of your new green coat?
> And might you not break a bone?
> It never occurred to me before—
> That perhaps we shall never go down any more!"
> And Mrs. Discobbolos said—
> Oh! W! X! Y! Z!
> What put it into your head
> To climb up this wall?—my own
> Darling Mr. Discobbolos?"

Mr. Discobbolos replies in proper choric order in the third verse:

Mr. Discobbolos answered,—
  "At first it gave me pain,—
And I felt my ears turn perfectly pink
When your exclamation made me think
  We might never get down again!
But now I believe it is wiser far
To remain for ever just where we are."
    And Mr. Discobbolos said,
    Oh! W! X! Y! Z!
    It has just come into my head—
We shall never go down again—
  Dearest Mrs. Discobbolos!"

In the last verse they stand up together and sing a defiant song, like the Broom, the Shovel, the Poker and the Tongs:

So Mr. and Mrs. Discobbolos
  Stood up, and began to sing,
"Far away from hurry and strife
Here we will pass the rest of life,
  Ding a dong, ding dong, ding!
We want no knives nor forks nor chairs,
No tables nor carpets nor household cares,
    From worry of life we've fled—
    Oh! W! X! Y! Z!
    There is no more trouble ahead,
Sorrow or any such thing—
  For Mr. and Mrs. Discobbolos!"

They are trapped, but determined to be happy.

Just as in the versions of the courtship voyage poems of *Laughable Lyrics*, Lear moved from a study of the feelings of confinement to an investigation of what happens when his heroes have at last put home behind them, so here he begins with an escape in the first two lines, and then looks at the consequences of its success. He is writing, again, of his San Remo predicament, but in slightly different terms. He has made good his escape from domestic England, only to find himself stuck in a paradise which turns out to be just as domestically confining. What can he do but resolve to bear it bravely? This is what the brave song of the Discobboloses expresses, with its hysterical tenacity and reckless fervor.

The domestic has, once again, reduced the sublime: the spiritual wings of the poet, already clipped in "Mr. and Mrs. Spikky Sparrow," now refuse even to sprout. The Discobboloses themselves are half ideal and half matter-of-fact: only a "b" distinguishes their name from that of the famous discus-thrower whom Lear drew as part of his tiresome training in the Antique School at the Academy. He failed then to master the human figure, and he fails now—his creatures are nonsensical, half-perfect. Given their nature, the Discobboloses are bound to stumble in their attempt to escape a drab plain life for a brilliant sublime one. They ascend their wall and gaze on the sunset sky, in the hope of sharing the secret of the Young Lady historian of mysteries at the end of the limericks. But what do they see? Only half-perfect creatures like themselves: the Nupiter Piffkin, a new and possibly Brummagem Jupiter, a god but also a mere "piffkin"; and the Biscuit Buffalo, a creature of the prairie and the tea table, half wild and half comestible. If only they were Discobboloses they might see the wild buffalo and real gods, and then leave their wall for higher and freer perches. But they are stuck, like Lear, halfway between a despised home from which they have escaped and an unattainable sublime. They are left spiritually sitting on the fence, and they have only their courage to depend on.

The tension in this poem is fierce, especially in the nonsense swearing—"Oh! W! X! Y! Z!"—and in the precariousness of the Discobboloses' position and the instability of their mental state. Their fuss is comically deflating, but also a sign of profound distress. Unlike the Table and the Chair, who also peep at the sublime, they have no friendly animals to rescue them and lead them home. Nor can they make a bright and deceitful retreat like Mr. and Mrs. Spikky Sparrow. They have put home behind them forever. They cannot turn back and they cannot advance, nor can they stand still. Something has to give, and in the sequel the grief and fear and yearning explode with a huge nonsensical bang.

"Mr. and Mrs. Discobbolos, Part II"[19] is nearly identical in form, although it was not written till 1879, when the new hotel, which Lear called the Enemy, was being erected in front of his Villa Emily. The Discobboloses live on the top of their wall for twenty years:

> Mr. and Mrs. Discobbolos
>   Lived on the top of the wall,
> For twenty years, a month and a day,
> Till their hair had grown all pearly gray,
>   And their teeth began to fall.
> They never were ill, or at all dejected,

By all admired, and by some respected,
Till Mrs. Discobbolos said,
"O, W! X! Y! Z!
It has just come into my head,
We have no more room at all—
Darling Mr. Discobbolos!"

Just as before, everything is going well when the wife starts to have doubts.

"Look at our six fine boys!
And our six sweet girls so fair!
Upon this wall they have all been born,
And not one of the twelve has happened to fall
Through my maternal care!
Surely they should not pass their lives
Without any chance of husbands or wives!"
And Mrs. Discobbolos said,
"O, W! X! Y! Z!
Did it never come into your head
That our lives must be lived elsewhere,
Dearest Mr. Discobbolos?"

Family life is too limiting. Her children have never had the chance to come out in society:

"They have never been at a ball,
Nor have even seen a bazaar!
Nor have heard folks say in a tone all hearty,
'What loves of girls (at a garden party)
Those Misses Discobbolos are!'
Morning and night it drives me wild
To think of the fate of each darling child!"
But Mr. Discobbolos said,
"O, W! X! Y! Z!
What has come to your fiddledum head!
What a runcible goose you are!
Octopod Mrs. Discobbolos!"

It is curious to hear that the Discobboloses have eight feet—why have they not been able to climb down the wall? And it is alarming to find that this time Mr. Discobbolos, instead of agreeing with his wife, calls her a fool, and takes swift and decisive action:

Suddenly Mr. Discobbolos
  Slid from the top of the wall;
And beneath it he dug a dreadful trench,
And filled it with dynamite, gunpowder gench,
  And aloud he began to call—
"Let the wild bee sing,
And the blue bird hum!
For the end of your lives has certainly come!"
    And Mrs. Discobbolos said,
    "O, W! X! Y! Z!
    We shall presently all be dead,
On this ancient runcible wall,
  Terrible Mr. Discobbolos!"

Pensively, Mr. Discobbolos
  Sat with his back to the wall;
He lighted a match, and fired the train,
And the mortified mountain echoed again
  To the sound of an awful fall!
And all the Discobbolos family flew
In thousands of bits to the sky so blue,
    And no one was left to have said,
    "O, W! X! Y! Z!
    Has it come into anyone's head
That the end has happened to all
  Of the whole of the Clan Discobbolos?"

The pun on "mortified" is a nonsense pun, since it has been dislocated and made to refer to the mountain, not the wall.* "Pensively" is a nonsense understatement, expressive of the indifference in the face of calamity which we so often find in the limericks and in modern comic conventions. The catastrophe is the most devastating in all Lear's poems, and this is the only occasion in the mature work where death is openly admitted—and not just death, but murder, and three kinds of murder: suicide, wife murder and infanticide.

The catastrophe ends at least two tragedies. The first is the particular tragedy of Lear's own childhood. He suffered both the constraints of the bourgeois family and the atomization of home life when, because of his father's insolvency, the family was dispersed and the close bonds of child-

*The wall, composed of brick and mortar, has been mortared, mortifying it mortifyingly.

hood life were cruelly snapped. We have some idea of his feelings from a diary account of his last visit to Bowman's Lodge in 1863:

> Some of the steps were gone:—a woman showed me in to the hall. The parlour at once annihilated 50 years. Empty—but—there were the two bookcases, and the old "secretary" my father used to write at. I saw every possible evening for years. Would I could see the pictures as they were!!—then I went upstairs—the Drawing room is really a fine good room—but spoiled now by the back buildings. *My* room—ehi!—ehi!—Henry's, Mary's, mother's, and the spare room. Down stairs again—the Nursery, a large low room—just as it was—only with no view. Dear Ann's—& the painting room—the happiest of all my life perhaps—the "dark room"—and the "play ground." The little parlour was shut—& the study & greenhouse now extinct. Gave the woman 2 shillings—a cheap & wonderful lesson."[20]

His childhood had been undone twice—once by insolvency, and once, in the ordinary way, when his father had retired and he and Ann moved into rooms together in London.

But this is not the only tragedy, and it hardly explains Mr. Discobbolos's nihilistic behavior. We can understand what he dislikes about both home and polite society, and we sympathize. Mrs. Discobbolos is a cowardly figure, if she really wishes to return to the ordinary world. Perhaps she deserves to be blown up. But why kill himself and the children? Isn't he going too far?

Another, darker tragedy is suggested in the first Discobbolos poem. The home that Lear blows up is not merely home, it is also paradise. But it is a fake paradise, or rather, a nonsense purgatory. The social tragedy of domestic confinement is real, but it is also a nonsense cover for the spiritual tragedy which befalls those who, having the courage to escape from home and social conformity, still lack the vision to find their sublime. They watch the sun go down from their new home without understanding its secret. Their perch is not only a prison, it is also dangerously insecure. Instead of seeing the wild Buffalo and Jupiter, they see only their pathetic counterfeits. Enough! the poet exclaims, and blows them all sky-high.

In this splendidly riotous death joke there is a great deal of relief. The home that smashed the child's spirit has itself been smashed. The delusive hopes that misled the grown-up's spirit have at last been dashed. The catastrophe purges the reader and the poet, and makes the way clearer. Again, the main work of the nonsense has been to make sense. The familiar strategies—displacement and paradox (domestic/sublime)—coax out the hidden fears and scatter them; the nonsense makes the trouble intelligible. The "awful fall" is really a happy one, since at the end we share with the poet a clear-sighted joy that the household prison and the fool's paradise have been "mortified." The ending is not a disaster but a triumph, because the nonsense in the real life of which the art speaks and in the fiction which real life has informed is shown to be nonsense, and only nonsense. The nonsense celebrates its own moral, and clarity prevails.

True, there is no place here for the expression of wonder. But these three family poems have done some necessary spring-cleaning, uncluttering the house so a fresh life may be lived in it. And they have dispelled some wintry feelings about the sublime which had bewildered the poet for too long.

"Calico Pie,"[21] the first of two cloth poems, is a kind of negative of "The Quangle Wangle's Hat" and "The Scroobious Pip." It describes the desertion of the poet-hero by birds, fish, mice and insects; in fleeing his home, they ruin his paradise. It is a poem of pivotal significance not only because it stands halfway in *Nonsense Songs and Stories*, but because it presents in the most succinct form the poet's darker feelings—lovelessness, alienation, bewilderment. Like "My Uncle Arly," it is one of a few key poems which show Lear's fears and joys for what they are.

It is unique in form. It is composed of trimeter and dimeter lines stitched together in a seesaw form. The fulcrum of the stanza is the seventh line:

Calico Pie
The little Birds fly
    Down to the Calico tree,
Their wings were blue,
And they sang "Tilly-loo!"
Till away they flew.—
And they never came back to me!
    They never came back!
    They never came back!
They never came back to me!

"And they never came back to me!" extends by one line the second triplet and forms the first line of the refrain. With its seesaw and its brevity, the poem is like the limericks.

It is an obsessive piece. Each new verse is a simple variation on the essential situation of desertion, with only a new name at the start to ring the changes:

Calico Jam,
The little Fish swam,
  Over the syllabub sea,
He took off his hat,
To the Sole and the Sprat,
And the Willeby-wat,—
But he never came back to me!
  He never came back!
  He never came back!
He never came back to me!

The nonsense world is made up of familiar, obsessive substances—cloth and clothes, food, music, trees, the sea and, as we see in the drawing, staring eyes and a mysterious smile:

The tree is made of cloth, the cloth is in a pie and in the jam, the sea is made of food, and so on. Calico is especially mysterious stuff, and the word is used almost as a neologism, to which it is impossible to attach a specific meaning other than "desertion" or "desolation."

Calico Ban,
The little Mice ran,
  To be ready in time for tea,
Flippity Flup,
They drank it all up,
And danced in a cup,—
But they never came back to me!
  They never came back!
  They never came back!
They never came back to me!

Is Calico Ban a version of Caliban? And why is the poem called "Calico Pie"? There is the joy of a purely nonsensical rhyme, of course, but beyond that, what is Lear thinking of? The Quangle Wangle's Hat was also made of cloth, and Lear made a title of that. A pie, like a hat, is round. Was the

Quangle Wangle's Beaver Hat made of calico, perhaps? The last verse has a ring-dance, performed this time to the beat of a round instrument:

> Calico Drum,
> The Grasshoppers come,
>   The Butterfly, Beetle and Bee,
> Over the ground,
> Around and round,
> With a hop and a bound,—
> But they never came back!
>   They never came back!
>   They never came back!
> They never came back to me!

The conclusion provokes more of the same questions—why this obsession with circles? Why a drum made of cloth?

To look for specific answers is, of course, only to chase one's tail. The poem is as mysterious and baffling as the most tight-lipped of the limericks, and we should expect only general answers. They are nevertheless firm ones, because of the obsessiveness. Indeed, the poem is, for all the elusiveness of its detail, almost self-explanatory. The creatures stand for all of creation, natural and social. "Me"—and this is the only time Lear writes poetry in the first person—is the poet. A paradisal home is taken, and nothing is given in its place. What reason is there behind such loss? Nowhere else in the long poems is the sense of desolation so complete. The fish and mice can be sociable, but not with "me"; the insects can do their circle dance, but not for "me." There is no voyage, no courtship; neither love nor adventure, company nor hope. The alienation is total; the only movement is one of the world vanishing. Here, in the middle of the courtship voyage series, Lear pauses to suggest the motive fear behind the whole nonsense. At the heart of each poem there is the cry, "I alone am left!" The world is evacuated of wonder. In this sense, "Calico Pie" is a negative of the whole work.

In *Laughable Lyrics*, there is also a cloth poem, "The New Vestments."[22] It is another obsessional piece, composed in a reductive manner, but less intensely. It has a brusque amphibrachic line, like the limericks, and a cathartic ending. It begins just like a limerick, except one foot is added:

> There lived an old man in the Kingdom of Tess,
> Who invented a purely original dress;
> And when it was perfectly made and complete,
> He opened the door, and walked into the street.

The next six couplets describe his strange dress. The hat is made of food, the shirt of mice, the drawers and shoes are of rabbit skin, stockings also of "Skins,—but it is not known whose" (an untypically macabre touch). Waistcoat, trousers, buttons, coat, girdle and "cloack" are all made of food too. So attired:

> He had walked a short way, when he heard a great noise,
> Of all sorts of Beasticles, Birdlings, and Boys:—
> And from every long street and dark lane in the town
> Beasts, Birdles, and Boys in a tumult rushed down.

They attack him, and in ten riotous couplets, they strip him naked:

> They speedily flew at his sleeves in a trice,
> And utterly tore up his Shirt of dead Mice;—
> They swallowed the last of his Shirt with a squall,—
> Whereon he ran home with no clothes on at all.

He ends up like the Table and Chair in full retreat:

> And he said to himself as he bolted the door,
> "I will not wear a similar dress any more,
> "Any more, any more, any more, never more!"

The beasts have flocked to him, not to nest and make a paradise of home, but to strip him. No wonder so many of the heroes and heroines of the limericks concealed themselves in their clothes or strutted defiantly, making exhibitions of themselves.[23] Here the Old Man has ventured out again to face the enquiring and conventional horde. "The New Vestments" shows that there was need of courage and of concealment: They have proven a ferocious enemy, and have driven the hero back into the secure solitude of his eccentricity, his alienation. Instead of love and a voyage, there is vengeance and a chase. The Old Man has tempted Their appetites, of course, by wearing food, but the real reason They attack him is that he has "invented an original." His crime is the same as Mr. Spikky Sparrow's.

Lear was himself an original, half willing and half reluctant. He was also the inventor of originals, his "nonsenses," which often describe the punishment inflicted when an independently minded man dares to stand alone and test, with tiresome curiosity, the limits of ordinary understanding and tolerance. The Sparrows and the Old Man of Tess—the first hesitantly, the second outrageously—try the patience of social convention and are beaten back within bounds. The Discobboloses, who have the temerity to declare society unacceptable only to discover that the sublime is unattainable, prove troubling not just to the social censors but to the poet himself, who has risked his social place for his spiritual advancement. They must be destroyed because they reveal the essential condition of the "me" of "Calico Pie," where social and spiritual alienation are most plainly depicted, and where it is made clear that the original, in leaving home and society behind, must be prepared to face the possibility that his separation will be permanent and—worse—that his search for the wonders of the spirit may be in vain. He must be ready to give up everything and trust that the absurdity of letting go of the absurd world around him will somehow show him a better way.

In the family and cloth poems, Lear is a seeker who abandons his home only to mistake the way; and the fool is there at his elbow to explain how he went wrong and to tell him that there can be no turning back. But if there is no retreat, and no moving ahead, and no standing still—what then?

Paradise

In the paradise poems—"The Jumblies" in the second book, "The Quangle Wangle's Hat" in the last*—Lear at last carries out his views. However briefly, he makes some sense of the sublime, the strange, the free, the exalted. Here the poet is no longer confined at home, or lost abroad, or frozen in between. He finds a way of expressing his spiritual aspirations joyfully and honestly. The two poems are not totally happy; there is always a sad note. But they describe the gaining or fashioning of a paradise, a real and heartfelt figure for the poet's views and feelings. Love between a couple is replaced by love among people of a community, and the exile finds a home for himself abroad, in places which lie beyond ordinary comprehension. The fool's trust in the absurd is rewarded, the original's way of seeking is vindicated.

"The Jumblies"[24] is a forerunner of the general concerns of the final poems for two reasons. It is formally mature, the first real nonsense ode—two five-line stanzas bound by a running "b" rhyme, and a refrain of great beauty—at once lyrical, dramatic, narrative, modestly epical and comic. Secondly, it is probably Lear's earliest full-length investigation of the sublime. Like all the courtship voyage poems of the last books, it starts in one paradise and moves to another. But where they all end in disaster, with the hero still isolated in his nonsense paradise, the Jumblies, happy and

*See also Appendix, section 2, on "The Scroobious Pip," an unfinished paradise poem.

triumphant, return home to the first paradise, bringing the good news of the second.

With a pea-green flag and faces that express anxiety, anger, fright, daring, joy, calm, bright expectation and cheerful determination, the Jumblies set sail, the bold mariners of a nonsense epic:

They went to sea in a Sieve, they did,
  In a Sieve they went to sea:
In spite of all their friends could say
On a winter's morn, on a stormy day,
  In a Sieve they went to sea!
And when the Sieve turned round and round,
And everyone cried, "You'll all be drowned!"
They called aloud, "Our Sieve ain't big,
But we don't care a button! we don't care a fig!
  In a Sieve we'll go to sea!"
  Far and few, far and few,
    Are the lands where the Jumblies live;
  Their heads are green, and their hands are blue,
    And they went to sea in a Sieve.

Two possible epigraphs come to mind.[25] The first is the traditional nonsense jingle:

Three Wise Men of Gotham
Went to sea in a bowl;
If the bowl had been stronger,
My tale would be longer.

Lear's tale unfolds in comical contradiction of the accepted folklore. The second epigraph is a limerick we have already discussed:

> There was an Old Man in a boat,
> Who said, "I'm afloat! I'm afloat!"
> When they said, "No! you ain't!" he was ready to faint,
> That unhappy Old Man in a boat.

"The Jumblies" also contradicts the opinion of Them and vindicates the Old Man. If only he had had the courage of the Bò or the Jumblies!

In the second verse, their vessel is described, and They, that is, "their friends" or "every one," repeat their warning:

> They sailed away in a Sieve, they did,
> In a Sieve they sailed so fast,
> With only a beautiful pea-green veil
> Tied with a riband by way of a sail,
> To a small tobacco-pipe mast;
> And everyone said, who saw them go,
> "O won't they be soon upset, you know!
> For the sky is dark and the voyage is long,
> And happen what may, it's extremely wrong
> In a Sieve to sail so fast!"
> Far and few, far and few,
> Are the lands where the Jumblies live;
> Their heads are green, and their hands are blue,
> And they went to sea in a Sieve.

It is both dangerous and against conventional propriety to set sail in a sieve. However, neither They nor the Jumblies seem to understand why a sieve is a poor vessel: in the first verse the Jumblies say they do not care that it is small, and in the second, They are alarmed that it goes so fast. But the poet understands well enough that a fast, small sieve soon lets the water in, like any other sieve:

> The water it soon came in, it did,
> The water it soon came in;
> So to keep them dry, they wrapped their feet,
> In a pinky paper all folded neat,
> And they fastened it down with a pin.
> And they passed the night in a crockery-jar,
> And each of them said, "How wise we are!

Though the sky be dark, and the voyage be long,
Yet we never can think we were rash or wrong,
  While round in our Sieve we spin!"
  Far and few, far and few,
    Are the lands where the Jumblies live;
  Their heads are green, and their hands are blue,
    And they went to sea in a Sieve.

And all night long they sailed away;
  And when the sun went down,
They whistled and warbled a moony song,
To the echoing sound of a coppery gong,
  In the shade of the mountains brown.
"O Timballo! How happy we are,
When we live in a Sieve and a crockery-jar,
And all night long in the moonlight pale,
We sail away with a pea-green sail,
  In the shade of the mountains brown!"
  Far and few, far and few,
    Are the lands were the Jumblies live;
  Their heads are green, and their hands are blue,
    And they went to sea in a Sieve.

Evidently they are *periploi* and hug the coastline in the classical tradition. But here is a fresh contradiction—they are far out to sea and yet close to land, "in the shade of the mountains brown." No wonder they consider themselves in no danger—the sieve is not a sieve, they have not set out to sea! Of course, it is, and they have, and their courage, in the fifth verse, is at last rewarded:

They sailed to the Western Sea, they did,
  To a land all covered with trees,
And they bought an Owl, and a useful Cart,
And a pound of Rice, and a Cranberry Tart,
  And a hive of silvery Bees.
And they bought a Pig, and some green Jack-daws,
And a lovely Monkey with lillipop paws,
And forty bottles of Ring-Bo-Ree,
  And no end of Stilton Cheese.
  Far and few, far and few,
    Are the lands where the Jumblies live;
  Their heads are green, and their hands are blue,
    And they went to sea in a Sieve.

Perhaps they met the Old Man of the Isles, and the Bò, if he was successful, and King Crane and his Queen Dell Pelican. Perhaps they also met, and were able to console, the Dong and the Daddy Long-legs and the Fly. Certainly Gromboolia and the Chankly Bore seem transformed by the Jumblies' exemplary high-spiritedness into a real paradise:

> And in twenty years they all came back,
> In twenty years or more,
> And every one said, "How tall they've grown!
> For they've been to the Lakes, and the Torrible Zone,
> And the hills of the Chankly Bore;"
> And they drank their health, and gave them a feast
> Of dumplings made of beautiful yeast;
> And every one said, "If we only live,
> We too will go to sea in a Sieve,—
> To the hills of the Chankly Bore!"
> Far and few, far and few,
> Are the lands where the Jumblies live;
> Their heads are green, and their hands are blue,
> And they went to sea in a Sieve.

The wistful, valiant refrain concludes their adventure.

The refrain is sad not because the poet is unhappy, but because the happiness he and his Jumblies have won may be beyond most people. We can only hope with "every one" else that "if we only live," we may be able to follow their example. They have lived as if miracles were true, they have put their trust in the unintelligible and incredible. They have believed where they could not see; and the rest of us look, in comparison, like Doubting Thomases. Sieves do not float, as we have said, and it is not possible to cross the ocean to the Western Seas by hugging the coastline, unless you are willing to risk your common sense.

The nonsense works because the figures of love and quest have new and elevating meaning. Love no longer has its anxious sexual character, the couple has been replaced by a team or crew, a community which will cooperate in the adventure. The quest is now consciously absurd. The new formula works, because for Lear it is obviously the right one. He had to admit that ordinary love would not satisfy him, and that his search could succeed only when he bowed to the unintelligibility of the way, persevering without the tourist's guides.

The nonsense also works by blind faith. If we look back to the wonder limericks we see that their revelations were really make-believe. Nothing was revealed there; they were only pictures of revelation. The Old Man and the Young Lady knew what lay beyond, but the poet and the reader were not let in on the secret. But if we did not understand, we at least felt an exalting and joyful sense of mystery. The poet gave radiant and intense representations of the state of revelation, make-believes which seemed to prove the rewards of believing. But he could see no more than we could—only his nonsense heroes had been blessed with the vision to *really* see. This, perhaps, is the final joke, and point, of the nonsense. It is a make-believe which makes belief, where faith is brave enough to be blind, and the mind understands its own limits.

Religion did not matter to Lear, but faith did. Love, belief, make-believe: they all somehow depended on each other.

> Nluv, fluv bluv, ffluv biours,
> Faith nunfaith kneer beekwl powers
> Unfaith naught zwant a faith in all.

So he had written in a note sent round one morning to Baring, after they had been up late reading and singing and weeping over Tennyson. The nonsense spelling mocks their indulgence but it also allows Lear to speak from the heart.

> In Love, if Love be Love, if Love be ours,
> Faith and unfaith can ne'er be equal powers:
> Unfaith in aught is want of faith in all.

It is Lancelot's song in the *Idylls of the King*, but it might as well be the song of the Old Man in a tree to the Young Lady of Lucca, or more truly the Jumbly lover's warble to his silly maid.

"The Quangle Wangle's Hat"[26] shows Lear at his happiest. The Beaver Hat of the title looks very much like the Jumblies' Sieve.

Both are a sort of nonsense aureole, crowning the poet's nonsense faith with joy. Perhaps the best epigraph for the poem is the limerick about the Old Man of Dee-side who invited his neighbors in under his hat:

There was an old man of Dee-side
Whose hat was exceedingly wide,
But he said "Do not fail, if it happen to hail
To come under my hat at Dee-side!"

The vessel or hat is really a huge nest and shelter, the paradise home Lear has been searching for all his life. We might recall, too, the limerick about the Young Lady whose bonnet became untied.

There was a Young Lady whose bonnet
Came untied when the birds sat upon it;
But she said, "I don't care! all the birds in the air
Are welcome to sit on my bonnet!"

Now all the beasts of the nonsense field and all the birds of the nonsense air flock to Lear's hero, the Quangle Wangle, to live with him.

The poem's structure is roughly that of "The Yonghy-Bonghy-Bò," but it is simpler, more clipped. Two quatrains, the first trimetrical, the second tetrametrical, are patched together with a trimeter name-tag as a one-line refrain. It is the briefest and perhaps the most perfected of Lear's ode forms:

> On the top of the Crumpetty Tree
> The Quangle Wangle sat,
> But his face you could not see,
> On account of his Beaver Hat.
> For his Hat was a hundred and two feet wide,
> With ribbons and bibbons on every side
> And bells, and buttons, and loops, and lace,
> So that nobody ever could see the face
> Of the Quangle Wangle Quee.

We may well think of all the limericks about treetops and concealment, especially when we see from the drawing that the Quangle Wangle's head is hidden by the hat. In the second stanza the poet associates loneliness with nursery teatime food, as he has so often done in the limericks and in "Calico Pie." The tree itself has something to do with crumpets:

> The Quangle Wangle said
> To himself on the Crumpetty Tree,—
> "Jam; and jelly; and bread;
> Are the best food for me!
> But the longer I live on this Crumpetty Tree
> The plainer than ever it seems to me
> That very few people come this way
> And that life on the whole is far from gay!"
> Said the Quangle Wangle Quee.

Salvation is at hand, however:

> But there came to the Crumpetty Tree,
> Mr. and Mrs. Canary;
> And they said,—"Did you ever see
> Any spot so charmingly airy?
> May we build a nest on your lovely Hat?
> Mr. Quangle Wangle, grant us that!

O please let us come and build a nest
Of whatever material suits you best,
    Mr. Quangle Wangle Quee!"

Cloth, food, a married couple, nesting, a search for home and happiness, a cure for loneliness—all the themes and materials of Lear's poems are gathering. Without waiting for the Quangle Wangle's assent, the creatures flock toward him:

And besides, to the Crumpetty Tree
    Came the Stork, the Duck, and the Owl;
The Snail, and the Bumble-Bee,
    The Frog, and the Fimble Fowl
(The Fimble Fowl with a Corkscrew leg);
And all of them said,—"We humbly beg
We may build our homes on your lovely Hat,—
Mr. Quangle Wangle, grant us that!
    Mr. Quangle Wangle Quee!"

And the Golden Grouse came there,
    And the Pobble who has no toes,—
And the small Olympian bear,—
    And the Dong with a luminous nose,—
And the Blue Baboon, who played the flute,—
And the Orient Calf from the Land of Tute,—
And the Attery Squash, and the Bisky Bat,—
All came and built on the lovely Hat
    Of the Quangle Wangle Quee.

Many of these nonsense creatures are by now familiar to us, and Lear probably thought of the poem as a summary. Again, reading these verses we may think of the limericks where the Old Man either led nature like a Pied Piper:

There was an old person of Shields,
Who frequented the valley and fields;
All the mice and the cats, And the snakes and the rats,
Followed after that person of Shields.

—or found himself in entranced harmony with it:

There was an old man in a tree,
Whose whiskers were lovely to see;
But the birds of the air, pluck'd them perfectly bare,
To make themselves nests in that tree.

The poem ends with the usual celebration, but feasting and singing for once are absent. There is a simple magical dance:

And the Quangle Wangle said
  To himself on the Crumpetty Tree,—
"When all these creatures move
What a wonderful noise there'll be!"
And at night by the light of the Mulberry Moon,
They danced to the Flute of the Blue Baboon,
On the broad green leaves of the Crumpetty Tree,
And all were as happy as happy could be,
  With the Quangle Wangle Quee.

It is a masterful ending, by virtue of its reticence. The Baboon plays his flute, and for the rest, it is only a "wonderful noise," a blissful nonsense shuffle.

In the drawing, most of the creatures are arranged on the brim of the hat from left to right in the order in which they arrived, except for the Blue Baboon who has settled behind the crown to play his flute, the Bisky Bat (perhaps a relation of the Biscuit Buffalo) who is about to land on his right side, and, on his left, that entranced Cockney, the Attery Squash, whose presence ensures that in the blissful dance there will be much squashed-hattery. The creatures look as though they are about to start an ecstatic treetop paradisal ring-dance.

Where the movement of "Calico Pie" was centrifugal, with all the creatures fleeing the circular home at the center, here the movement is centripetal. Lear's nonsense creatures seek the circular home at the center. With their help, he overcomes his fears of separation. Their company satisfies what he has sought in love, and their gathering inward completes his quest. As in "The Jumblies," the figures have new and elevating meaning, and finally the "views and feelings" of the sublime that Lear knows to exist within him are fully carried out. Again, there is no revelation, only the representation of a make-believe one; and again, the poet believes where he cannot see, and depends on nonsense strategies of displacement (food/loneliness) and paradox ("small Olympian"). But if the revelation is only make-believe, the faith is strong and the sense of wonder resonant, "a wonderful noise." If we lift the Quangle Wangle's Beaver head-dress, we see it is really Lear's own wideawake hate, and there beneath it is his smiling face and enormous nose and those "very bright eyes that seemed to be watching a pleasant comedy all the time."[27]

Uncle Arly

My reading of Lear has been biographical. Without the life, we cannot easily understand how his nonsense works or what it is trying to say. He composed three openly autobiographical poems, which help correct and reinforce my interpretation.

He wrote the plainest of them, "How Pleasant to Know Mr. Lear" in tandem with a young admirer, and perhaps for this reason it describes only the surface of his life in playful and untroubling terms. Here and there, however, it does touch some deeper aspects of his character. It mocks, for instance, his self-pity ("He weeps on the side of the ocean, / He weeps on the top of the hill"), and hints at the failure of his art ("Long ago he was one of the singers / But now he is one of the dumbs"). But the poem is much too close to its subject to risk self-revelation.

The second autobiographical poem is the title-page limerick in *A Book of Nonsense*. While it too tells us nothing deep about Lear's character, it reminds us of a very important aspect of his art, one we are apt to lose sight of in the seriousness of our survey. Lear gives himself a whimsical Irish nom de plume:

> There was an Old Derry down Derry,
> Who loved to see little folks merry:
> So he made them a book, and with laughter they shook,
> At the fun of that Derry down Derry.

He tells us what inspired the nonsense in the first place. He wanted to make children, his real friends, laugh; and indeed, "with laughter they shook." In other words, the motive and the effect of his poems have greatly to do with the comical surface. While it is true that the laughter has lasted over the years because it is provoked by the deeper tensions of nonsense, we should not fool ourselves that the surface is unimportant.

Take, for instance, the Pobble's Aunt Jobiska. We should be dull readers if, having observed the hidden and savage aspect of her character, we ceased to be moved by the benign and charming role she plays on the surface. It is not that she is a hypocrite, but rather that she really is two people. We have to believe in the good Aunt as wholly as we believe in the bad. How, indeed, could we think ill of someone so magical? How could we slight a lady capable of concocting lavendar water tinged with pink? The nonsense works only when we read every surface detail with the same respect. Unless we take it all at its happy face value, we miss the point.

The third autobiographical poem, "Incidents in the Life of My Uncle Arly,"[28] is much more revealing, once we spot Lear hiding "unclearly" in "UncLE ARly," and realize that it is a very exact piecing together of his whole life. He wrote it while recovering from a severe bout of pleurisy and bronchitis in the winter of 1884–1885. He had come close to dying and had taken the chance to look back, this time with a fairly detached mind, without his usual nostalgia. The Uncle is himself, of course, the "Adopty Duncle" of his many "little folks," among them Emma Baring, to whom he formally presented the piece. Rough drafts survive from the 1870s and are to be found on the fly leaves of the copy of *Spectator* essays which he read and reread during his last years. He was very pleased with the poem, and sent a copy to Ruskin, who had recently declared publicly that *A Book of Nonsense* was his favorite reading. He also sent copies to Wilkie Collins, whom he greatly resembled, and to Tennyson, from whose "Lady of Shalott" he had taken the form of the poem and a few images as well.

It opens with an invocation:

> O My agèd Uncle Arly!
> Sitting on a heap of Barley
>   Thro' the silent hours of night,—
> Close beside a leafy thicket:—
> On his nose there was a Cricket,—
> In his hat a Railway-Ticket;—
>   (But his shoes were far too tight.)

Here the nonsense poet is stripped to his nonsense essentials. He finds himself in a desolate pastoral landscape, benighted. He is ill at ease both with nature and with society; he seems to be torn between hiding in a thicket and running away in a train. He has no real home and no loved ones, and his emotions—so the enclosed refrain tells us—are greatly cramped. The style is as dense and reductive as in the cloth poems, and as resonant and elegiac as in "The Yonghy-Bonghy-Bò."

In the second verse the poet begins to recount his uncle's history in a flashback reminiscent of "The Dong":

> Long ago, in youth, he squander'd
> All his goods away, and wander'd
>   To the Tiniskoop-hills afar.
> There on golden sunsets blazing,
> Every morning found him gazing,—
> Singing,—"Orb! you're quite amazing!
>   How I wonder what you are!"

"Tin" was Victorian slang for money. Lear refers here to his setting out in the world and his search for the sublime, the practical and the spiritual struggle of his life. Perhaps he is also thinking of his father's imprudence and of the generation of Victorian misfits who went off to seek their fortune in the gold diggings in California and Australia. Certainly he was thinking of his own travels in golden and exotic countries where, as a painter of fabulous landscapes, he hoped to make his living. It is pleasant to see him working in a piece of Jane Taylor's nursery song "Twinkle, twinkle, little star / How I wonder what you are!"—just as Carroll did in *Alice*.

The third verse tells how he fared:

Like the ancient Medes and Persians,
Always by his own exertions
He subsisted on those hills:—
Whiles,—by teaching children spelling,—
Or at times by merely yelling,—
Or at intervals by selling
Propter's Nicodemus Pills.

It is clear that the Tiniskoop hills are not really in California or Australia, but where the Medes and Persians traveled and explored—in the Mediterranean. Lear's life was indeed one of "subsistence," and in his letters he constantly complained of "tinlessness." The grammatical disconnection of "whiles" suggests the strain the poet undergoes in putting these broken memories together. The spelling lessons refer perhaps to his nonsense alphabets, the yelling to the nonsense poems ("O, W! X! Y! Z!") and the Pills to the advertisements—"uncommon little shop sketches"—by which he had first made a living before he became an ornithological draftsman.

Then, there is disaster:

Later, in his morning rambles,
He perceived the moving brambles—
Something square and white disclose;—
'Twas a First-class Railway-Ticket;
But, on stooping down to pick it
Off the ground,—a pea-green Cricket
Settled on my uncle's Nose.

Never—never more,—oh! never
Did that Cricket leave him ever,—
 Dawn or evening, day or night,—
Clinging as a constant treasure,—
Chirping with a cheerious measure,—
Wholly to my uncle's pleasure,—
 (But his shoes were far too tight).

What are we to make of this Cricket? The Cricket is associated with the First-class Railway-Ticket, and hence with Lear's aristocratic friends and his traveling. It is also fixed to his nose. Perhaps the Cricket and his ticket are figures for Lear's oddity in high society, or for the pain and the pleasure of his wandering, or for his homosexuality. Perhaps the Cricket represents, more simply, the plain fact of his ugliness. Or, perhaps it is his epilepsy, "the demon," and also his depressions, the morbids. When we remember the limericks in which the Old Man of Quebec and the Old Person in black[29] are plagued by hideous insects, we are likelier to favor the more anxious of these possibilities:

There was an old Man of Quebec,
A beetle ran over his neck;
But he cried, "With a needle, I'll slay you, O beadle!"
That angry Old Man of Quebec.

There was an old person in black,
A Grasshopper jumped on his back;
When it chirped in his ear, he was smitten with fear,
That helpless old person in black.

On the other hand, the fourth verse says that the Cricket is "a constant treasure" and that it chirps "with a cheerious measure, / Wholly to my uncle's pleasure." Perhaps it is Lear's muse. This seems to be the best interpretation, if only because it easily accommodates all the others. The Cricket is the nonsense muse inspiring the poet to write about his alienation in high society, his wandering, his ugliness and homosexuality, his epilepsy and depression. Ridiculous yet natural, ungainly but magical, the Cricket sings cheerfully of the poet's joy, and honestly of his emotional constriction. And the pain returns with the tight refrain at the end of the fifth verse.

The penultimate verse ends the flashback:

So for three-and-forty winters,
Till his shoes were worn to splinters,
    All those hills he wander'd o'er,—
Sometimes silent;—sometimes yelling;—
Till he came to Borley-Melling,
Near his old ancestral dwelling;—
    (But his shoes were far too tight).

In 1827, Lear left Bowman's Lodge; in 1871, he settled at San Remo. For forty-three years he had wandered over the hills, sketching and painting. Sometimes, in his solitude, he was silent, and sometimes he shouted out in rage at his fate. At last he returned—and here Lear seems to prefer fiction to life, for he has Uncle Arly settle not in a nonsense San Remo but in Borley-Melling, a nonsense village near his ancestral home. Lear, of course, had no ancestral home, and those he visited he mostly disliked: they were, indeed, "really more barely and merely boring" than even the name Borley-Melling may suggest. His shoes worn out, with aching feet, Uncle Arly limps home to some nightmare abbey of boredom.

Here he dies on his heap of Barley:

> On a little heap of Barley
> Died my agéd Uncle Arly,
>   And they buried him one night,—
> Close beside the leafy thicket;—
> There,—his hat and Railway-Ticket;—
> There,—his ever-faithful Cricket;—
>   (But his shoes were far too tight.)

He is buried with his hat (was it the same one he had shown to the gentleman in the train in 1866?), his railway ticket, the token of his wandering and the symbol of his freedom, and his Cricket, his nonsense muse.

Appendix

"The Pobble Who Has No Toes"

The longer version of "The Pobble Who Has No Toes" starts with the first three stanzas of the shorter version. Then come the following stanzas:

> The Pobble went gaily on,
> To a rock by the edge of the water,
> And there, a-eating of crumbs and cream,
> Sat King Jampoodle's daughter.
> Her cap was a root of Beetroot red
> With a hole cut out to insert her head;
> Her gloves were yellow; her shoes were pink;
> Her frock was green; and her name was Bink.
>
> Said the Pobble—"O Princess Bink,
> A-eating of crumbs and cream!
> Your beautiful face has filled my heart
> With the most profound esteem!
> And my Aunt Jobiska says, Man's life
> Ain't worth a penny without a wife,
> Whereby it will give me the greatest pleasure
> If you'll marry me now, or when you've leisure!"
>
> Said the Princess Bink—"O! Yes!
> I will certainly cross the Channel
> And marry you then if you'll give me now
> That lovely scarlet flannel!
> And besides that flannel about your nose
> I trust you will give me all your toes,
> To place in my Pa's Museum collection,
> As proofs of your deep genteel affection!"

The Pobble unwrapped his nose,
And gave her the flannel so red,
Which, throwing her beetroot cap away,
She wreathed around her head.
And one by one he unscrew'd his toes,
Which were made of the beautiful wood that grows
In his Aunt Jobiska's roorial park,
When the days are short and the nights are dark.

Said the Princess—"O Pobble! my Pobble!
I'm yours for ever and ever!
I will never leave you my Pobble! my Pobble!
Never, and never, and never!"
Said the Pobble—"My Binky! O bless your heart!—
But say—would you like at once to start
Without taking leave of your dumpetty Father
Jampoodle the King?"—Said the Princess—"Rather!"

They crossed the Channel at once
And when the boats and ships came near them,
They winkelty-binkelty-tinkled their bell
So that all the world could hear them.
And all the Sailors and Admirals cried
When they saw them swim to the farther side—
"There are no more fish for his Aunt Jobiska's
Runcible cat with crimson whiskers!"

They danced about all day,
All over the hills and dales;
They danced in every village and town
In the North and the South of Wales.
And their Aunt Jobiska made them a dish
Of Mice and Buttercups fried with fish,
For she said—"The world in general knows
Pobbles are happier without their toes."

"The Scroobious Pip"

"The Scroobious Pip," an unfinished poem published first in *Teapots and Quails*,* is about a mysterious creature to whom many other beasts flock:

**Teapots and Quails* (London: John Murray, 1953), ed. and intro. by Angus Davidson and Philip Hofer, pp. 60–62.

The Scroobious Pip went out one day
When the grass was green, and the sky was grey.
Then all the beasts in the world came round
When the Scroobious Pip sat down on the ground.
  The cat and the dog and the kangaroo
  The sheep and the cow and the guineapig too—
  The wolf he howled, the horse he neighed
  The little pig squeaked and the donkey brayed,
  And when the lion began to roar
  There never was heard such a noise before.
  And every beast he stood on the tip
  Of his toes to look at the Scroobious Pip.
At last they said to the Fox—"By far,
You're the wisest beast! You know you are!
Go close to the Scroobious Pip and say,
Tell us all about yourself we pray—
For as yet we can't make out in the least
If you're Fish or Insect, Bird or Beast."
The Scroobious Pip looked vaguely round
And sang these words with a rumbling sound—
  "Chippetty Flip; Flippetty Chip:—
My only name is the Scroobious Pip."

The couplets have clearly not been reworked, perhaps because the poet thought them unpromising. They lack energy, and the relative clauses in the first quatrain are clumsy, though "When the grass was green" is good nonsense.

The poem is fraught with anxiety about identity and deformity. Lear placed a drawing of the Scroobious Pip above the first verse, and when we see it we understand why the Quangle Wangle Quee prefers to stay hidden under his hat. The Pip is a monstrous creature:

It is part beast, bird, fish and insect, with many arms and legs, wings and fins, antennae and ears, and an aquatic beak. The drawing, like the verse, is unfinished: a disembodied parrot's head with rabbit's ears floats under the Pip's breast, and below, there is a beaked rabbit with a fishtail and insect wings, and under the Pip's boot another faint and half-formed creature that looks like an owl with a rabbit's head and a strange vestigial tail. Perhaps the most ghastly features of this nonsense hybrid are its long and definite smile and the large blank eye, with its clearly marked, drooping eyebrow. It is one of the few Lear cartoons that can properly be called grotesque.

Each of the first four stanzas has four parts. In the first quatrain the Pip appears on the grass, on a treetop, in the sea, and under a tree on the seashore. He is either in or near the "Jellybolee," the shores of which the Duck had wished to reach in "The Duck and the Kangaroo." To each place beasts and birds, fish and insects come, and from each group one is singled out as the wisest, who must ask the Pip who or what he is. A fox, an owl, a whale and an ant in turn ask him, but to no avail. In the last part of each verse, a couplet with a rhyming refrain name-line, the Pip gives them a nonsense answer:

> The Scroobious Pip looked vaguely (gaily/softly/quickly) round,
> And sang these words with a rambling (Chirpy/liquid/whistly) sound,
>   "Chippetty Flip; Flippetty Chip;-
>   (Flippetty chip—Chippetty flip-/
>   Pliffity flip, Pliffity flip-/
>   Wizzeby wip—wizzeby wip-)
> My only name is the Scroobious Pip."

The fifth and last verse ends, like "The Quangle Wangle's Hat," with a ring-dance performed by all the creatures:

> Then all the beasts that walk on the ground
> Danced in a circle round and round—
> And all the birds that fly in the air
> Flew round and round in a circle there,
> And all the fish in the Jellybolee
> Swum in a circle about the sea,
> And all the insects that creep or go
> Buzzed in a circle to and fro.
> And they roared and sang and whistled and cried
> Till the noise was heard from side to side—
>   Chippetty tip! Chippetty tip!
> Its only name is the Scroobious Pip.

Like the drawing, the poem is exuberant but grotesque. It is not fair, perhaps, to say it is contrived; doubtless, if Lear had worked on it, the corners would have been rounded off and the drawing, too, might have taken a more benign form, resembling possibly the Scroobious Bird, which Lear included in his *Coloured Bird Book for Children.** But as it stands, the poem is too bright and bustling, too foursquare a summary, too busy a list, and its final circling and humming are too manic. "The Scroobious Pip" is like a mechanical toy. It is full of whirring, buzzing energy, but its expression is fixed and blank. A comparison with "The Quangle Wangle's Hat," which in situation and form it so closely resembles, shows that Lear has tried to steal a march on the sublime—only to have it once again vanish before him.

Unfinished Nonsense Sonnet

Lear left behind him many fragments, among them the following untitled sonnet, which was published sixty-five years after his death in *Teapots and Quails:*†

Cold are the crabs that crawl on yonder hills,
Colder the cucumbers that grow beneath,
And colder still the brazen chops that wreathe
  The tedious gloom of philosophic pills!
For when the tardy gloom of nectar fills
The ample bowls of demons and of men,
There lurks the feeble mouse, the homely hen,
  And there the porcupine with all her quills.
Yet much remains—to weave a solemn strain
That lingering sadly—slowly dies away,
Daily departing with departing day.
A pea green gamut on a distant plain
When wily walrusses in congress meet—
  Such such is life—

It is fitting that Lear should break off in mid-sentence, his thought unfinished, the form unrevised, the whole broken and baffling; and even

*Printed in *Queery Leary Nonsense*, ed., Lady Strachey (London: Mill & Boon), 1911.

†Angus Davidson and Philip Hofer, eds., *Teapots and Quails* (London: John Murray, 1953), p. 63.

more fitting when we see, on closer reading, how deliberately he has created these effects. It is really a very complete work, a nonsense ballad-sonnet made out of three ballad quatrains and an octave and sestet, with only three feet missing at the very end. It is dense with literary allusions and echoes,* which gather most thickly in the eleventh line, where the elegiac note, sustained throughout, is sounded most loudly, movingly and absurdly. It is, in fact, Lear's most literary composition, keenly calculated, exactly slight.

In the first quatrain Lear complains of the indifference of the world. Neither nature nor society nor philosophy affords him any comfort or consolation. He is out in the cold. The second quatrain explains why. Even when life's illusory reality is at its sweetest, man's sense of the sublime is undone by his essential timidity and domesticity—"the feeble mouse, the homely hen." Not even "demons,"† the Romantically adventurous, escape the conformism, confinement and pettiness of modern life. Man is out in the cold because he is afraid to give up what he knows for something he cannot be sure of. He is not a Jumbly or a Bò, to take risks. He does not dare put his faith in the absurd, renounce the world and reach beyond what he knows toward the unintelligible.

The sestet complicates and extends these statements. On the surface, it provides consolation. Man is dying and the world with him, but slowly and solemnly, with as much delay as a refrain allows. He can die with dignity. Beneath this, the poet extends the sense of deprivation. The repetition of the assurance that he is dying slowly is bathetic. Are we being comforted, or teased? The feeling of consolation survives this undercutting, and we are left—"Daily departing with the departing day"—in a state of suspense between a faint and honest hope and an exhausted but honest grief.

*Possible echoes and allusions. Line 1, Pope: "Cold is that breast which warmed the world before." Lines 1–3, Tennyson: cf. adjectival constructions in *In Memoriam*, progressing like "Cold . . . / Colder . . . / And colder. . . ." Line 4, Wordsworth: "And years that bring the philosophic mind." Line 5, Keats: "But when the melancholy fit shall fall." Lines 6–7, Burns: "The best laid schemes of Mice and Men / Gang aft agley." Line 8, Shakespeare, *Hamlet* I, v. 20, direct echo. Lines 9–11, Tennyson: cf. "Ulysses"—"Tho' much is taken, much abides;" "Tithonus," "Tears, Idle Tears" especially of line 11. Line 11, Gray: "The curfew tolls the knell of parting day." Line 11, Wordsworth: "At length the Man perceives it die away / And fade into the light of common day." Lines 12–13, Arnold: "Dover Beach," especially the last lines. Doubtless the reader will discover many other echoes for himself. I suspect, but have been unable to place, echoes of Milton and more of Tennyson.

†Since Lear called his epilepsy "the demon," "demons" may also mean "men who suffer epilepsy like me."

The last mysterious image unfolds just as the nonsense begins literally to repeat itself:

> Daily departing with departing day.
> A pea green gamut on a distant plain
> Where wily walrusses in congress meet—
>   Such such is life—

There is, from the rhythm, an overall sadness in these lines. But it is not deeply felt. "Pea green," for one thing, has always signified happiness in Lear's imagery.* A gamut suggests teeming and sociable life. The plain is distant, true; but walruses meet on it in congress. Evidently the gamut comes to order. On one level the image merely prolongs the suspension of joy-in-sadness. But on another it distracts from the irresolution of this position by placing great weight (like the weight on the epithet in the last line of the limericks) on the final adjective "wily," a word which implies neither sadness nor joy. Significantly and happily, the last impression is of a happy and diverse group of creatures who live in two elements and who, though they are on their guard, curious about danger and doubtful of what they are told, nevertheless come together.

Lear throws up his hands with a gesture that reminds us of many of the limericks,† and utters, with exhaustion but also wry humor, the cliché "Such such is life." In the first eleven lines he has argued that life is on the whole lonely, cold, dead. In the last three he does a volte-face and shows us a vivid, companionable, puzzlingly active world. The sonnet swells with a fresh life at the end. This feeling is emphasized by the syntax. In line 11 Lear ends a sentence, when we expect it to continue to the end of the quatrain. In line 12 he starts a fresh sentence for his last image. The syntax conspires with verse and image to buoy us up at the final moment. "Such such is life" is not, consequently, a throwaway line but a declaration of bewilderment and—possibly—of joy. Lear has tried to recreate, unconsciously, the expansive movement of the limericks of wonder. Even at his most inconclusive and fragmentary, he tries to make sublime sense of the nonsense of life.

*See "The Owl and the Pussy-cat," "The Pelican Chorus," "The Jumblies," and "There was an old person of Bar." It is a nonsense version of the Homeric "sea-green."

†See Dover, pp. 198.1, 187.1, 186.2, 181.2, 174.1, 172.2, etc.

Notes

Abbreviations used in notes

Davidson	Angus Davidson, *Edward Lear*
Diary	Edward Lear's Diary, Houghton Library
Dover	Holbrook Jackson, ed., *The Complete Nonsense of Edward Lear*. Numbers indicate the location of the limericks: the first number denotes the page; the second, the position on the page, 1 for top, 2 for bottom.
EL	Edward Lear
LEL	Lady Strachey, ed., *Letters of Edward Lear*
LLEL	Lady Strachey, ed., *Later Letters of Edward Lear*
Noakes	Vivien Noakes, *Edward Lear*
Opie	Iona and Peter Opie, eds., *The Oxford Dictionary of Nursery Rhymes*

Chapter One

1. Lady Strachey, ed., *Later Letters of Edward Lear* (London: T. Fisher Unwin, 1911), pp. 78–79.
2. Diary, 9.10.1862. His diary is in Houghton Library, Harvard University. The entry for 31.7.1882 tells us more about "the demon": "I suppose the ever-presence of the Demon since I was 7 years old would have prevented happiness under any sort of circumstances. It is a most merciful blessing that I have kept up as I have; and have not gone utterly bad mad sad."

3. Diary, 19.6.71. Vivien Noakes, *Edward Lear: the Life of a Wanderer* (London: Collins, 1968), pp. 250–251.
4. Edward Lear to Fanny Combe, about July 15, 1832. Houghton Library. Noakes, p. 24.
5. EL–C. Empson, 1.10.31. Pierpont Morgan Library, New York. Noakes, p. 24.
6. Lady Strachey, ed., *Later Letters of Edward Lear* (London: T. Fisher Unwin, 1911), p. xxii. Also *Nonsense Songs and Stories*, intro., Sir Edward Strachey, p. 6 (London: Warne, 1894). Noakes, p. 29.
7. Angus Davidson, *Edward Lear: Landscape Painter and Nonsense Poet* (London: John Murray, 1938), EL–Miss Combe.
8. Edward Lear, *More Nonsense, Pictures, Rhymes, Botany, etc.* (London: Robert John Bush, 1872), Preface, p. 17.
9. Privately printed.
10. EL–Ann, 3.11.37. Noakes, p. 51.
11. For a sensitive account of Lear's paintings and drawing, and their influences, see Philip Hofer, *Edward Lear as Landscape Draughtsman* (Oxford University Press, 1968).
12. Lord Carlingford, Diary, 1.5.46. Quoted LLEL, p. xxiii. Noakes, p. 66.
13. Howard M. Nixon, "The Second Lithographic Edition of Lear's *Book of Nonsense*," *British Museum Quarterly*, 28 (1964), pp. 7–8.
14. Davidson, p. 47.
15. EL–Fortescue, 25.8.48. Lady Strachey, ed., *Letters of Edward Lear* (London: T. Fisher Unwin, 1907), pp. 12–13.
16. EL–Fortescue, 12.2.48. LEL, pp. 8–9.
17. EL–Ann, 3.6.48. Noakes, p. 87.
18. EL–Ann, 14.5.48. Noakes, p. 86.
19. EL–Fortescue, 25.8.48. LEL, p. 13. Noakes, p. 30.
20. EL–Ann, 21.4.49. Noakes, p. 99.
21. *Poems of Alfred Tennyson*, illus., Edward Lear (Boussod, Caladon & Co., 1889).
22. Marianne North, *Recollections of a Happy Life*, ed., Mrs. J. A. Symonds (London: Macmillan, 1892), I, p. 29. Noakes, p. 115.
23. EL–Tennyson, 9.6.55. Noakes, p. 127.
24. Emily Tennyson–EL, 17.8.55. Noakes, p. 128.
25. Emily Tennyson–EL, 30.8.55. Noakes. p. 129.
26. EL–Emily Tennyson, 28.10.55. Noakes, p. 130.
27. EL–Fortescue, 25.8.48. LEL, p. 13. Noakes, p. 90.
28. EL–Ann, 8.10.56. Noakes, p. 145.
29. Diary, 27.3.58.
30. Diary, 28.3.58.
31. Diary, 30.3.58.
32. H. Van Thal, ed., *Edward Lear's Journals: A Selection* (London: Arthur Barker, 1952), p. 244. Noakes, p. 160.
33. Diary, 12.5.58.
34. Diary, 5.4.59.
35. Diary, 16.6.60.
36. Diary, 18.6.60.
37. Diary, 17,6.60. Noakes, p. 179.
38. Diary, 19.6.60.
39. EL–Fortescue, 7.3.61. LEL, p. 183. Noakes, p. 183.

40. Diary, 10.3.61. Noakes, p. 183.
41. Diary, 11.3.61. Noakes, p. 184.
42. Diary, 10.1.63. Noakes, p. 193.
43. Diary, 15.5.64. Noakes, p. 202.
44. Diary, 15.5.64. Noakes, p. 202.
45. Diary, 2.12.64.
46. Diary, 11.1.66. Noakes, p. 207.
47. Diary, 18.4.66. Noakes, p. 209.
48. Diary, 1.10.66.
49. Diary, 26.11.66.
50. Diary, 18.8.67.
51. Diary, 18.1.67.
52. Diary, 13.2.67.
53. Diary, 30.1.67.
54. Diary, 3.2.67.
55. Diary, 30.3.67.
56. Diary, 30.3.67.
57. Diary, 21.1.67.
58. Diary, 5.4.67.
59. Diary, 3.11.67.
60. Diary, 7.11.67.
61. EL–Fortescue, 5.10.66. Noakes, p. 222.
62. Diary, 26.9.69.
63. Diary, 27.9.69.
64. Diary, 17.10.64. Noakes, p. 237.
65. Diary, 29.3.68. Noakes, p. 241.
66. Published by Field, Boston.
67. Mrs. W. Chanler, *Roman Spring* (Boston: Little, Brown & Co., 1934), pp. 29–30. Noakes, p. 243.
68. Mrs. Hugh Fraser, *A Diplomat's Wife in Many Lands, II* (London: Hutchinson, 1911), p. 333. Noakes, p. 245.
69. Diary, 20.6.71.
70. Diary, 13.1.73.
71. Diary, 3.4.73.
72. Diary, 3.4.73.
73. Diary, 3.4.73.
74. Diary, 20.9.73. Noakes, p. 259.
75. Diary, 20.9.73. Noakes, p. 259.
76. EL–Fortescue, 12.9.93. Noakes, p. 260.
77. Diary, 22.11.73. Noakes, p. 261.
78. Diary, 14.12.73.
79. Diary, 13.12.73.
80. Diary, 13.12.73.
81. Diary, 14.12.73.
82. Diary, 9.1.74.
83. Diary, 17.1.74.
84. Diary, 20.1.74.
85. Diary, 18.1.74. Noakes, p. 265.

86. Diary, 21.1.74.
87. Diary, 2.8.77. Noakes, pp. 276–277.
88. Diary, 9.8.77.
89. Diary, 7.8.77.
90. Diary, 2.8.77.
91. Marianne North, *Recollections,* II, p. 83. Noakes, p. 283.
92. Holbrook Jackson, ed., *The Complete Nonsense of Edward Lear* (New York: Dover, 1951), p. 250.
93. EL–Mrs. Stuart Wortley, 26.2.82. Noakes. p. 293.
94. Dover, p. vii.
95. Diary, 28.3.83.
96. Diary, 12.5.83.
97. Diary, 22.5.83.
98. Diary. 5.8.83.
99. Diary, 13.1.74.
100. Diary, 4.4.87. Noakes, p. 309.
101. Lushington–Fortescue, 6.2.88. LLEL, p. 362. Noakes, p. 312.

Chapter Two

1. W. S. Baring-Gould, *The Lure of the Limerick* (London: Rupert Hart-Davis, 1968). I am indebted to his account for the broad historical outline here.
2. See "Hush thee, my babby" and "Hush-a-bye, baby," Nos. 14 and 22 in *Oxford Dictionary of Nursery Rhymes* (Oxford University Press, 1951), eds., Iona and Peter Opie.
3. See especially nursery rhymes, such as "A little old man of Derby" and "There was an old woman / Who lived in Dundee." Opie, op cit., Nos. 120, 145.
4. Holbrook Jackson, ed., *The Complete Nonsense of Edward Lear* (London: Faber and Faber, 1947). Reprint (New York: Dover Publications, Inc., 1951). Referred to below as Dover. In identifying the limericks, the first number refers to the page, the second to the position on the page, 1 for top, 2 for bottom.
5. See Brian Reade, ed., *Edward Lear* (London: Arts Council Pamphlet, 1958), item 87, pp. 43–44 and item 92, pp. 45–46. He states that the gathering of the leaves in both parts of the first edition was random. Lear was so involved in the publication of the Routledge edition that it seems unlikely that he did not arrange the limericks in some order of his own, however unconsciously.
6. Angus Davidson and Philip Hofer, eds., *Teapots and Quails* (London: John Murray, 1953). Vivien Noakes and Charles Lewsen have collected many more for a new and more complete edition of Lear's nonsense, to be published by Oxford University Press in 1978.
7. See Randall Thompson's discussion of the music for "The Yonghy-Bonghy-Bò" in Part II of Philip Hofer's article of the same name, *Harvard Library Bulletin,* XV (1967), pp. 229–237.
8. J. St. Loe Strachey, ed., *The Lear Coloured Bird Book for Children* (London: Mills & Boon, 1912).

9. See the nursery rhyme "Hush-a-bye baby, on the tree-top." Opie, op. cit., No. 22. Lear's preoccupation with treetops may well come from nursery rhymes, especially lullabies. See the discussion of "Calico Pie" and scaring rhymes. p. 204.
10. Dover, 165.1, 180.2, 198.2, 162.1, 189.2.
11. See the nursery rhyme "Baby and I / Were baked in a pie." Opie, op. cit., No. 15. Nursery rhymes are full of pies. See also the discussion of "Calico Pie," p. 204.
12. Dover, 16.2, 57.2, 45.1, 10.1, 17.1
13. Dover, 4.1, 7.2, 26.2, 44.2.
14. Dover, 178.1, 196.1, 192.2, 200.1.
15. Dover, 202.1, 168.2, 185.2.
16. Dover, 199.2, 192.2, 207.2, 179.2, 193.2, 162.1, 169.1, 189.2, 169.2, 163.1, 202.1, 188.2, 206.2, 160.2, 159.2, 181.1, 178.1, 200.1, 174.2, 175.2.
17. See the nursery rhyme "Leg over leg, / As the dog went to Dover, / When he came to a stile, / Jump he went over." Opie, op. cit., No. 144. This is a finger-game rhyme. The limericks seem often to echo these and other game rhymes.
18. EL–Alfred Tennyson, 9.6.55. Noakes, p. 127.
19. Diary, 29.3.68. Noakes, p. 241.
20. I use "sublime" according to Samuel H. Monk's usage in his definitive study *The Sublime* (first published, Modern Language Association of America, 1953; University of Michigan, 1960), p. 8.
21. See the nursery rhyme "Gregory Griggs, Gregory Griggs, / Had twenty seven different wigs. / He wore them up, he wore them down. / To please the people of the town." Opie, op. cit., No. 195.

Chapter Three

1. Houghton Library, Harvard.
2. Ibid.
3. Noakes, p. 321.
4. W. M. Parker, ed., "Edward Lear, Three New Poems," *The Poetry Review* (June 1950), pp. 81–83. The original manuscripts are in the National Library of Scotland.
5. Ibid.
6. Dover, pp. 61–63.
7. Ibid., pp. 64–66.
8. Ibid., pp. 67–70.
9. Ibid., pp. 75–77.
10. Ibid., pp. 85–86.
11. Ibid., pp. 87–89.
12. EL–Fortescue, 25.8.48. Noakes, p. 90.
13. Dover, pp. 225–228.
14. Davidson, p. 200.
15. Dover, pp. 242–244.
16. Ibid., pp. 232–235.
17. Ibid., pp. 81–84.
18. Ibid., pp. 247–248.

19. Ibid., pp. 249–251.
20. Diary, 10.9.63. Noakes, p. 198.
21. Dover, pp. 78–80.
22. Ibid., pp. 245–246. See Dover, limericks, 5.1, 15.2, 56.2, 165.2, 166.1, 94.2.
23. See Dover, limericks 5.1, 13.2, 15.2, 16.1, 16.2, 17.1, 26.2, 38.1, 41.2, 44.2, 49.2, 54.1, 160.1, 161.2, 163.2, 165.2, 167.1, 167.2, 168.1, 176.2, 188.2, 191.2, 193.1, 194.1, 194.2, 205.1, 206.1, 206.2.
24. Dover, pp. 71–74.
25. Compare Thomas Love Peacock's "Seamen three! What men be ye ? / Gotham's Three Wise Men we be. / Whither in your bowl so free ? / To rake the moon out from the sea." Peacock's mariners also survive, giving the lie to tradition and commonsense.
26. Dover, pp. 252–254.
27. Noakes, p. 245.
28. Dover, pp. 275–276. Published posthumously in *Nonsense Songs and Stories* (1895).
29. Compare an unfinished poem in his diary for 30.10.73: "The Attalik Ghazee / Had a wife whose name was Gee / And a Lady prosperous was she, / While residing by the Sea. // Said the Attalik Ghazee / Who resided by the sea, / "My own beloved Gee! / I am suffering from a flea / Which has settled on my knee." // Said the Begum Lady Gee / (Who resided by the sea,) / "Why! What is that to me! / Do you think I'll catch a flea / That has settled on your knee?"

Bibliography

Works by Edward Lear

A Book of Nonsense, by Derry Down Derry (Edward Lear). London: Thomas McLean, 1846.

A Book of Nonsense. Routledge, Warne and Routledge. Enlarged edition, 1861.

Nonsense Songs, Stories, Botany and Alphabets. London: Bush, 1871.

More Nonsense, Pictures, Rhymes, Botany, etc. London: Bush, 1872.

Laughable Lyrics, a Fourth Book of Nonsense Poems, Songs, Botany, Music, etc. London: Bush, 1877.

Nonsense Songs and Stories. Intro., Sir Edward Strachey, London: Warne, 1895.

Queery Leary Nonsense. Ed., Lady Strachey. London: Mills & Boon, 1911.

The Lear Coloured Bird Book for Children. Foreword, J. St. Loe Strachey. London: Mills & Boon, 1912.

The Complete Nonsense of Edward Lear. Ed., Holbrook Jackson. London: Faber & Faber, Ltd., 1947. Reprinted by Dover Publications, Inc., New York, 1951.

Teapots and Quails. Ed., Angus Davidson and Philip Hofer. London: John Murray (Publishers) Ltd., 1953.

Illustrations of the Family of Psittacidae, or Parrots. Pub., R. Ackermann and E. Lear, 1832.

Gleanings from the Menagerie and Aviary at Knowsley Hall, Knowsley. Privately printed, 1846.

Tortoises, Terrapins and Turtles. Drawn from life by James de Carle Sowerby, F.L.S. and Edward Lear. London: Henry Sotheran, Joseph Baer & Co., 1872.

Illustrations, *Poems of Alfred Tennyson*. Illustrated by Edward Lear. Boussod, Valadon & Co., 1889.

Views in Rome and Its Environs. London: Thomas McLean, 1841.

Illustrated Excursions in Italy. Vols. I and II. London: Thomas McLean, 1846.

Journals of a Landscape Painter in Greece and Albania, etc. London: Richard Bentley, 1851.
Journals of a Landscape Painter in Southern Calabria and the Kingdom of Naples. London: Richard Bentley, 1852.
Views in the Seven Ionian Islands. Pub., Edward Lear, 1863.
Journal of a Landscape Painter in Corsica. London: Bush, 1870.
Lear in Sicily. Intro., Granville Proby. London: Duckworth, 1938.
Edward Lear's Journals: A Selection. Ed., H. Van Thal. London: Arthur Barker, 1952.
Edward Lear's Indian Journal. Ed., Ray Murphy. London: Jarrolds, 1953.
Edward Lear in Southern Italy. Intro., Peter Quennell. London: William Kimber, 1964.

Natural History Books to which Lear Contributed

The Gardens and Menagerie of the Zoological Society Delineated. Vol. II. Ed., E. T. Bennett. 1831.
A Century of Birds from the Himalayan Mountains. J. Gould. 1831.
Illustrations of British Ornithology. Vols. III and IV. Sir William Jardine, Bart., and Prideaux John Selby. 1834.
A Monograph of the Ramphastide, or Family of Toucans. J. Gould. 1834.
The Transactions of the Zoological Society. Vol. I. 1835.
Birds of Europe. 5 Vols. J. Gould. 1837.
The Zoology of Captain Beechey's Voyage. 1839.
The Zoology of the Voyage of HMS Beagle. Ed., Charles Darwin. 1841.
The Naturalists Library. Ed., Sir William Jardine, Bart., Vol. IX, Pigeons, and Vol. XVIII, Parrots. Henry G. Bohn, 1843.
The Genera of Birds. Vol. II. G. R. Gray, 1849.

Letters

Letters of Edward Lear. Ed., Lady Strachey. London: T. Fisher Unwin, 1907.
Later Letters of Edward Lear. Ed., Lady Strachey. London: T. Fisher Unwin, 1911.

General Works About Lear

Davidson, Angus. *Edward Lear: Landscape Painter and Nonsense Poet.* London: John Murray. 1938.
Hofer, Philip. *Edward Lear as Landscape Draughtsman.* London: Oxford University Press, 1968.
James, Philip (ed.). *Edward Lear, 1812–1888.* An Exhibition, etc., Arts Council of Great Britain, 1958.
Noakes, Vivien. *Edward Lear, the Life of a Wanderer.* London: Collins, 1968.
Osgood, Field, William B. *Edward Lear on My Shelves.* New York: privately printed, 1933.
Parisot, Henri. *Limericks et Autres Poèmes Ineptes.* Paris: Mercure de France, 1968. Translations.

Reade, Brian. *Edward Lear's Parrots.* London: Duckworth, 1949.
Richardson, Joanna. *Edward Lear.* Writers and Their Work Series, No. 184. London: Longmans, Green, 1965.

Lear: Victorian and Edwardian Articles and Reviews

Review of *A Book of Nonsense.* "Christmas Books II." *Saturday Review*, December 21, 1861, p. 646.
Review of *Lispings from Low Latitudes.* Murray, 1863. *Athenaeum*, April 11, 1863, p. 486. Mentions *A Book of Nonsense.*
Review of *Our Favourite Nursery Rhymes.* Warne, 1865. *Athenaeum*, November 25, 1865, p. 727. Mentions *A Book of Nonsense.*
"The Nursery and Modern Thought." *Spectator*, December 9, 1865, p. 1376. Mentions Lear and *A Book of Nonsense.*
Review of *Journals of a Landscape Painter in Corsica.* Bush, 1870. *Athenaeum*, April 1870, pp. 521–522.
"The Science of Nonsense." *Spectator*, December 17, 1870, pp. 1505–1506. Review of *Nonsense Songs.*
Review of *Nonsense Songs, Stories, Botany and Alphabets.* Bush, 1870. *Athenaeum*, December 24, 1870, pp. 838–839.
Review of *Nonsense Songs*, etc. *Saturday Review*, December 24, 1870, p. 814.
"A Book of Nonsense." *Judy*, January 18, 1871, p. 114. Review of *Nonsense Songs.*
"Mr. Lear's New Nonsense." *Spectator*, December 23, 1871, pp. 1570–1571. Review of *More Nonsense.*
Colvin, Sidney. Review of *More Nonsense. Academy*, January 15, 1872, p. 24.
Review of *Laughable Lyrics. Athenaeum*, November 18, 1876, p. 664.
Review of *Laughable Lyrics. Spectator*, December 2, 1876, pp. 1516–1517.
Review of *Laughable Lyrics. Saturday Review*, December 9, 1876, p. 734.
"Lear's Nonsense-Books." *Spectator*, September 17, 1887, pp. 1251–1252.
"Lear's Book of Nonsense." *Saturday Review*, March 24, 1888, pp. 361–362. Review of twenty-fifth edition of *A Book of Nonsense.*
"Lear's Nonsense Songs and Botany." *Athenaeum*, September 1, 1888, p. 288. Review of sixth edition of *Nonsense Songs.*
"Nonsensical Books." *Saturday Review*, October 5, 1889, pp. 388–389. Review of *The Secret Doctrine*, by Madame Blavatsky, and other occult works, with prefatory comments on Lear's nonsense.
Review of *The Nonsense Birthday Book.* Warne, 1893. *Athenaeum*, February 4, 1893, p. 152.
"Nonsense Songs and Stories." *Athenaeum*, December 22, 1894, p. 868. Review of the ninth edition of *Nonsense Songs.*
Review of ninth edition of *Nonsense Songs. Saturday Review*, December 22, 1894, p. 691.
"Art for the Nursery." Warne, 1900. *Athenaeum*, December 15, 1900, p. 800. Review of *The Pelican Chorus.*
Review of *Nonsense Songs, The Jumblies and The Pelican Chorus.* Illustrated by Leslie Brooke. Warne, 1900. *Academy*, December 8, 1900, p. 560.
Review of *Letters of Edward Lear*, ed., Lady Strachey. T. Fisher Unwin, 1907. *Athenaeum*, December 14, 1907, pp. 760–761.

Review of *Queery Leary Nonsense*, ed., Lady Strachey. Mills and Boon, 1911. *Academy*, December 9, 1911, p. 728.

"A Humorous Letter Writer." *Academy*, December 9, 1911, p. 5 (supplement). Review of *Later Letters of Edward Lear*, ed., Lady Strachey. T. Fisher Unwin, 1911.

Obituary Notices

Athenaeum, February 4, 1888, pp. 154–155.

Saturday Review, February 4, 1888, pp. 130–131.

Academy, February 11, 1888, pp. 97.

Reviews of Lear's Travel Books

"Lear's Illustrated Excursions in Italy." *Athenaeum*, October 31, 1846, p. 1120. Review of *Illustrated Excursions of Italy*.

Review of *Journals of a Landscape Painter in Albania*. *Athenaeum*, May 3, 1851, pp. 471–473.

Review of *Journals of a Landscape Painter in Albania*. *Spectator*, April 19, 1851, pp. 374–375.

Index of Limericks